THE PORTAL

THE SAGA OF
THE FARMHOUSE ON CEMETERY HILL RD. CONTINUES.

CYNTHIA HERBERT-BRUSCHI ADAMS

ISBN: 978-1-64184-612-7 (Paperback)
ISBN: 978-1-64184-613-4 (Ebook)

DEDICATION

To Easton and Dalton who make the sun come up

CONTENTS

PART 1

BONES BEYOND THE GRAVEYARD

PART TWO
FINDING PEOPLE
2020 - 2021

ACKNOWLEDGEMENTS

Every writer needs readers. Not just to enjoy our final product but to review and criticize the early editions of a manuscript to insure readability. Roger Adams has faithfully read every word, chapter by chapter, as I wrote it, to catch spelling errors, typos and phrases that required more explanation. He was also kind and tactful allowing our long marriage to endure and flourish!

Next, each chapter was also read, one at a time, by Ann Aulerich. As a retired principal and English teacher, her knowledge of construction and punctuation offered a living correction system. I am responsible for any errors you may find for I would persist that the author's "literary license" could take precedence over "rules", sometimes. Ann certainly makes me look good in many places and I very much appreciate her efforts.

Then, a special thank you to the readers who, once the manuscript was completed, gave it a thorough review with feedback primarily on the storyline to be sure the intended messages came through. Those wonderful folks are Sharon Cormier, an author herself; Edith Posselt, Ed.D., a well read psychologist; Andrew Adams, a former journalist and consumer of the written word as well as a sometime movie critic; and W. Hagan, an author from Southern California who helps jump-start my occasional writer's block. Thank you all for your time and input.

Last, I must again acknowledge Priscilla D. Douglas, Ph.D.; a friend who continues to encourage me to reach out and write. She truly seems to enjoy the successes of a friend which is so lovely.

And to Stephen King, for years of inspiration from afar.

PART 1

BONES BEYOND THE GRAVEYARD

1

TEDDY 1869 ON

Teddy awoke just before dawn. Although the rooster had not yet crowed, and his bed felt comfortable, he could no longer sleep. Soon it would be time to milk the cows and feed the animals. But the reason he had awakened so early was the dread which filled his heart as though he was trying to pump molasses instead of blood; at the least sign of waking his mind sent him a jolt that signaled worry, terrible worry. He knew this was the day he had promised his grandmother that he would bury her in the cellar.

Matters were complicated as she wasn't yet dead, and further, she wanted her final resting place to be a secret from the rest of the family. He reluctantly got out of bed, dragging each leg out, and commenced his routine: dressing, going outside to wash his face, and grabbing his work gloves. He first entered the cow barn, and pitched hay in front of the girls so they would be content while he milked them. Milking was a fairly relaxing, methodical process, pull and squeeze, eliminate the first few ounces for cleanliness sake, then with the right tension the milk made a heavy squirting sound as it hit the sides of the bucket. This rather mindless repetitive action allowed Teddy's mind to wander.

Heretofore Teddy had led a happy life raised by a loving family in this town of East Apple, Connecticut. His parents Levy and Woodard Mills had three sons of which he was the youngest. Because of this birth order and the fact his mother might have wanted a daughter; his brothers said he was coddled. It was true that Mother kept him close to herself for many years but this had offered advantages. Teddy could read at an early age, he never had to depend on anyone else to prepare a good meal for he knew how to cook, and he wasn't shy when it came to talking with girls.

It was his kind and somewhat gentle ways that must have impressed his grandparents, Reverend Ben and Emily Harrison Wilbur. They were slowing due to old age and needed to employ a trustworthy and reliable helper. These grandparents asked his mother if he could work for them part-time and they would see that he got to school every morning. Naturally she said yes as she would do anything for her dad and stepmother. This also somewhat decreased the burden of serving three meals a day to three hungry, growing men.

In addition to being a young man, Teddy had the advantage of size as he had grown to nearly six feet tall by the time he was thirteen years old. Since he had just finished 'filling-out' it was easy to see that he was strong and able. This had helped to deter his brothers from making more fun of him than they had already done as he began to mature. In fact, he was taller than his middle brother had been; the brother who was named Ben after their grandfather. Thus Teddy was happy and received enough respect, even when a youngster, to live well as the 'baby' in the family.

Before he started working for his grandparents Teddy had been trained to do all the basic chores on the farm from animal care to thrashing wheat and cleaning the equipment; simple though it was at that time. The brother's were accustomed to taking turns or assisting each other when the work was more challenging so it was good that they each knew how to do all the chores. It was anticipated that as they matured they would each become farmers, of at least their own property, for their own families, if not in order to harvest and sell products. Most families would strive to be self-sufficient and did what was called subsistence agriculture. It wasn't until shortly after the Civil War, which ended in 1864, that commercial farming played a major part in agriculture. This commercialization doubled the area of farmland used in the United States. The cause of this growth was related to population growth and industrial growth.

As products were manufactured for general sales to the public, such as clothing and all cotton products, there was a demand for more cotton to be raised. This was a commercial product from the southern region of the country. Tobacco was primarily a Southern product as well with the exception of the larger tobacco leaves which were used for wrapping cigars, and which were grown in Connecticut. New England also produced fruit that was not readily found in the South but the problems of rapid transportation prevented much success in exporting these items out of this region, and in receiving perishable foods from the warmer climates during long New England winters. Also crops in New England had a short growing season limiting their commercial potential.

Thus Teddy was limited to thinking about how to produce and store enough food for his future family and what, if anything could be a cash crop to allow him the money necessary to purchase the things he could not grow himself. His grandparents had sold a few eggs each week and dried herbs which they had raised and preserved. Along with a few sheep, a few pigs and a cow they could manage to eat fairly well as long as grandmother had pickled, dried, and or cured sufficient fruits and vegetables to last them through the winter. But because of the crop production limitations, a large labor pool emigrating from Europe and the good harbors in New England, it became more industrialized. Cities grew rapidly in New England and this industrial growth triggered a need for food from other regions and thus the transportation to bring produce east.

So these were the thoughts of a young man with regard to how he could earn his own way in the world. What could he do in a city? His grandfather on his mother's side had been a pastor but his own parents and paternal grandparents had all been farmers. Then one day Teddy had been invited to work for his grandparents while he still attended school. And during this time his grandparents started showing him things which had been collected and studied by his now deceased Uncle Will.

His late uncle's collection of bones and sea creatures made him think of becoming a naturalist or even a biologist; the books about the Amazon encouraged him to think about travel and exploration;

maybe even writing books. But the fact was his educational opportunities were already limited when he started to think about these things, and his life was going along a course which would pretty much keep him in East Apple working on a farm.

His brother Ben had decided to seek adventure and see the world and could not wait to sign-up to fight the Confederates during the War Between the States. Of course he was a Union soldier. Unfortunately this cost him his life. His family had to find and hire embalming surgeons which were both rare and expensive, but they wanted him brought home. Eventually he arrived in East Apple in a box pulled by a wagon with a flag draped over it. No one looked inside as he had been dead too long, no matter what preservative had been used, but his mother was comforted as she had a portrait painted of him before he had left for the war the last time. In the portrait he is wearing a dress jacket of black with a bowtie. The sleeves of the uniform have gold buttons down both sides but these are not visible in the portrait. He has a small neatly trimmed mustache and short beard covering his chin; an extremely handsome man whose loss would be felt by his young wife for many years. Even Teddy dearly missed his brother.

Now Teddy had to deal with another loss, and his years of working for his grandparents, and then just his grandmother had drawn him very close to her. That was part of the problem; he loved her and hated to see her go even though she had tried to prepare him for this occurrence. For years his grandmother had been saying she was getting ready to die so that she could be borne again right next to her long gone son Will. She believed that Will and his pet arachnids would be coming back to life some 150 years from now, and she could join the resurrection party. This burial, she believed, would provide her an opportunity to reunite with her son, although try as he might, Teddy could not quite figure out how this would happen.

It seemed these spiders of Will's would have dormant periods, like cicadas, and then be active again. Will initially had lost the right to return with them each time, but Grandmother knew he would be back around 2020 or 2021. Thereafter she expected that they would have frequent periods of active life.

6

He might not be the smartest kid in the family but he knew enough about life and death that he had determined she must be wrong about miraculously coming back. Still, she had requested that he not speak about this with anyone, not even their pastor. So Teddy felt very alone with what was coming tonight, the helping her to die and letting her go.

The other part of the problem was that she had warned him when he digs the hole for her body he might unearth some other objects: human bones and giant spiders; either could be living or dead.

2

GRANDMOTHER

Teddy completed his chores after prolonging them as much as he could. He was most reluctant for the remainder of the day to unfold in which his grandmother would disappear for all time, and he must assist her in making this happen. The day continued like every other day on the farm: Teddy came into the kitchen from the barns, and greeted his aunt and cousins who were busy with breakfast preparations. He left his boots by the back door, washed his face and hands with water from a pitcher poured over a bowl also setup near the back entry and walked into the kitchen.

The kitchen was a large room whose most prominent feature was a grand fireplace that could burn logs as long as four feet. There were kettles of water heating on the hearth. This hot water would be mixed with water straight from the pump to facilitate cleaning pans and plates and the washing of clothing. Making tea was also easy if the fire was going or the woodstove could be lit to heat a small amount of water. Keeping warm water available was a major chore and on Saturdays, when most members of the household would take their weekly bath prior to going to church the next day, the work was so time consuming that many elected to take their bath in the same water someone else in the family had just used. While this also conserved on water there were obvious disadvantages.

The fireplace itself contained andirons for holding roasting pots and occasionally spits containing game birds. There was also a gap at the back wall of the bricks for dropping ash down to the cellar to save for making soap. Finally, the most glorious sight was that of the beehive oven just to the right of the fireplace.

A beehive oven was shaped just like a beehive with a rounded dome and contained its own flue which entered the chimney just above the larger opening for the fireplace. The fire burned toward the back of this oven where the air exchange occurred. When the fire was new but very hot it would be used to roast meat so that it was seared on the outside and then removed from the oven when the internal heat of the meat appeared to reach a desired temperature. As the day wore on the coals would form and spread out over the bottom of the beehive and the women would make pies and slowly roast a chicken. Finally, the coals would dissipate but the stones making up the beehive would hold the heat for hours, long enough for corn muffins, some cakes and breads to be baked without burning. After running the oven late yesterday the family was producing warm biscuits this morning which were being served with a jar of honey and placed on the long harvester table at which all sat for meals. The men would often add a few eggs in the morning prior to beginning hard labor.

Teddy's uncle was in the kitchen by now and announced he would be heading way out back to take some trees down which would be left to dry for next year's fires. Ordinarily Teddy would go with him but everyone knew he couldn't leave the house before his grandmother made her appearance and let him tend to her needs for a bit. She had become particularly dependent upon him for several years and all accepted that. Generally she appeared in the kitchen as Teddy was finishing his breakfast, which she did this day, joining him at the table. It was expected that after Teddy took care of his grandmother he would then join Uncle John out back.

Emily, Teddy's grandmother, did not seem to have much appetite this morning, a fact that worried her family. She nibbled a bit and sipped her tea and then said she wanted Teddy to take her for a walk. That was typical of their routine although she could never go far. Yet today, Teddy knew, she planned to go far enough that there would be no coming back. He let her sit for awhile over her tea believing she might need to say good-bye to her old place. The others could think her mind was drifting but he knew she was planning to disappear.

When they got outside she needed his support. She was such a sweet old thing that he was happy to hold her or carry her if she preferred. He asked her how she had slept and she said better than she had in a long time. Then she surprised him by saying she might want to wait another day or two before "concluding things." He advised her that this made him extremely happy and she should take lots of time to consider this move. He set her on a bench his grandfather had made years back so she could see her herb garden and consider what might need harvesting. He brought her a cup of water and told his Aunt where she was before he headed out to join his uncle.

He was so relieved that he almost forgot his hatchet and the midday meal the cousins had put in a large piece of cloth for him to carry along. Still the feeling of dread did not leave him. He knew she didn't have much time left if they were to enact her plan, for it necessitated that she be able to wander away and "get lost" in the woods. Her ability to walk at all was rapidly diminishing.

And by the next morning, when she joined Teddy for breakfast, she told him it was time to take her out near the stand of pines where she could linger in a pleasant setting until the Lord took her. After they had only walked a short distance she did ask that Teddy carry her and, while in his arms, she thanked him for ensuring the success of her plan. She said although she wouldn't be able to thank him later she was dying with a happy heart knowing she could lay in eternity, or until resurrection, with her son Will. She assured Teddy that he had made that possible by agreeing to her plan. She had already been most kind to Teddy and had recently given him a beautiful ring with two diamonds in it that he was to sell or otherwise put to use as part of his future plans.

Her regard for him gave the young man more confidence even though he was both frightened and heartsick over the things he must do that very night. She had certainly warned him many times that the gravesite he was to dig might present surprises. He now told himself he must be brave and not recoil from whatever the remainder of this day and night might present to him. He must be strong.

10

By supper time Teddy was nearly twitching with anxiety. Although he had worked hard in the field all day he could only think about finding his grandmother's dead body and having to carry it home in the dark and into the cellar. They asked at this meal if he had seen his grandmother and he had to react with surprise that she wasn't yet home. Then he added "It is getting harder for her to walk each day. I hope she hasn't lost her way again but I will bring a lantern and leave in just a few minutes." He did leave almost immediately but knew he would be out until full nightfall and until they should all be fast asleep.

At first Teddy wandered somewhat aimlessly just to kill time. Before he was out of view from anyone potentially trying to spot him from within the house, he acted out a sort of pantomime of calling out to his grandmother and looking behind a few bushes. Once he was out of view he slowed down until the thought entered his head that she might still be alive and needing help. "What if Grandmother had not been as ready to die as she thought?" he wondered now in a panic. He turned himself toward the stand of pine where she had requested he leave her this morning. In the dwindling light he could still make out the form of the pine grove but nothing on the ground, at least from this distance, resembled a person. He started running for those woods and was soon shouting "Grandmother, Grandmother!"

Then he thought "Please let her be alright. Please Lord, I pray she changed her mind and is patiently waiting for me." And as he thought these words his lips began to tremble and grown man or not he was crying. What he had agreed to do months before: to let her pass away peacefully in the woods, then after all in the house were fast asleep he would smuggle her into the cellar, and quietly dig her grave where she had requested it, now seemed a more daunting task. He felt torn to pieces by wanting things to go the way grandmother Emily had wanted them to and at the same time wanting her to live forever.

She had also warned him he might not like everything he found there in the cellar dirt but he was to ignore whatever there was and simply add her body, cover her with the dirt he had removed and clean the area so that all looked as it had. Then the final challenging part would be in the morning when he would have to convince the family that he did not find her although he had hunted for hours. He knew he must appear anxious to look for her and lead a search party toward that end while hoping not to waste their time too long as he would know where she lay; but first to find her tonight.

He continued running to the pines and cursed himself for starting off in the opposite direction when he was attempting to throw the family off course. By now he was winded but had arrived close to the spot where he had left her. He called her name several times surprising himself with just how shaky his own voice sounded. There was no response as well as no light as the sun had set and the moon must be behind clouds. His desperation was such that he got down on all fours and began crawling around the area where he expected to find her, the lantern slung around his shoulders on a rope. He had several moments of false hope when the ground or a rock felt like it might be some part of her but turned out not to be. He bumped into a tree with his head and felt dazed for a few moments and had to lean back. When he did, the hand he stretched behind him for support felt another hand. It was a small very cold hand; he knew before he turned around and groped the ground that this would be grandmother. He turned toward her finally lighting the lantern and gazed at her face. She looked peaceful and calm but there was no life left in her body. Grandmother was gone.

3

BURYING EMILY

Teddy cradled his grandmother for what seemed like an hour. During that time he told her all the sweet things he wished he had said while she could still hear the words; he just needed to put his love on the record for her. He told her he hoped she had had no pain and had not been fearful or wished he had come to find her sooner. Then he kissed her cold check and declared out loud "I guess we'd better do this!" He was big enough and strong enough that there was no problem for him to standup while holding onto her. Teddy began to make his way back home. Fortunately, farmers go to bed early so that they can glean enough rest by daybreak to feel ready to begin again. He was counting on everyone at the farmhouse already being asleep.

One of the dogs barked a greeting as he came up the wagon path from Rattlesnake Hill Road. He tried to shush her and as soon as she had sniffed his leg she was quiet until she also scented his grandmother and then the dog did a little whining; but she was a trusting old girl and settled down as Teddy was on the scene. When they arrived at the back of the house there was a lantern still lit in the kitchen. Teddy froze and moved stealthily toward the kitchen window keeping his arms containing grandmother's body held down low. Slowly he peaked through a lower corner of the kitchen window and spied his cousin sitting at the table doing a little mending. She was a person who hated to mend things and would much rather walk around with holes in her clothing than to run a needle and thread through a piece of material. Teddy had to conclude that she must purposely be trying to stay awake waiting to see if Grandmother was alright.

"Ah, such a nice girl" he thought and then, "Darn her, how long will I have to stand around before she tires and goes to bed!" So he sat right down below the window in order to not lose sight of the light: a dog at his side and his dead grandmother in his arms. He might have dozed off a bit himself but when he next looked up the light was off and it was still early in the night. He quietly got up and made his way around to the cellar door. The door only squeaked a bit as he opened it and then he retrieved grandmother's body from the grass and headed inside the cellar. Fortunately, he had prepared for this night by placing a tarp to hold Grandmother Emily, and the tools he would need for grave digging, out of view, inside a corner of the large base of the chimney.

The ground was hard packed where she had requested to have her final resting place: the day had been long and worrisome; Teddy felt the burden of too much grief and stress just as an older person might; he was exhausted. Half in a daze he began hacking at the soil with the pickaxe reminding himself not to make noise or he'd soon be discovered. He'd swing the axe a few times then he'd set it down and see what dirt could be moved out of the way before he had to again loosen it with the chopping action of the axe. In this manner it was not too long before he was down in the earth about three feet. That was when he observed some motion.

There were definitely skeletal remains in this area of the cellar and these bones intended to have something to say to Teddy. A hand and an elbow pushed a little on the side of the hole, and then another hand and elbow were free and, before Teddy knew what was happening a woman's voice was addressing him from the mouth of a skull! She said "Before you think to disturb me you had better consider the horror of my death in this house and how I have no qualms in retaliating whether or not you are related to the Judge!" The bones were barely sheathed in black clothing.

Teddy had thought of many things since his grandmother had tried to warn him that anything might happen at this gravesite, but it had never occurred to him that he would be confronted by a resident of the grave; he simply thought he would perhaps see something disgusting. This was beyond his ability to cope. He stammered "please rest, I will fix it" and that was all he could get out.

With that, the skeleton lay back down, crossed her arms over her chest, and allowed Teddy to cover her back up with soil. Teddy worked as silently as he could, and made things look as undisturbed as possible, while his primary concern was to be as quick as possible. He wanted to cover up this mess and get out of the cellar with his dead grandmother's body. And as soon as he was again outside he leaned against the house and said out loud "Now where do we go?"

The only thought that jumped into his mind was that he must take grandmother to the church. She and his grandfather had spent many years working in the church. If she couldn't be buried with Will because someone else was there, and she did not wish to be buried in the cemetery up the hill because his grandfather's first wife was in that ground, then he would make her a fresh spot unique to herself. He thought about the surprise he had just had and reasoned perhaps Will's body had been laid to rest a few feet away and he had had bad luck; but he wasn't going to chance running into that person/skeleton/creature, again if he could prevent it.

He set grandmother gently down and wrapped her lovingly in the tarp. He then took the shovel, with which he had run out of the cellar, and tied the tarp so that it made a hammock for grandmother. He then balanced the shovel along his broad shoulders and carried the shovel and body in that manner along Snake Hill Road until he reached the bend where the church sat. He did not dare to light the lantern again nor had he managed to bring it along. Instead he felt his way to the right of the entry stairs and around toward the plaque on a tree which commemorated his grandfather's years of service to the church. He knew this spot from gazing at the plaque many times. This would be a fitting place for his dear grandmother, under the sign honoring her Ben.

Fortunately, the digging was easy as this ground was well cultivated. He carefully cut out squares of the grass, grateful that the moon was finally out from behind the clouds so he knew what he was doing. After he removed the sod he then dug for what seemed like hours, but in fact he was faster than he had imagined; there was a sizeable hole at about four feet depth before he even required a break. Seeing this opening he said a final prayer to his grandmother and gently worked her body into the depths of the soil, tarp and all. He then covered her with the loose soil and carefully reassembled the hunks of grass on top of that. Reluctantly he pressed it all down trying not to think of possibly squishing her but needing to mask the disturbance he had created. He then fled the scene for home hoping to get a few hours sleep before he would have to lead a "mock-rescue" team to look for her.

He got back and returned the shovel to its proper shed but was so exhausted he simply crumbled to the grass, leaned against the house and fell into a deep sleep. Only the dog understood his hard work that night and she simply joined him next to the house. They slept until the rooster awakened them and Teddy's cousins came running out asking about Grandmother Emily.

They could all see how exhausted Teddy looked so it took no convincing for them to believe he had searched all night. His Aunt Esther insisted he come in for coffee and oatmeal, believing but not saying out loud, that her step-mother must be dead. She knew they would all spend the day searching for Emily but she no longer saw it as an emergency. They were saddened by this loss and they would do their duty by looking for Emily, but the poor old dear was probably happier in her own private graveyard wherever she might have wandered. Esther sent the girls out to do the milking and began preparing food to sustain them as they hunted for grandmother.

Little did Esther know how right she was in thinking that Emily enjoyed a private spot. But, who knows what transpires in the thoughts of the dead. While Emily was indeed in her own private grave her mind told her she was lying beside her son, Will, for all eternity, thanks to the plan she had made with Teddy. And the only exception she had to that thought was that she and Will would wake up in or around the year 2020 and enjoy their old life together on this very farm. She also allowed for the possibility that some of the giant arachnids might be among them but this was not her preference. She had mused that a new plan might well be made for those nasty creatures when the time came. Yet this was but a story with which she had died, and her grave remained private, even from herself.

Following his breakfast, Teddy led the girls and his aunt around "likely" places for Emily to have traveled the day before. They tried the backsides of several gardens because Emily had enjoyed seeing those crops grow; or one wooded area because it held a bench which she and Ben had put in place for afternoon teas; or a stone in the herb garden which Emily often dried a few sprigs on; all with no results. Then Teddy mentioned Emily's interest in the stand of pines just above their farm. Although the trees were at enough distance that it seemed a less viable option and, indeed, when they got to the edge of that area it was clear that Emily was not under the pines, it still had to be considered, as the obvious places had already proved fruitless.

For one frightening moment Teddy caught sight of his grandmother's kerchief blowing near some leaves a few yards into the pines. He rushed to that spot meaning to retrieve the scarf before others spotted it and asked questions, only to discover the colors were those of an old kite someone had lost in the woods. His relief was palpable but he hoped only to himself. He brought the kite out laughing at himself and portrayed the sighting of the kite as a moment of "false hope".

Finally they walked in one more direction to complete a full circle around their home. They called Emily's name whenever they entered a new area and all grew despondent as the hunt for her seemed to conclude with no hint of the missing grandmother, not even a handkerchief or a shoe print. Uncle Woodard had remained at the farm to take care of all necessary chores and had promised to let the constable know of the disappearance if they had no luck. And so, reluctantly, but with some acceptance, the little team of searchers moved toward the farm; further and further from the body of their grandmother lying in a grave near the center of town within the churchyard.

4

TEDDY'S PLANS

Before the death of his grandmother, Teddy had been a fairly laid back fellow. He enjoyed the farming and family life with only a few troubles in his mind when he thought too long about what might be the purpose of his life. He had also known losses, as when his grandfather Ben had died, and of course his brother being killed in the war. Now with Emily gone he both wanted to reexamine his own purpose, or future, and decide what he must do regarding the broken promise to her: after all he had essentially accepted payment from her when he took the ring she offered yet had not fulfilled his commitment. These thoughts began to wear on Teddy's mind especially at night when the house was quiet.

Their preacher often spoke of the plight of the slaves who had just been emancipated at the end of the War Between the States. Some of these folks didn't even know that they were free to leave their original homes and to work for themselves. Most did not know how to read or write and were often taken advantage of and tricked into not realizing their rights; those who left the South often ended up homeless in the East and did not know about cold weather. The Church was asking every week for donations and time commitments to assist with serving the needs of these former slaves. That sounded like a most important cause to Teddy. His grandparents had spoken often of charitable deeds and living life as Jesus would want you to.

He wasn't so sure he had a calling from God, but Teddy knew he owed the world a debt for the good fortune he had to be healthy and strong and not to have faced his brother's fate on the horrible battle-fields of the Civil War. If his brother, a Captain in the Union Army, had died to set the slaves free then maybe it was a clear message for him to honor his brother's sacrifice by committing himself to the cause of helping to support the newly emancipated slaves. It was a mandate: He knew he could ask the pastor what help was needed.

Then he thought about Victoria, his brother's widow. He'd be lying if he denied feeling an attraction to her but he had never shown her a hint of his desire. First, she and his brother had been newly-weds, establishing themselves on her parents' farm as her parents moved into a smaller house on the property. Then, for several years, she had been a dutiful wife waiting for her husband to return from the war. Finally, she was a grieving widow and, other than offering to help on her farm if she needed anything, he had stayed away: afraid of her grief; afraid of doing the wrong thing around her; and most afraid of commitment.

But Victoria was more on his mind especially now that the needs of his grandmother were no longer part of his daily chores. Teddy was lonely and longed for the company of a woman with all that might lead to, including children. Teddy was nearly 26 years old and knew very few females in his own age group who were still single or not cousins. The more he thought about Victoria the more he convinced himself that she might also be interested in him. His brother Ben had been intending to run Victoria's family farm as her parents were elderly, but then the War and tragedy intervened. Wasn't this also a duty calling to him?

Those thoughts ruminated in Teddy's mind for several days while he tried to formulate a plan. When he wasn't planning what he should do, he was feeling depressed because he had let Emily down. It wasn't long before he realized that thoughts of Victoria were a good deal more pleasant than were thoughts of having cheated his grandmother out of her promised burial. He had even become so concerned some days that he played with the idea of going back to the church one dark night and exhuming her remains. Once he had her out of the ground and in the tarp again, the next part of what he would do with her wasn't so clear, but it probably involved returning her to the farmhouse for interment in some other part of the cellar. That part of his thought process almost caused him to weep at which point he would quickly recall thoughts of Victoria.

And so, approximately two weeks after the family marked a little grave for Emily at the top of Cemetery Hill Road, even knowing full well she was not at that site, Teddy went to call on the widow of his late brother Ben. He made certain not to arrive at meal time and brought good wishes from his parents and some of Emily's chamomile tea which she had packed tightly into envelopes so that they might be stored in a dry place until used.

Victoria was surprised but did not seem disturbed by this interruption of her gardening, which that day, was in a small plot not far from the house. Teddy was nervous but polite and Victoria took the lead by offering her condolences for his grandmother's loss as she had meant so much to the entire community of East Apple. He felt a sudden stab of guilt at the mention of Emily but if Victoria noticed him flinch she assumed it was still his grief which she understood all too well. She offered him tea, as he had brought some for her, but he instead expressed interest in walking out to see her garden. Victoria seemed delighted with this suggestion as she always preferred to be out-of-doors and she would not be required to wash dishes later.

Before Teddy left her they had both found themselves laughing in a way neither had done in recent times. Victoria mentioned out loud how she thought Theodore resembled her late husband and that gave her comfort. Teddy allowed how flattered he was by that and then he awkwardly said he had always thought Ben had excellent taste when he had fallen in love with Victoria. At this point they were both a bit embarrassed but also feeling pleased.

On his way to the door Teddy asked if he might call for Victoria to walk to church two days hence on Sunday morning. Victoria said that would be fine and her mother might join them if she felt up to the walk. Teddy replied that was an excellent idea and he would drive his late grandmother's buggy to fetch them if that would be of help. And so, after years of no actions but many thoughts, Teddy began a courtship with Victoria, his late brother's widow.

It amazed Teddy how easy she was to speak with, not at all the way he had recalled the giggling girls of his childhood. She was reasonable and thoughtful and cared about others as he had been taught to care. She and her mother had already been knitting warm clothing for the "refugees from the South" as they referred to the former slaves. So it did not take Teddy long to realize that if his goal was to farm and to serve this population, Victoria would be right by his side. She even mentioned believing that she "owed it to Ben". If they could both dedicate themselves to the same issues how could a life together be wrong?

Then he became bolder and started to see her as a true confidant; he broke his promise to his grandmother and revealed part of their secret, but only a small part. He didn't lie to Victoria but he didn't give her every detail of how he came to acquire a ring with two large diamonds in it as a gift from Emily. He recalled the time when he was still a schoolboy and Emily had needed him to come by their farmhouse both every morning and again right after school, as she and Grandpa Ben could no longer manage the farm work by themselves.

He had gone willingly and happily helped them each day. They fed him a large breakfast and sent him along with food to eat for his midday meal; that had seemed like payment enough. Then one day Emily insisted he accept her mother's engagement ring and not tell the other grandchildren about it. She said she only had one such piece of jewelry and too many grandchildren. She and Grandpa Ben felt the closest to him and wanted him to have the ring. She said it would help him when he met the right woman or when he needed to support himself, but asked that he not discuss it with his brothers or cousins to prevent hurt feelings.

Victoria said that made sense and she could understand why he was his grandmother's favorite. After he stopped blushing Teddy took the ring out of his pocket where he had it wrapped in a piece of velvet. He showed it to Victoria and her eyes grew wide as she admired the beauty of it. Then his heart took control of his tongue and he asked her if she would like the ring and to become his wife. She quickly said "no" and his heart sank with a fierce thud louder than dropping a stone into a hollow well.

"No" she said again, "I will gladly become your wife but I will not wear that huge and fancy ring." And Teddy was just able to control his joy and not toss her in the air. After a few moments he asked "Then what do I do with this ring, find a woman who will accept it?" "Not on your life" she replied. "How would it be to take one of the diamonds and have a simple setting designed for me and we put the sale of the other stone and the gold to use for others?" And so they began to formulate a plan that they hoped would define the rest of their lives; although, Teddy did have a fleeting thought about possibly needing to tell his future wife all of his secrets, he decided to stop where he was.

5

GETTING ON WITH LIFE

Teddy wanted to place a ring on Victoria's finger before they made an announcement to their families. Due to their age, and the fact that Victoria had already been married, neither of them felt a need to ask parental permission. However, Teddy did think it prudent to speak with his parents privately and let them know he was becoming serious in his courting of Victoria. Naturally, as Victoria was the widow of his late brother, he knew this was bound to bring up certain painful emotions especially for his mother. But to his great relief Levy was very happy for them both and probably tickled by the new potential for more grandchildren.

The following week the young couple traveled into Hartford where arrangements were made to make a ring for Victoria with a solitary diamond. The remainder of Emily's family ring was placed for sale through the jeweler. They were to return in two weeks to collect the engagement ring and would then announce their plans. As Victoria's first marriage took place at the start of the War Between the States there had been no extra funds available for Ben to use in purchasing a ring for Victoria making this ring very special.

Victoria urged Teddy to move out of his Grandmother's farm, which was now Aunt Esther's, and to live with Victoria and her parents. She admitted they had been struggling to keep up with the chores even though they hired a man part-time to help them. Teddy agreed that he would move in right after the wedding, and as Victoria had been married in the church the first time, Teddy's parents would provide a small wedding at their home.

The pastor performed a brief service at this ceremony and the only problem for Teddy was when he emphasized the two of them would now be as one. The pastor gave examples of their "oneness in the eyes of God" and provided examples of this holy bond. Teddy wanted to ask if this meant he must tell his new wife every secret he knew for he did not think she would choose to hear about the skeletons in his aunt's cellar. Instead he said nothing; just let it go, although it continued to trouble him.

There were also moments of doubt when he thought he owed his cousins and aunt a warning of some kind regarding possible spiders, as well as skeletons lurking beneath them, but his grandmother had known and really told no one. Teddy reasoned that if those creatures remained undisturbed they would cause no problems so he would do everyone a favor by leaving this topic alone. He began working days on Victoria's farm and realized he would be too busy to think of the dead.

Soon after the wedding the pastor asked Victoria and Teddy to meet with him. There was an organization trying to start-up for the expressed purpose of assisting more families in relocating to the Northeast. The pastor did remind the couple that, not so many years back, and not far away within Connecticut, a woman named Prudence Crandall had tried to run a school for former slaves. She had not been accepted well by the community, and eventually her school had been forced to close after much hostility. Still, that was prior to the Civil War and hopefully the abolitionists were more highly regarded now than in the past.

Teddy said he would be honored to add this work to his current life, that he would see it as a mission and could probably give it more time on Sundays but only if Victoria had no objections. Victoria said she would be Teddy's partner in this for as long as she could be. Both she and Teddy were hoping their lives would soon be changed by a child, but that didn't mean she couldn't still serve this cause. So as their married life began, and Teddy lived on the Chase Farm as was Victoria's family name, the name Mills was now added to

24

the sign on the farmstead and to a list of individuals supporting the emancipated slaves.

Little could they have known what strange thoughts and feelings this might generate among the neighbors, for a few of the people who opposed their work were soon stricken with a mysterious ailment. It all began to happen in the spring after heavy rains caused piles of snow, nearly big enough to look like mountains, to melt very rapidly. It happened that three homes on the downhill side of the cemetery on upper Snake Hill Road not only flooded, but the families living in those homes became ill; gravely ill. By summer's end many of the children and the elderly within those homes had perished, and most of the women were quite ill. The husbands were ill too but somehow fared better than the others.

No one before this time had ever become ill in those homes except when very elderly. In addition to location, the only other commonality among these families was their vehement protestations against support of the newly released slaves from the South. They had formed an opposition group to the one in which Teddy Mills gave so much of his time, and they believed that rather than integrate the "slaves," as they still called them, into normal New England culture, they should instead be sent home to Africa, and other islands along the way. They would not donate money, food or even old clothing to this cause, and they forbade any instruction set-up through their local schools, to support the needs of the Africans to learn to read. In fact, they saw no need for "these people" to have such skills. In truth many of the farmers themselves lacked the ability to read or write more than their own names.

There had been many angry words and public protests even leading to some of the protesters dropping out of Church and beginning one of their own. All this was painful enough and gone was the sense of harmony the community had enjoyed when it was smaller. Then more rain, melting and flooding came: week after week there were increasing numbers of dead. A few joked that the Lord must have sent the rains to wash these protestors away, but as tiny children were dying, the number of jokes soon gave way to major concerns.

How were the dead in East Apple Valley dying? Accusations flew back and forth. At the same time Teddy and Victoria were welcoming their first child, a daughter named Jane after Victoria's mother: they were also being accused of poisoning the crops of this group living in the Valley. It was terrible that their joy could be so overshadowed by evil suspicions which anyone who really knew Teddy would never believe. But talk in a small town, and the surrounding tragedy, led to near hysteria. When babies were dying in considerable pain then many were insisting that someone should pay.

Teddy and his organization made a magnificent gesture by using a considerable sum from their funds, meant for the training and support of the new citizens, to instead bring in a doctor who was familiar with "environmental issues". It was hoped that he might discover what was causing the illness in the Valley. The ill citizens remained skeptical, and did not believe that the Mills' group would do anything to help them, but they were desperate enough to listen to the doctor's findings. Sadly he said that he suspected their well water was contaminated but had no idea what might have happened to it, if indeed it were contaminated. He said that the best advice he could give, and which he himself would follow if in their situation, was to move – to abandon their homes and farms and especially their wells; to do whatever they could to start over somewhere else.

The doctor had sufficient evidence, based upon the manner in which most deaths occurred, to suspect arsenic poisoning. But try as he might he could find no evidence of an excessive amount of arsenic in either the dust these farmers used on their crops or in any particular poison used to kill the local vermin; he just knew it was somehow getting into their wells. Since the folks in this valley were the only ones so affected he surmised that getting them to move might change their lives.

Hearing this message was not easy. People who were sick and had already lost such precious family members were now being advised to leave their homes. At some level they must have known this was true and necessary but at other levels they wanted someone else to blame. It was a most difficult time. Among the effected families were the children and grandchildren of Edwin Thompson. Due to old age

Edwin had just left the farm he had originally attained from his sister and had moved in with his son's family. His sister had been Mrs. Alice Bridgefield, the mother of Wilbur, who became the adopted son of Emily Harrison and the Reverend Benjamin Wilbur.

And Edwin Thompson still had a sharp mind. He easily figured out who Theodore Mills was and that Teddy had inherited property from his 'grandmother' but that grandmother had originally left all her land, through her will, to her adopted son. That son was really Edwin's biological nephew. Now, under these circumstances, wasn't it only fair, he reasoned, that Edwin claim his nephew's land for himself? And so he presented his theory and claim to the young Mills couple.

Initially Teddy was quite taken aback and Victoria was simply shocked having never known the details of Will's birth. Teddy had not actually known the details either but had surmised much of it from what he heard transpiring in conversation between his grandparents. Now, he was a bit shocked himself but also pleasantly surprised to realize that Will had actually been a blood relation as Will was his grandfather's biological son.

Apparently, Reverend Ben Wilbur, the father of Teddy's mother and aunts, had fathered this son, Will, out of wedlock. This had occurred due to the brazen behavior of Edwin Thompson's widowed sister and the weakness of the Reverend. Edwin's sister died following the birth of her son, and Emily Harrison had adopted the infant and raised him as her own, even deeding all of her land to him. But fate had worked against this plan, and Emily lost her son when he was but twelve years old.

The Reverend's wife had died shortly thereafter, and eventually he and Emily had wed. Emily helped the Reverend with his girls bringing them all to live in the farmhouse on Snake Hill Road which she had inherited from her parents. Now Edwin believed that, as the biological uncle of Will, he had some claim to the property, and was trying to shame or frighten Teddy into giving a portion to him.

Teddy and Victoria told Edwin that they needed time to think about this arrangement as they now had their own and future children to consider. Having a child and hoping to have more, coupled with their commitment to supporting the emancipated slaves, made them especially want to guard their finances and property. If they needlessly turned land over to the Thompson family, what would it cost them as they tried to help others?

Not a week had gone by when one of Edwin's kin was again knocking on the Mills' door. Victoria was alone, but he stated she could pass on the message. He said Edwin and he didn't think that there was time to waste as their families continued to be ill, and they needed a decision about where they could move; then he seemed to become a bit aggressive and almost threatening. He said it would be easy to build a case that Teddy had poisoned the wells in their area because they opposed his liberal thinking in wanting to educate the Africans and help them to become a part of the local community. He stated that Teddy and Victoria had best take care of Edwin's clan if they didn't want real trouble; personal trouble.

Victoria was quite aghast. She thought of her baby and her two elderly parents; she had already lived through the loss of one husband, and this truly frightened her. She was used to a sedate life, perhaps of hard work but genteel evenings and only thoughts of doing 'good' by her neighbors; she had no capacity to take in the crude threats of this Thompson family. Victoria invited the fellow to leave but asked that he return the next day right after milking time in the evening, and they would have an answer for him. When he left she bolted the door closed and was visibly shaking.

Once Teddy realized that his wife had been threatened, he wanted to get a gun, and an uncle or two, and pay a call on the Thompsons. But, Victoria convinced Teddy that that family had a point. They were all suffering from something. Maybe it was the right thing to do to help them out, to give them land to build on with enough extra acreage for a subsistence farm and to wish them well. Teddy said she made sense and he would sleep on it. He would give them an answer before they had to come back for it. That night would be the second time he ever dealt with the remains in his late grandmother's cellar.

6

CONFESSIONS NEEDED

Victoria was making dinner after the Thompson men left their house. She usually enjoyed preparing the evening meal for her family. This night was different as she was still too shaky from having to make serious decisions about giving away some of their land to appease these angry people. First she nicked her finger with a sharp knife as she sliced into a hard cheese, and then burnt her thumb, although not seriously, while stirring the soup. Her parents were contentedly playing with the baby in the corner of the room, and Teddy was looking at the map of his Grandmother Emily's land reviewing the portions that he believed would soon be deeded to him. He didn't want to give away land that other members of his family were expecting to be theirs. This would require a discussion with Uncle John, a banker, and possibly someone in the town office. He would go see his uncle in the morning to get things started.

Eventually they all went to bed, with Victoria having the cradle next to her so that the baby could easily be fed during the night. Teddy thought "what a peaceful scene" as he climbed under the quilts. He did not know how much he was about to rock that idyllic moment when his unconscious mind returned to his grandmother's cellar.

All the talk of Will, and inheriting what was "rightfully Will's", had disturbed the tranquility that Teddy held so dear. He would have appreciated his grandmother's advice but when his mind fell into deep slumber, Teddy was transported, not to Emily's gravesite at the Church, but into the cellar of Emily's farmhouse where he had encountered the anger of a woman's skeletal remains. What could that angry widow need from him, and indeed what could he do for her?

When he found himself down in the dirt, next to the spot Emily had wished to be in, his thought was that she, Emily, must be pulling him there to remind him that he had not completed his promise to her. But in just a moment the angry bones themselves began pushing up through the soil and confronting him. Her hollow tube-like, raspy voice sounded as though it had dirt in its throat yet, there was no throat in evidence, only bones. She wanted him to know something. She said she "Could not rest in peace until he helped her."

She told Teddy "I did not end up in this hole in the cellar floor out of choice, but rather was forced to lay here because my murderer has so placed me. I was hidden away where it had been thought that no one would ever think to look. I was discarded with less concern than was given to old unwanted glassware; I was considered disposable trash!"

She had been angry, she went on to tell Teddy, and now she was beyond livid, if a dead person might use that expression, she had added. "A man of laws, who sat in judgment upon others and was thought to enforce laws, had gotten rid of me, and he had been helped by another man of laws elected by the Town. "This is no riddle," she yelled at Teddy. "I am speaking of the judge who built this house and the sheriff with whom he worked! I was trouble and the judge could not control me so they thought it best to kill me, bury me, and say nothing. I would simply disappear, and what could my little girls do to generate the help needed to try and find me? Nothing, because I was already dead and the chief culprit, the judge, would be long gone! So I waited for someone to look for me, to ask questions that would get others to wonder where I had literally disappeared to, but no one came!"

"Now I need you to ask questions; to find out 'whatever happened to the Widow', and how was it I never returned for my children nor contacted my kin? Doesn't anyone wonder why the judge left town so fast, and I simply disappeared?"

Of course the Widow didn't seem to realize that many years had elapsed since she met her end. Her children were probably dead of old age, and certainly the men she was accusing of murder were deceased, but Teddy did not know how to say these things to an angry skeleton.

He said "I cannot blame you for your rage; this is a horrible and grim tale which you and your family did not deserve to have happen. I pray that these evil men met their own sad endings, but I do not know. I will try to discover what became of them and find a way to report it to you. And if it is at all possible I shall pursue any likely stream to allow me to clear your good name. The story that the judge left behind him in this town should not be what others believe, and your reputation and that of your daughters' should be cleared. Your only crime was fighting unrealistic harshness which was placed upon you. When authority has no restrictions and no checks, it frequently destroys the boundaries which are necessary for the safety of the weak. You were the victim of greed by an all powerful force."

Then Teddy started yelling "I must find a way to help you!" for those words were being repeated in his head when the whole world began trembling. Actually, it was Victoria shaking Teddy's arm and repeating "Wake-up Teddy, please wake-up!" as she tried to get him to become quiet and to leave what must be a most unpleasant dream. Teddy was sweating profusely, and Victoria was a bit frightened for him. Her Uncle Ebenezer had died of a seizure, and she did not wish to see her husband begin convulsing. He was soon able to assure her that it was but a bad dream.

"Then what, pray-tell, were you dreaming?" she whispered, for somehow the baby continued to sleep. Teddy tried to tell her that he had no idea, kidding that he had been asleep at the time, but she began by repeating much of his dream back to him. Apparently, although initially not loud, he had been talking in his sleep throughout most of the dream.

Finally, he took a deep breath and said he did have secrets, several secrets, and he wanted to confide in Victoria about them, but he did not want to burden her. He cautioned her that she might be wise to ask that he spare her the information that was pounding inside his head at night and squeezing his heart by day. He said she would either judge him to be crazy, thus demanding her freedom from him, or she would be trapped in a world of horror with layers of pressure in every direction she turned.

"When is death simply and sadly just the end of someone's life?" he added; "or" as he was now experiencing, "when was it the beginning of hopes for the impossible and wishes for connections and continuations which would only cause fear and terror for one's family? How could anyone rest in peace if a corpse was expected to finish some of its business and even make amends or restitution for wrongs it may have committed during life? Or, must it demand justice for wrongs done to it? These are the types of things you are asking me to share. Do you really want this burden?" he ended.

Victoria drew Teddy close, and resting her head on his shoulder as they sat in bed, she said "Yes, I am your wife, and I must know what is going on for you or it will always be between us." Then she added, "You might even consider giving me credit for the possibility that I will be of help to you in solving some of these dilemmas although I am certain they are most serious and currently beyond my comprehension." Teddy simply kissed her and said "We will attack this together and knowing you are with me has already helped me to feel better." Then Teddy told the rest of the story.

"I will begin by saying that there are two sets of skeletons buried in my Grandmother Emily's cellar and the night of her death I had a brief conversation with one of them. It is she that I dreamt of this evening and she that I believe I must help. Do you still wish me to continue?" he asked. Victoria took a few minutes to digest this unexpected information before she responded with a slow but emphatic "Yes, if you believe this, and are worried about it, then it must be shared."

It was now nearing dawn, and tiny Jane was beginning to make sucking motions with her mouth as her dream informed her that she was hungry and must find her mother. Soon the little hands would begin frantic motions, and then the baby would commence to cry out demanding that her mother provide the breast milk which would sustain her. There were but moments of peacefulness remaining.

Teddy took this bit of time to assure Victoria that in the evening they would indeed talk, and he would answer all of the questions he possibly could: that until then they should carry on as normal and hope to enjoy the day before them.

Victoria had a sudden sense that this might be her last calm moment for a long time and that very soon she could possibly wonder if she, herself, were insane. She hoped she would not suffer the loss of another husband, for Teddy was a very dear man, but she could not understand how he believed the dead were having conversations with him and, even why he felt he owed land to that terrible Thompson fellow, but she would stand by him; at least for now.

The day seemed to drag along, but once the evening chores and the meal were prepared, Victoria arranged to have her mother bath the baby so she and Teddy could take a walk. He led her down the hill and across toward the church. As they walked he informed her that he had met with Aunt Esther and Uncle John about how Emily's acreage would be divided among the various family members. They had understood that he was not anxious to push them out of any land, but needed a piece of property to help the group from up the hill who were being poisoned. With that charity in mind they carved out a generous piece for Teddy. They thought it was his due after all they knew he had done for his grandmother.

He told Victoria that he stopped in, and left word for Edwin that the land-gift was in progress, and he would have more information after he met with the town. Then they arrived at the church, and he resumed the story begun the night before. He pointed over toward the sign honoring his grandfather and said "My dear Grandmother Emily is actually resting in that spot." And thus he started to unravel the mystery with which he lived.

7

VICTORIA'S RESEARCH

Teddy continued telling Victoria details of the death of Will, who had been adopted at birth by his Grandmother Emily. How Will had actually been the son of Edwin Thompson's sister, and how his grandfather, Reverend Benjamin Wilbur, was Will's biological father. Victoria had recently learned some of this but Teddy found it essential background in order for her to comprehend the rest.

Teddy then discussed how interested Will had been in natural science and how this eventually led to his acquiring a Goliath Bird Eating Spider, actually an arachnid, which ended up escaping, invading the farmhouse, and taking Will's life. His Grandmother's grief had been unrelenting and she believed she had communicated with Will after he was in the grave.

The grave, by the way, was not at the top of Cemetery Hill, but actually in the dirt floor of the farmhouse basement, as were the hiding places of the spiders. This had led his grandmother to further conclude that Will would return to the world by rising from the dead with the spiders at some future point. Initially this resurrection was thought to be 100 years from the date of Will's death but, due to Will making demands, so that he could communicate with his mother, the spirit world pushed the date forward to something like 2020 or soon thereafter.

Grandmother Emily had not planned on Will's return based solely on superstition but due to some facts about insect life. She knew that many of these critters became dormant following critical attacks on their nests, or were simply cyclical. Will had been bitten to death by these arachnids leading Emily to conclude that the venom in his veins would react to dormancy as it did with the spiders: when the spiders returned, so would Will.

Out of a profound desire to rest with her son, and the hope of joining him when he would again live, Emily had negotiated with Teddy to make extraordinary arrangements for her burial. First, the location of her body would be most private; no one but Teddy should know she was in the cellar next to Will. Also, as far as Emily knew, Teddy was the only living person to know where Will was actually buried so this would keep the matter extremely private. The only hitch was that when Teddy went to complete his grandmother's bidding, and lay her in the ground with Will on the night of her death, a different and very angry skeleton was in the place Emily had expected to occupy.

Teddy had carried his grandmother's corpse around most of that night before he finally found a suitable place in which to bury her. Then Teddy tried to digest his guilt at having let his grandmother down by not honoring his promise to her. He also experienced the horror of now knowing that a widow had been murdered in the farmhouse by its original owner, a judge, who took her life for his own convenience. These were the nightmares he faced, and needed Victoria to understand, if not also help him to sort out. How and when should they begin to handle these disturbing matters? He certainly didn't want others aware of the 'ghosts' in his head.

Victoria could not say that she accepted completely the horrors that he had told her, but she did agree to help him begin sorting things out. First, she said, let us complete the land-gift so that those poor people suffering from poisoning may make a new start, and cease disturbing us. Teddy agreed, but said it was his intention to give the Thompson family half of the parcel. This would leave a plot of land so that one day they might have a farmstead in that location perhaps to give to a child.

Next, Victoria wondered how they might find anyone who would have a written record, or good legends about, what had happened to the widow in question. "Perhaps there is an older solicitor who took over a business for an even older one?" Teddy mused. "Maybe they stored older records?"

"Or, someone who kept records when a person was arrested by a town official back then?" Victoria added. They decided to see what their respective parents might know about this old case and would begin that evening with Victoria's parents. Teddy would also do what he could to expedite matters for the deed to the Thompsons' future land-gift. And, at least for the time being, Teddy knew it was up to him to manage his guilt over his failure to accommodate Grandmother Emily. It did help that he was no longer alone with this secret. Victoria seemed to remain kindly toward him, even with all his strange tales and dreams. He thanked his lucky-stars that Victoria would now advise him, and would share the burden of the worries, and that she appeared to do so very lovingly.

That evening Victoria and Teddy told her parents that there was a rumor from long ago regarding a widow having died in Teddy's Grandmother's farmhouse before the place actually belonged to grandmother's family. Both of her folks looked blankly at each other and began to shake their heads indicating that they knew nothing. Then her dad paused and said, "Now was that the old judge that this story is about?" When Teddy said "Yes", the older gentleman began to talk.

"That was Judge Rider, and I never knew him. He left town, I think, just before the time your grandfather arrived to take over the church. I wasn't yet born, but when I was a youngster there were stories about old Judge Rider. There was even a poem about him, gosh, how did it go? *Be careful what you promise and of the bills you make because Judge Rider wants your farm to take. If you argue with his honor, or ask him "please be nice" he'll take your last penny and leave you only rice. If the bank does not get money and your promises are fake, then Judge Rider wants your farm to take.* Or something like that," her father said sounding a bit embarrassed.

"Anyway, he didn't have a good reputation for being kind to folks who were down on their luck, and may even have taken someone's life over a financial dispute, but I really couldn't say. These were old stories. My father would have known, but he is long gone, of course. Is someone still talking about him?" asked Victoria's dad.

"Well," said Teddy, "I heard something about the unsolved disappearance of a widow, with whom the judge had a major dispute, but there was no conclusion; I just wondered if someone knew what really happened."

"You could try the town office as they might have records. Also, for a short period, the Town of Apple had its own little newspaper, but that only lasted a couple decades; we didn't have enough population to sustain a paper. The newspaper in Windham might have been in operation by then, it seems like a disappearance would be a big story around here. Someone should know," he concluded.

After chores were caught up the next morning, Teddy headed over to the town office which was actually a shed connected to the Feed and Grain Store and the Post Office. Here he intended to find out what paperwork he must produce to deed a portion of land to a "distant relation". He thought it would raise fewer questions if he simply referred to Edwin Thompson as some sort of kin. He wanted to have this deed move forward expeditiously to smooth things over with that family as quickly as possible. Fortunately, John Farmer, Aunt Esther's husband, had already filed the papers giving Teddy his portion of the property so that Teddy had the legal right to do this.

Teddy then sauntered into the area filled with record books and asked how far back their information went. He was told that once the Town of Apple was incorporated they had kept a copy of all land records; all probate matters, and any correspondence so related. Teddy was then invited to have a look. He asked to see information pertaining to his Grandmother Emily Harrison Wilbur's farm. He was handed a log book and told to look for the place by date, if he knew it, or by name of the owner. Teddy started with the name Harrison, as he knew Emily's parents had acquired the place directly from Judge Rider, and then he worked backwards.

What he found out about the judge was the date he had purchased the land and began building the farmhouse, the amount he had paid, and the date of completion. Then he read forward a bit and saw the dimensions of the house, the number of outbuildings

CYNTHIA HERBERT-BRUSCHI ADAMS

and a tax figure. Finally he came to Emily's father's name and the date he had purchased the property from the judge plus the amount he had paid. The judge had completed the farmhouse in 1785 and sold it in 1800.

Fifteen years seemed a very short period of time to keep a home one has built unless there were extenuating circumstances. Of course Teddy knew that there were likely several things that had happened, but nothing, other than dates and dollars, appeared in this record book. When he asked the clerk about information that coincided with the timing of transactions, he was told such details were not recorded by the Town unless there were some criminal elements. Teddy was then referred around to the back corner of the building which was the constable's portion of the town office.

When he spoke to a man in that area he was told to come back the next day around 8 AM to catch the constable before court in Windham. Teddy thanked him and headed home to complete more chores and to provide Victoria with the details of all that had transpired. He could see that there would not quickly be details for the 'widow'.

The next morning Victoria was given the opportunity to meet with the constable as Teddy still had heavy chores at 8 AM, and Jane could be left with her grandmother. Victoria was pleased to participate in this hunt for answers and hoped to find something which would allow Teddy to rest better. When she entered the town offices she was amazed by just how little the Town had put into these buildings by way of amenities; they truly appeared to be sheds with poorly hung doors and rough-hewn boards for counters and desks. The constable worked alone much of the time thus leaving long gaps in service; if he was out on one call all others would have to wait in line until he was again free.

This workload did not enhance Victoria's chances of learning things from the man. He was pretty overwhelmed and had enough problems in the here-and-now on which to focus, never mind questions from 1800. He was probably a man of 50, a little overweight, and moved as though his feet hurt. Still, Victoria, was a very attractive brunette in her late twenties and capable of putting a twinkle in the older fellow's eye by just smiling. He began to act like he wanted to please her, and she played up to him expressing her understanding of how numerous his responsibilities must be. Before an hour was up she had agreed to come back each morning for an hour or two to help him organize the records by date, as a volunteer, in exchange for his pulling up the boxes of information pertaining to her in-laws' farm on Rattlesnake Hill Road. When she left the town office both she and the constable were smiling.

8

DUST

Victoria brought Jane with her, wrapped in a soft hand-woven shawl, when she went to help out in the constable's office the next day. The baby was still at an age where most of what she did was sleep, eat, and require a few diaper changes. Constable Brewster was pleased to see that Victoria had kept her word by coming in to help. He set up the boxes she was interested in from the earlier days, and showed her which, more recent records, were disorganized. He did not seem to object to the sleeping baby looped around her neck and shoulders. This method of holding the baby helped her to sleep and yet left Victoria's hands free for sorting files. With this arrangement Victoria did not need to rush home for feedings. The constable also felt free to leave her alone in the office when he was called out, or had meetings, as she could remain there for awhile. Day one was a great success in terms of beginning their work.

Day two permitted Victoria to complete more of the sorting and organizing that the constable had wished to see accomplished, and it provided a little opportunity for her to look through the old record books. Once she found the dates in question, and the signature of Judge Alexander Rider, she scanned this log intently. She learned that The East Apple Farmers' Savings and Loan had pressed charges on the widow, named Beatrice Loudon, for failure to make her mortgage payments over a period of six contiguous months, and they were demanding at least partial restitution immediately. In the judge's chambers, which were located at his Rattlesnake Hill Road home, she met with a representative of the bank, His Honor and she brought her oldest child, a son, along as he was pledging to provide help for his mother and sisters.

No one could imagine how this boy would accomplish anything resulting in cash, within the next two weeks, but that was what Judge Rider insisted they must do. They must accept this offer from the court, or immediately forfeit their small farm. The son spoke again in a most determined manner pledging he could achieve this phenomenal feat. The boy had just lost his dad in a haying accident, and his sisters' were little children, but neither the judge nor the bank offered a hand in the challenge before him.

A reporter, William Edwards, for the little town paper amusingly called the Cider Press (for East Apple) wrote the following, and it was clipped to the town's record book. "The son and his mother both 'worked like ants before a hailstorm', and at the end of thirteen days the boy brought a sow to market. They had tried to fatten this pig for the profit her weight might provide them. But thirteen days was not long enough to have gained the desired girth. Once the sow made the long walk to the marketplace she had probably lost a couple of those precious pounds resulting in a minimal gain, hardly worth the price of the corn they had sacrificed to feed her."

Edwards went on; "The judge had been clear that, failure to produce the portion of the money in question would result in eviction from the farm. The boy's apparent guilt over not having helped his dad with the haying on the day of his accident and death, coupled with his failure to provide the needed income to sustain his family at this time, resulted in tragic consequences. He did not even seem to return to the farm from the market, but rather he left the money between the backdoors of the farmhouse, without entering. He apparently then went to their barn and took a strong rope, and proceeded to the judge's home; then, shortly after dark, he snuck into the judge's chambers, which were in this home, and made a noose which he strung from a lantern hook. It was there, in the morning, that the judge's wife found him hanging. 'His face was purple and his tongue was bloated and protruding from his mouth, his legs and

CYNTHIA HERBERT-BRUSCHI ADAMS

feet were filled with fluid, huge, and distended, and the smell of his excrement filled the air,' stated Dr. Barrett who is the local doctor, 'A terrible sight for Mrs. Rider.' And a suicide of one so young is the saddest kind of news," added the reporter.

"When notified of this horrific event, the Widow Loudon appeared to lose her mind, which was reportedly fragile from the recent death of her husband, and the pressure the court and bank had put her under. Yet, while her behavior deteriorated, the judge, the bank, and other local officials softened their views out of sympathy for this second loss. Only the judge's wife was reportedly unable to forgive the violation of her home. In any case, the bank agreed to further delay calling in its loan, and members of the community began working at the widow's farm, on a rotating shift for part of each day, so that they could still manage their own chores.

"But, according to the authorities, it was too late for Mrs. Loudon. Her mind was fractured, and she did not wish it to be repaired. She was consumed with vile anger and hatred. She could only think vengeful thoughts. Many nights she repeatedly harassed the judge and his family by placing a crude hangman's scaffolding outside of the judge's kitchen window. This was precisely the first place Mrs. Rider looked when she came downstairs to prepare breakfast each morning. Then one morning Mrs. Rider beheld the sight of the widow's son having been exhumed, in a decaying state, and hoisted into the scaffolding.

"Naturally, Mrs. Rider screamed and fainted, only to wake up and learn that her husband and children were by her side and all were well. Still, each of these events took a toll, and they were adding up for poor Mrs. Rider. She began demanding that they move from this 'God forsaken town'.

"According to Town Clerk, Ezra Wilson, Judge Rider went to see the constable. He explained how fair he had tried to be, how understanding, but the widow was clearly deranged and insisted upon harassing and threatening them day and night; that Mrs. Rider could take no more. The judge insisted that this widow be taken away. The constable would not speak on the record as this is an on-going case but Wilson continued.

'Unfortunately the constable could think of no place a woman could be housed, especially with two young girls, where she could be supervised and allowed to heal. He said there was really no place to confine her.' "But the following day the constable and judge met together with this reporter and stated a person had come forward to care for the children, and the children would be made 'wards' of the town. Further, this permitted the removal of the widow from the area. The town breathed a sigh of relief."

However the next day's Cider Press ran this headline (ordinarily it was a weekly paper but this story was too big for the Town of East Apple to keep from printing) "Widow Escapes Town Jail!" Mrs. Loudon, widow of the late Henry Loudon, and much embroiled with the constable and other town officials, has left the town jail and disappeared into the night!"

"Of course she was found by afternoon and dragged through the town in an open cart. Before the constable could take her behind closed doors for removal from this area, she cursed the judge and his family and predicted that evil and death would befall any male child by the age of 12 if he were born in the judge's house."

The reporter's printed story ended here, but there was a hand written note attached to the backside of the record book and signed by William Edwards. It stated that his paper would not print the remainder of the story because there were no corroborating witnesses but that a workman had seen Widow Loudon attack the judge in his own barn with a knife. His honor had fought back, first with a whip and then with the knife. Before he had finished with her it seems he had raped and then killed the widow. But no one would stand up against the judge. He and the constable buried her in a portion of the judge's cellar where the floor was made of dirt. One advantage to this was that they did not have to transport her dead body anywhere; another advantage was that the judge would soon move far away, at a great distance from this rotting corpse.

Edwards went on to say that the judge and constable stuck to the story that they had removed the poor woman to an out-of-state working farm which sought to rehabilitate such persons while seeing that they received the proper exercise, diet and religious support. Of course this meant that the children were placed in alternative homes, but in safer places than the widow's care. This would also insure the safety of local families, especially the judge's.

Victoria was overwhelmed with all this information, but she suddenly understood why the Widow Loudon was so angry. She knew the widow could be told that much of her story was credible, but Victoria could not say if it would be fully appreciated and believed by others. Victoria also did not know if this somewhat speculative information would make the widow feel exonerated. Could exoneration be enough without retribution, she wondered?

She planned to tell all to Teddy that evening and see if they should try to explain what they had found to Widow Loudon.

9

ASHES

Following dinner, Victoria recited to Teddy all she had read in the town office. It was very astounding to them that these officers of the court, a judge and a constable, had acted in such brazen disregard not only of the laws, but of human decency. Still, there was no actual proof available for Teddy and Victoria to use, nor was this even noted as an "unsolved crime" within the town records. As far as those records indicated, the Widow Loudon was placed out-of-state for rehabilitation, and had to pay her own way laboring on that state's farm. How do you clear the name of some- one who appears not to be accused? How do you accuse those who have long been gone? And how does a skeleton make accusations or provide testimony? These three questions seemed like the meat, potatoes and onions a broth would simmer around. The soup might not be worth eating if these staples are not good.

The thought which occurred to both Victoria and Teddy was that the Widow Loudon might be the only one to whom this infor- mation mattered: and she was essentially dead! "But what about her daughters" asked Victoria? "You mean where did they end up? Who raised them?" replied Teddy. That is still a mystery and one the widow is likely to inquire about.

"Dear Lord," said Victoria, "it is impossible to know how to pro- ceed after all this time." "Perhaps I should check with the church," said Teddy. "If a family took the girls in, it is most likely to have been a family associated with the church." And so they ended this discussion for that night with Teddy planning to ask about old records at the church.

Later the next day, Teddy did inquire at the church regarding the entire story, but predominantly about the fate of the two young Loudon girls. It was a very old tale, of course, at the church too, for it had happened well before Teddy's grandfather, the first real minister, had served the church. The current pastor had known Grandfather Wilbur and wanted to be of help to Teddy. He said that an elderly spinster named Adelaide had confided to him that she and her sister had been adopted. The story was that their mother had been sent to a poor house when they were little. Adelaide said that their brother and father had both died shortly before this and they remembered their mother as screaming and crying all the time.

The girls, according to Adelaide, had been very sad, and kept expecting their mother to get better and come and bring them home, but she never did. Eventually the younger one, not the sister speaking to the pastor, forgot about most of what had happened, and started using the name of the people who had taken them in, and calling the adults there "mother" and "father". She eventually married and moved to Hartford. Adelaide stayed with her "parents" and cared for them throughout the remainder of their lives but she claimed she was still half waiting for her mother's return which was why she never wanted to marry and move away. The pastor remembered this story as it was so poignant.

Teddy asked if Adelaide was still living, but the pastor reported she had been gone about ten years, and was quite elderly even when he first met her. He also added that she made an effort to be certain he knew her adoptive parents had been very kind, and loving to them, as had been their older sister from the new family. Teddy asked if the pastor remembered their adoptive name, and he said yes, he believed it was Edwards. So when Teddy saw Victoria that evening he did have one pleasant piece of news that might be helpful to the Widow Loudon. The reporter who had seen the evil in the judge and the constable had done what he could to help, as he and his wife had adopted her two little girls.

Heartened by this good news, and ever curious about what really went on in that cellar on Rattlesnake Hill Road, Victoria decided to pay a call on Teddy's aunt and cousins at the family farmstead. She caught the ladies as they were preparing tea while waiting for a few more muffins to bake in the beehive oven; then they built the fire back-up. They were very happy to see Victoria and to have a look at Jane who was in her usual place hanging around Victoria's neck in that beautiful shawl. After fresh muffins and tea, Victoria asked if she could have a look around the place as Teddy spoke of the house so lovingly from his many years there with his grandparents. Aunt Esther said "look all you would like, and be sure to stop back in before you head home. We'd like to send some muffins to Teddy." Then the cousins giggled a bit and went back to their chores.

Victoria took her time pretending to be very interested in all aspects of the house. She admired the curtains, the hand-hooked rugs, and the spice rack with fresh herbs hanging in fragrant clusters from the kitchen beams. Then she felt it would not look awkward for her to surreptitiously go down the cellar stairs. Once in the cellar she felt a chill, and sensed, rather than observed, a presence of spiders, but no one had mentioned Will's Goliaths since the time of his death or when Teddy had been learning of his dead uncle's collection.

Putting the creeping crawling things out of her mind, she walked to the place in the dirt of the cellar floor where Teddy had described the intended burial spot for Grandmother Emily. Of course she knew he had been forced to abandon this spot, as the Widow Loudon was lying there. She approached this area with mincing and gentle steps. Once her feet touched the edge of what she believed to be this soil, she stopped, and forcing her voice to sound confident, stated who she was, and that she was there with information the Widow Loudon would want. Then she stood very reverently by, as though visiting a tomb, which she was. After a few moments the dirt appeared to crack, and then a skeletal head seemed to roll forward to face Victoria.

It required all the courage Victoria had to stand there waiting to address this skull in which she wasn't even sure she believed. But there was certainly motion, and then the horrible dirt-clogged sounding voice Teddy had described. This was the terrifying and angry Widow Loudon. "And what information might you have" gurgled the creature?

"We know that you were murdered by the very men who pressured you and your son for money, and eventually drove the boy to his death, and drove you to rage at the judge. We suspect that very judge of raping you before he murdered you, and we know that the judge and the constable colluded to cover-up your murder. Further they passed themselves off as having done charitable deeds on your behalf when, in fact, you were lying dead in this very cellar. Some were aware of this, but only after your death, and none dared to take the judge and constable on to prove any of this."

"The good news is that we did find out what happened to your girls. They were adopted by a family named Edwards and they were raised with love and caring. Additionally, Adelaide never gave up hoping for you to return and loved you throughout her life. She never left East Apple telling confidants that she must be accessible so you would find her. She deeply loved you." Here Victoria paused and waited.

The Widow Loudon had, for a moment, appeared to accept the information calmly. But the calm phase passed quickly, and then she apparently was in one of her classic rages. Dirt began to bubble up at her sides and she commenced to sputter. "I want those men to pay! Don't they know what they cost me, my son and my daughters? Adelaide spent her whole life pining for me, did she? And whose fault is that? And nothing can be proven? You are as crazed as are they! You stand there with your lovely little babe and tell me how sad my girls were to lose me, and what do you know of loss? What?" she continued to rant concluding with "I deserve to have that baby!"

Then a lightning fast claw of bones reached out from the dirt-heap and tried to snatch dear Jane from her mother. There was a frantic scuffle for a few moments ending with Victoria clutching Jane and running from the graveside toward the staircase, and Widow Loudon collapsing back into the grave only pulling with her the beautiful shawl to rest with in the dirt. When Victoria was at a safe distance she gathered herself, took several calming breathes, and then proceeded up to the kitchen to bid adieu to Aunt Esther and the girls.

As Victoria exchanged parting pleasantries with the Farmer family, she was relieved that no one asked her where she had dropped her shawl, and that they did not seem to have heard any noise while she was in the cellar. There was no need to involve them, she prayed, in this horror that she and Teddy may have compounded by thinking they could be of help.

She described her afternoon to Teddy as soon as she ran home: it took all of her strength not to collapse in tears from the fear of almost losing Jane. Shortly after dinner she went up to bed and relied on Teddy and her mother to take care of things. It would not be until late the next morning that they were disturbed by one of Teddy's cousins rushing over to tell them the news.

It seems that after Victoria left, and while they were all preparing a large supper awaiting Teddy's Uncle John to come in from the fields, there had been an apparent explosion of sorts in the fireplace. Aunt Esther said if she didn't know better she would have said it was a 'spirit', but as she bent to baste the rabbit on a spit the fire leaped up, and her skirts were quickly ablaze. If the girls had not immediately covered their mother with flour they would have lost her, but the flour smothered the flame. Poor Esther had a burn on her thighs but it seemed as though she would be fine and the doctor wasn't needed. Still, the girls thought, Teddy would want to know.

10

WADDLE AND DAUB

Once Teddy was certain that Victoria and Jane were unharmed, he was most concerned about his Aunt Esther. He feared the widow might be threatening her or the entire Farmer family, as they lived in what she thought of as the judge's house. He decided it was his duty to at least go check on the chimney and the mortar in his Aunt's home. If there were a breakdown in the workings of the chimney then maybe he could take care of those repairs, and prevent any further harm from befalling them. If the chimney was in perfect shape it might be necessary for him to say more about the 'widow' which he did not want to do.

Aunt Esther opened the backdoor for him with her usual broad smile. Aunt Esther never acted as though you were bothering her so Teddy felt right at home here especially since he had recently lived with them. And Esther, the daughter of a clergyman, had learned to be both welcoming and considerate, as was his own mother, her sister, Levy. Teddy told Aunt Esther how happy he was to see her feeling so well after being burned, and narrowly escaping a hideous fate. Accidental burning, while cooking, were a major cause of mortality in those days with most cooking being done on an open fire, the English style, and colonial era long skirts.

Esther admitted how lucky she had been to survive without a serious burn. The girls were right there with her when it happened, and they had been in the process of making bread. Naturally the bread making necessitated their having a good deal of flour in several bowls, thus providing an opportunity for them to instantly smother the flaming skirt, with almost one motion. She blushed, and said she also prided herself for the many discussions she'd had with them over the years, about how to respond if there was a fire in the kitchen. Teddy said he could see how the training had benefitted all.

"Today," he added "I would just like to inspect your chimney in case I find anything that would have predicted that flare-up and kept you safer. I notice you don't seem to be cooking today?"

Aunt Esther seemed to laugh to herself, "No" she said, "We decided to take one day off from baking just so all of us could gather a bit of strength after yesterday's fright. But the girls are out gathering apples for pies and preserves so tomorrow we shall be going full tilt again."

"Well that sounds like a good plan to me" said Teddy. And just as he was about to lean into the chimney at the great opening of the kitchen fireplace, he felt a hand on his arm. It was Aunt Esther, and she wanted him to know that there was something she had not dared to say in front of her family.

"Just as the flare-up leaped onto my clothing I could have sworn that there was a face in the flames. It was a horrid face, wicked, I guess you would call it, but it looked like a bony old woman half scornful, and half sneering at me. It made me want to scream more than did the sudden pain, but I refrained for the good of the household. Now, are you telling me that there may be a legitimate cause for this fire, not an evil one?" asked Esther.

"You are a good woman, Aunt Esther," said Teddy. "We will determine the cause of this mishap and I don't want you to be frightened." Then he turned back to the chimney and began his inspection. When many of the first fireplaces were built into homes in America the "Waddle and Daub" method was used. The "waddle" was a wooden framework which was rather woven together, and then held fast with "daub" which was a mixture of mud, clay, straw and dung. Clay was then fashioned within this frame and used as a chimney to move the smoke up and away from the fire. Of course the waddle and daub were quickly dried out, and in fact, became combustible, thus not always ending in the best result.

Teddy knew that this house had been constructed with bricks and mortar. In some homes the mortar was a mixture of limestone rich in clay, and mixed with ash and water, which could work well to bind the bricks together. There was not really a patent on this binding material until about 1824 when "Portland Cement" was concocted. Thus, this home built in 1785, could have very good mortar, very weak mortar, or different levels in different parts of the home depending on who mixed the batch for which area.

Teddy spent much of the morning reviewing the chimney at every level. He decided to reappoint the very top of the chimney that went above the roofline, as this was constantly exposed to the elements, and wore down faster than the rest. He found himself almost afraid of the inspection in the cellar. He knew the Widow Loudon might be able to sense his presence, and could, apparently if she willed it, rise up and cause him trouble. Thus he worked very quickly in this area, but the stone was strong, and the mortar true, so he had no problem.

He went back to his aunt's later that afternoon to complete the repairs, and told his cousins and aunt that all was well. But by evening of the next day his cousin Martha, the eldest sister, was again at Teddy's door. This time she was crying as her younger sister now had a severe burn. The burn was caused when her long-sleeved blouse burst into flame in reaction to a sudden and unexpected flare-up of fire. She was only reaching in to stir the stew. She swore on a bible to her family that she had done nothing different this time than she had done hundreds of times before. They all believed her, but this did not take away the awful pain of the burn, nor the grief and shock for them all, at having a child so injured.

Teddy felt terrible. After all, he had been the one who said the chimney was safe, and now another flare-up. He returned to the Farmer's house once more, where he and Uncle John together took stock of the chimney. After much deliberation the best they could conclude was that with the cooler weather the chimney was drawing very hard to pull smoke up to the rooftop from seven different flues.

There were two flues in the kitchen when both the large fireplace and the beehive oven were in use, then two more on the ground floor, one in each parlor. These fireplaces were all necessary for cooking and heating the sitting rooms, including the dining room, which was attached to the kitchen. The three fireplaces upstairs were also all lit by late afternoon to provide comfortable air for sleeping. But one of those fireplaces was in Teddy's former bedroom which no one used much anymore. Since the girls slept in the same bed, and Esther and John slept together in the other bedroom, it was safe to assume that no one would miss the heat generated by the empty guest room fireplace. It was decided that they were to cease lighting that fire. In fact, Teddy pointed out; it would really be a savings in wood to let this room stay chilly when there were no visitors. There were other rooms upstairs which only drew their heat from up the stairwells. The doors to these rooms could be closed when there were no visitors.

And so, the poor bedraggled Farmer clan now had a plan to alter the draw of the fireplace significantly enough, they hoped, to avoid any further flare-ups. But as Teddy left that day he warned them all to be careful for nothing was perfect. It seemed that the youngest sister would recover but the doctor believed she would always carry some scars from this burning, and she suffered through a few nights of feverish sleep from the whole matter.

Teddy told Victoria that they must pray that this last remedy would finally work. Unfortunately they didn't have to pray long before Martha was again at their door, this time reporting that she had been the victim. Her wounds were small, she told Teddy, as she had started to withdraw her hand the moment she saw a hideous face appear in the flames. "I did not allow myself to be mesmerized by it for I knew it bore me evil intent!" she exclaimed. Teddy said he believed her, and was so sorry for her worries and pain. If Uncle John was willing he would meet him at the house the next afternoon and bring enough men so that they might sink the hearthstone, and cover that area over.

Martha was surprised and responded "But how shall we eat without a kitchen fire?" Teddy said that they would have to find the resources to purchase one of the modern cook-stoves like Mr. Benjamin Franklin was writing about. "The chimney for this new stove will use your old flue but all the fire is contained in the box, the stove itself, and nothing can jump out. You place food within it to bake, or you cook things on top as you currently heat your tea sometimes. And until you get your new stove, Victoria and I will see that you are well fed" he added with a smile.

The work was strenuous, but none of the Farmer family, nor any of Teddy's clan, doubted its necessity. Before they finished they had removed the mantle, and boarded up even the beehive oven, to reduce the efforts of the chimney's draw. All of the remaining fireplaces worked beautifully and efficiently. No one was ever again, at least as long as these folks would know, plagued by flare-ups; and the great fireplace and beehive oven would remain covered for close to 180 years. Whatever evil lurked in the cellar would have to find a new means of accessing this family.

11

SEPARATING THE WHEAT
FROM THE CHAFF

Teddy and Victoria had spent weeks focused on the new baby, which was what they believed they should do, and which gave them great joy. Then they had both been consumed by the accusations and the needs of the folks near the graveyard who were being poisoned; followed by their efforts and sacrifice to see that at least some of those people had new land for farming and building. Before this was fully resolved, Victoria had attempted to comfort the Widow Loudon by telling her the results of their research in the town records.

The information given to the widow had not resulted in the reaction for which Victoria had hoped, and baby Jane was actually threatened. But the problem hadn't ended there with the widow simply angry at Victoria and the babe. When she could not get her claws into the baby, she had taken her pain out on the current residents of that house, the former home of her attacker, the judge. Aunt Esther and her daughters were terrified, and even suffered burns, as they worked in their own kitchen!

This grieved Teddy terribly. He felt responsible for being the catalyst of this horror which his dear family had suffered. He spent many hours trying to help his family resolve their problems with the chimney, and eventually helped them to switch to more modern methods of cooking. This proved successful, and his aunt's family was safe at last. But the upshot of all this, for Teddy, was that he had long delayed his commitment, through the church, to offer aid to the recently released slaves from other states. He had raised money for this purpose, and had put his name out as someone who would help others, but he had never delivered on that promise. Teddy told Victoria it was time for him to do more, and he proposed attending some church meetings in Philadelphia where he could connect with citizens needing help.

Victoria told Teddy that she was again with child. He was delighted, but after a day devoted to celebrating this blessing of theirs, he wondered if she would grant him two months to make that trip to Philadelphia, and then he would return fully involved with his own family, but also committed to this mission. At first Victoria was afraid, as she had lost her first husband when he went off to war, but she knew this to be a different situation, and she felt comfortable with her parents' help both on the farm, and with Jane. The new baby was not due for five months. So Teddy set about making his plans for this mission of outreach which should result in more emancipated slaves joining them in the East Apple area. Finally, he believed, his purpose in life would be fulfilled.

However, while Teddy was gone, there was evil brewing in East Apple. Not the evil of the skeletal remains in the cellar, but evil of the nature of man wishing harm on man; people were out to see harm come to Teddy. They did this for two reasons: 1) because they were jealous of Teddy's good fortune in both inheriting property from his grandmother, and marrying a woman with a farm; and 2) because he sought to share his riches with people who had been slaves, and make those people part of the East Apple community.

Teddy's trip involved him in meetings with people of the Quaker Faith, who did not believe in war, or violence of any kind. They believed in the good of each human, and acted toward all mankind with caring. They had been very much a part of the underground railway which helped slaves to escape, and find safety. Now that the war was over they helped to set up schools to educate the freed slaves, and fostered the integration of the former slaves into other areas where they might be treated fairly. Teddy hoped to be a primary contact for the purpose of relocating, and training the former slaves. He had great compassion for them, and all they had suffered at the hands of wealthy land owners. He knew his brother had died to free the slaves, and to help preserve the Union. This also bound Victoria to the cause of the ex-slaves, in memory of her first husband, and as she personally cared about their plight.

Not all people felt compassion for the former slaves. Many white Americans believed that "they should go back where they came from" not acknowledging that the former slaves had been kidnapped from Africa and many islands. Not admitting that these former slaves were innocent of knowing from where they had originated, or that many of them were by now second and third generation, making this the country "where they had come from". The superficial differences in language skills, and skin color allowed those from the slave-owner mindsets, to believe they were somehow superior. Preferences had long been given to slaves with lighter-skin color, but white families did not welcome even these former slaves, into their homes.

This racial problem did not end with the Emancipation Proclamation, nor has it truly ended even as of this writing well more than 150 years later. This may be the biggest horror within these pages. Certainly when Teddy returned to East Apple with two families of former slaves totaling four adults and eight children, he could not have imagined all that would occur to try and thwart his efforts and their freedom.

The first issue was one of housing. Where could these new friends be comfortable within their own family unit? One obvious place was the extra house Teddy and Victoria had on their property. Currently, Victoria's parents lived in this small house, but as they were requiring more and more support it made sense for them to now take the guest room on the ground floor in the main farm building. The little house would be tight for either family, but it did offer an open upstairs sleeping loft, and two bedrooms down, which seemed like luxury to either of these families. It also had the added benefit of sitting back on Teddy's property giving it a buffer from the roadway and, with that, a sense of protection.

The church met to discuss a location for the remaining family. No one seemed able to step forward and offer them a home, but the people who had relocated because their wells were found to be poisoned, were cruel enough to offer those empty homes. This was promptly rejected with the pastor then agreeing to take the former slaves into the parsonage, but he put the congregation on notice that they would all be expected to increase their offerings at church so that "the poor could be fed and clothed." And thus the grumbling among the less charitable picked up in volume.

Teddy's next efforts were put toward the inclusion of these new children in the East Apple school house. It was one room so that all the children could be taken in, and those that could not read, irrespective of age, would learn with all other children who could not read. While the older nonreaders may have felt embarrassed, it was also a golden opportunity for them to learn like every other child in town. For several weeks it appeared that this little community had made a proper accommodation, and everyone was progressing nicely. There had been an undercurrent of complaining as community funds supported the school, but it never reached a peak and, in fact, seemed to die down. Then some of the men from the poisoned well group began blocking the entry to the school and making it impossible for the new children to take their places.

Teddy dropped his hoe on the ground when a neighbor's child came to tell him how his friends were being treated. He ran into the farmhouse to tell Victoria what was going on and left for the school immediately. There was arguing, but Teddy managed to get the bigger men to give way, and the school day commenced although a little late in starting. But it wasn't over.

The next day, Teddy was approached by the constable who informed him that the men from the cemetery area of Rattlesnake Hill Road had pressed charges against him saying that they had been poisoned through their wells, and they knew him to be responsible. Teddy could not imagine how there would be charges for something he was so removed from, but the constable said they had significant documentation.

The documentation turned out to be that Teddy had purchased Rat Poison from the East Apple General Store, just a few months before this group had started getting sick, and that many people remembered seeing him in the graveyard just above this cluster of little farms. They put these two unrelated things together and their suspicious, small view mentalities, created proof from this. Then one of the wives reported seeing Victoria going in and out of the constables' office and determined that she might have been tampering with evidence or trying to sweet talk the constable into ignoring the misdeeds of the husband.

Whether you were in church, or at the General Store, there was little else about which anyone in town could find to speak. Initially Teddy found this reaction almost humorous, but when he realized it was upsetting Victoria, her folks, and even his own parents, he became angry. They didn't need to fight false accusations; the world was full of real problems and he wanted to resolve those for the good of others, not waste time on the make-believe. Talk even named the former-slaves he had brought to town as further proof that Teddy did not care about the citizens of East Apple.

Finally, Teddy turned to the son of an old friend of his grandfather's in Boston. This fellow, Gerald Magnolia, was an astute lawyer, who had handled criminal cases all over the country, and had a reputation of never failing his clients. His fee was anticipated to be hefty, but when he realized who would be his client, and the outrageous, unfounded charges Teddy faced, he insisted his fee would be a bushel of apples to take back to Boston. That gave Teddy and his family some real hope.

Before he came to meet with Teddy, the first thing Magnolia asked Teddy to do, via telegram, was to find out exactly what the poison consisted of, and if there were any people that it did not seem to affect. Teddy went back to the report his group had commissioned from the doctor some months back. Arsenic was suspected because people died so painfully, yet there were no visible traces of the substance. Also, smaller people seemed more affected than did larger people; and the young were hurt worst of all. But how to prove this, and once it was known to be a certainty, how to determine the point

59

of origin of this horrific chemical? Teddy wrote again to the doctor they had employed hoping for more information especially in light of the recent accusations directed at him.

One evening, before Teddy had the benefit of a reply from the scientist, the constable came to their home and arrested him in front of his family, his in-laws, and the former slaves he was struggling to assist. The constable seemed to apologize for the arrest, but stated another one of the folks from the cemetery area of the Rattlesnake Hill Road group had died, and the group was screaming "Murder." The constable felt his hands were tied.

The situation seemed dire to all. Poor Victoria was seven months pregnant and already with a small child, her parents now required some assistance, her husband was in jail accused of a terrible crime, and the recently emancipated slave families had been counting on him for help. She could barely eat or sleep as she was under so much pressure, and so worried about the eventual outcome.

One night, after having been without Teddy for a week, she awoke in the downstairs parlor holding onto a portrait, and seemingly engaged in conversation with her deceased husband, Ben. Shortly after the news of Ben's death, her in-laws had wanted Victoria to have the lovely portrait they had commissioned to be painted when Ben was first entering the Union Army. They hoped it would give the widow comfort. Teddy was happy to have it remain hanging in their home when he married Victoria, but now she felt almost bewitched by it, as if Ben had called her from a dream to stand by his side in the parlor.

12

BROTHERLY LOVE

Victoria had always worked hard on her parents' farm, but when she was still quite young, and Ben Mills had started to court her, she had been thrilled. She was excited by the attention, happy that such a handsome and agreeable person wanted her, and pleased that they would work together to care for her parents' farm and to raise a family. Her wedding seemed like a story one of her girlfriends had made up which they would all giggle over, complete with a white gown her mother had insisted on sewing. Even the church looked grand with the front stairs decorated by baskets of dried flowers. She was so young that her heart had never been broken by disappointments in love yet she seemed to grasp just how precious this time was.

As a newlywed she had not been well prepared for the "wifely duties" in the bedroom. Ben asked her if her mother had told her anything about her body or where babies came from. She said she knew from the farm animals that the male must ride the back of the female to plant the seed and that sometime later the female would squat and bleed and then produce a baby. He agreed that this was mechanically correct but he wondered if she knew anything about the physical pleasure of lovemaking by human beings. She did not, she said, but she had felt strong yearnings when he held her and kissed her and she knew this attraction, as she called it, must be an important component of lovemaking.

And so Ben began slowly, once they were married, to touch Victoria lightly on her breasts and then to increase the intensity of the touch until she felt a pull from deep within her groin as hormones were stimulating her, although she could not know that terminology. He then gently pressed his manhood against her hand and surprised her by how rapidly it became hard. He explained that this was the same experience she was having when he stimulated her breasts but now he was prepared to enter her and deliver seed.

She told him she was both interested in being entered, and afraid of the pain something so large and hard would cause her. He explained that was why it was also important for him to stimulate that area of her body where he would be entering. He began again with his fingers and also added some lanolin so that his touch felt soft and did not scrape her flesh. He took plenty of time and stimulated parts of her she had not heretofore known that she possessed. When Ben finally said it was time to enter her she was almost unable to wait. But once he was upon her and began to thrust into her she did feel pain. It did not last long, and mixed in with the pain there was also a wonderful feeling. Ben apologized promising that the next few times the sensation would get better and better for her and before long she would enjoy this time very much. She said she could see that she would and the couple entered a most happy and intimate phase of their marriage.

Then the war came and all that changed. Ben had gone off and trained and then returned. But the return was primarily to say good-bye, and then he was gone to war, never to return. And yet, in her dream that night she felt Ben's presence with such intensity it was hard to believe her imagination could alone create the sensation. He was pleading with her to help Teddy, his baby brother and her husband, which she very much wished to do. But Ben had something very specific he wanted her to understand, and try as she might, the only sense she could make of the dream was that Ben was saying that the poisoning was his fault. His fault, she asked herself, how could this false arrest of Teddy have anything to do with Ben? But in the dream Ben was determined that she must believe him, and he was as serious as she had ever seen him. He was so insistent that she must tell Teddy those words, "the poisoning is my fault" that she felt compelled to tell her living husband the command of the dead one. She stared into the portrait, now that she had awakened, and promised the image of Ben that she would do as he had asked. So intense was her focus on how realistic this conversation seemed that she actually thought her late husband had winked at her. While that was not comforting, given the circumstances, she put it out of her mind and began to get ready for the day so that she could go to the jailhouse early and provide the message to Teddy.

That day would also bring valuable information to Teddy's lawyer from the group who had hired the doctor to inspect the health of the cemetery's neighbors. There was now a method of examining the hair and bones of a corpse which would reveal if that body had contained arsenic. Arsenic is what was expected as the contaminant of those neighbors' wells and now proof could be found. The doctor's letter stated that the Civil War dead had been preserved with large amounts of arsenic in the embalming fluid. As the bodies decomposed and the rains came, this poison was washed into the ground and could easily find its way through the ground water and into wells. It had just begun to turn up in several other areas.

What would be needed to prove Teddy's innocence was an autopsy from a Civil War soldier buried at the Rattlesnake Hill Burial Grounds, and an autopsy of at least one of the poison's victims. If the arsenic occurred in both it would tell the story. The constable and judge decided, based on Teddy's commitment to the area, that he could be released while this investigation continued. And so he was able to return home to Victoria and his many responsibilities.

The first thing they did upon Teddy's release was to provide the necessary paperwork to exhume Ben Mills, Teddy's brother, and a known fallen soldier from the Civil War. Others quickly volunteered the bodies of their recently demised dead family members as they were anxious to determine the source of the poison, and perhaps find a way to return to their farms. Once the doctor who could test the bodies had arrived it should have been a simple matter, and it would have been, to identify arsenic in the hair of the corpses: but the person in Benjamin Mills' coffin was decidedly not Ben Mills. He was a much shorter man of Asian extraction.

Since this man had been exhumed, and appeared to have been embalmed as part of the Civil War recovery of bodies' effort, the review of his hair went forward. The doctor had his microscope; slides and reference books lined up, and compared all the hair samples to the reference material on arsenic. All were positive for arsenic: an exorbitant amount in the soldier and lethal levels in the farmers who had died. The science wasn't exacting yet amounts in the hair were quite significant. There was a sigh of relief among the committee and the doctor: although one of the group now asked "And who will tell the Mills family that they do not seem to have the body of their beloved Ben?"

Teddy was assisting the family in his guest house as they were learning to dress their first deer. They had spent their lives picking cotton and were now learning new ways to acquire and prepare food. The large buck would mean a lot of food to this household, and it was important to cure the meat and smoke some for when the ground was high with snow making hunting difficult. The father and his oldest son had shot the deer under Teddy's instructions and were enjoying a proud moment retelling the tale of the hunt; a universal ritual among hunters.

Teddy had been anxious to learn the findings of the doctor and the committee as it might be life or death to him. They needed to determine that the graveyard was the source of the poison for him to be exonerated. However, Teddy did not wish to be present when his brother's casket was opened. He had not wanted to see the badly wounded body at the time of the burial, and he certainly wouldn't choose to see it several years after it lay in the ground.

He called out to one of the men as they approached, "Tell me Samuel, may I remain free?" Teddy asked. "You may remain free from jail" Samuel shouted back, "but I hope you actually married a widow!" With that comment Teddy scowled, his eyes grew smaller, and he shook his head and walked away from the butchering in order to learn the details of what his friend was saying. When he was through listening he only said "Maybe his body was never recovered but I feel bad for my folks who were so happy to at least have his remains at home. I hope Victoria can handle this." And then he went back to finish the work he had been doing and to consider this new problem.

13

WHO WAS IN THE CASKET?

Teddy walked toward the main house with his head down appearing to ponder the ground. Victoria observed this approach, and caught her breathe thinking there must be bad news, but when Teddy came through the kitchen door he immediately put her mind to ease with the report from the committee. They had positive proof, he told her, that soldiers' bodies from the Civil War era were embalmed with arsenic, and as those bodies eventually began to decompose the arsenic was leeched into the soil and the ground water. The proximity of those farms to the graveyard had caused the poisoning of their wells. It was not a criminal act and there were considerations that could be made for digging wells deep enough that this ground water would not be a significant issue to the households, if anyone was brave enough to live on those farms in the future.

"That's good news!" Victoria replied.

"Yes," said Teddy, "but there is more. You know they exhumed Ben to use for this testing."

"Of course I know that," said Victoria, easing herself into a chair.

"Well," Teddy continued, "When they opened his casket they found the body of a different soldier."

"How can they be sure after so much time, and nature's corruption of the corpse?" she asked, looking stricken and confused.

"The person they found was a much shorter fellow, and there were several indications that he was Asian," replied Teddy.

It took Victoria a few minutes to absorb all this but she slowly nodded and said "I see."

She was thinking of all the times, before she and Teddy were courting, when she would go to this grave, and pray, and cry, and have conversations with her husband. It was extremely painful to think she had poured her heart out to a stranger. Almost as though he could read her mind Teddy said "I suppose somewhere in this country is an Asian woman praying over Ben's body with no idea it isn't her husband."

"What do we do?" Victoria asked. Teddy said that they must break the news very gently to his parents for his mother would be equally dismayed about praying over a stranger's body. Then perhaps they could contact the people who had "recovered and embalmed Ben's body" and ask them more questions in an attempt to undo the mix up. Eventually they might be able, he hoped, to exchange the caskets.

Then Victoria dropped a startling thought, and went into labor. "What if, somehow, poor Ben is still alive and has amnesia or some injury that does not permit him to communicate?" she asked. Teddy said after so very long that was highly unlikely, but they could send a drawing of Ben's face to see if anyone involved in these returns of soldiers had seen a man of his description. Then he gently led his wife to the birthing room, and called to his mother-in-law. This news about the body was upsetting to everyone, but now they would have a new blessing on which to focus. He would go for the midwife as soon as Victoria thought she was ready, and he would try to simply enjoy the good news of the day and their new baby.

When Teddy returned with the midwife, Victoria was rapidly progressing toward delivery. The midwife and Victoria's mother, boiled water and gathered fresh towels, but little fuss was needed. After having had one baby, Victoria was able to have this baby far more quickly, and with minimal pain. The baby turned out to be a very strapping, and healthy son. After the baby was cleaned and settled into his mother's breast, Teddy took the midwife home. When he returned, he, his in-laws, and even Victoria, ate a little soup, and then they went to sleep as all felt exhausted.

First thing the next morning Teddy rode out to see his parents, and to tell them the news. He gently explained to them how Ben's body had not been in the casket that they had received from the Union Soldiers Recovery group, and buried in their family plot.

Levy said "You mean I've shed all those tears on a stranger?"

And Teddy replied, "Yes we all have, but none so much as you and Victoria. It is a strange occurrence. Victoria now only hopes that some other family has poured love onto Ben's gravesite wherever that may be." And before his mom could give rise to the 'what ifs' concerning a possibility of Ben still being alive, but unable to communicate, Teddy said "And congratulations are in order for we have just had a baby boy around 12:30 AM. He is strong, large and healthy and Victoria is tired but fine!" Then his parents quickly turned to laughing for joy and congratulating them. When asked about a name Teddy replied that they were still considering but would soon decide.

Once home again, Teddy was overjoyed to spend a few minutes holding both his babies while Victoria had a few minutes to herself. He explained to her that it did not seem to be the right day to start searching again for Ben, but that he would discuss it with his folks when they were all used to the idea of the new baby; he did not want any conflict to interfere with the joy they were feeling.

Victoria appeared content to let it go, and only added "There may be another family searching for the man whose body we have although we do not truly know what he looks like." And then the discussion ended.

A few nights later, Victoria was up at two AM nursing her new baby boy, and walking around the house. She stopped in front of Ben's portrait, and facing him squarely, asked him where he was. She said, "We all love you, and want to know that you are able to rest in peace." There was no reply. Then she wondered out loud if the arsenic had been what he meant by something "being his fault?" There was still no reply. So she made light of her time in front of the portrait and said, "I want to introduce you to our new son, three days old. We plan to baptize him and give him your name to honor you." And she held the baby up. That was when she saw it, so clear that she knew she could touch it, there was a tear trickling down Ben's cheek.

Victoria drew in her breathe and said, "I am so sorry, Ben. I do love Teddy but I wish this could be our baby as it should have been." Then she kissed the portrait and hurried back to bed next to Teddy. She did not want to feel all the conflict which now crowded her head; she curled up against Teddy and gently cried herself to sleep. In the morning the portrait looked unchanged and Victoria began to question her memory. Had she really seen the portrait weep?

A few miles away it seemed that Levy could not let the matter go of where her son Ben's body might be. She had her husband send a telegram to the Union Soldiers Recovery Society who had reunified them with the wrong body. She apologized for taking so long to notice the error but explained how this had occurred, and wondered if there was anyone looking for an Asian soldier who might also have died at Antietam. If there was such a person they might possess his remains in East Apple Connecticut, although no longer specifically identifiable. Further they still hoped to receive the body of Captain Benjamin Mills.

The telegram was sent as mail was slow in those times, and no one expected a rapid reply, but Levy was hopeful there would be some word regarding her son; or at least an apology from the Army. She and Ben's father did not mention this request to anyone else in the family, as they wished to avoid hard feelings and conflicts especially as might occur in Teddy.

Teddy was also having the same concerns as his mother, although he planned to avoid delving into any further mystery surrounding his brother's disappearance. He thought it could only be disruptive to Victoria, and she now had her hands full with two little ones. But being a man of conscience he began to dream each night about his brother. By day he began to believe that perhaps he should go to the area where his brother had fought his last fight just to see what he could learn.

Victoria was not at that moment pregnant, and the friends living in their guest house were good, hardworking people, who now understood the farm and its responsibilities. He would pay them a small amount to help Victoria as the husband was extremely able and so were two of the children. With these thoughts in mind he began to prepare for another trip, even before he spoke with Victoria or his parents about it.

14

ANTIETAM

Teddy borrowed a saddle horse from his folks, who, in recent times, had only used a wagon which they pulled with a workhorse. This permitted him to leave both a workhorse, and a saddle horse for use by Victoria, and the friends on their farm. He carried a small tent, as many lightweight provisions as possible, and three canteens plus writing paper. He also carried a shotgun, thinking of it solely as a hunting rifle. He hoped to shoot available game along his journey. Victoria insisted he also take a map and a compass. While he thought he was able to find his way without these items for assistance, as he generally followed known streams and rivers, it soon proved auspicious that he had guidance. The world, and spaces between towns, was wider than Teddy had imagined.

He traveled through New York State from his farm in East Apple, Connecticut, and headed southwest aiming for Antietam Creek in Maryland, the location of the single bloodiest battle in United States history. It was believed that close to 23,000 lives were lost there in a single day. The family had been notified by the Office of the President that Captain Benjamin Mills had died on that September day in 1862. When they had learned more about the magnitude of that battle, Teddy had always wondered how Ben's body could possibly be identified and recovered. Ben was missing for several months before the letter had actually arrived addressed to Victoria. But knowing Ben had been in that melee had not provided them with much optimism during the period with no news from him. "He would have written if he could have" they all thought but no one said aloud.

The battle itself was strategically destined for failure and loss. General Lee had wanted to attack the Union States on their own territory, to give them a sense of the horror and disgust being experienced in the Confederate States. He planned a massive attack to take place in Maryland, along the Antietam Creek, near the heart of Union life. But President Lincoln knew the attack was coming, and refused to lose a battle in the states that were already part of the Union. He strategized with General McClellan, and more and more divisions of soldiers were brought to the sight knowing that their President did not want them to fail. The fighting was so fierce and bloody that it was like grabbing handfuls of young men, and just tossing them into a giant meat grinder then replacing them with more young men. The only way for victory to be declared was by body count; no land was actually given up or repossessed.

Finally, the Union declared victory, but scant proof can verify the veracity of this declaration. Rather the claim did allow President Lincoln to release his first Emancipation Proclamation, but without teeth in it, as the war continued for nearly two more years. The true effect of the battle was the desecration of the soldiers and grief to their families.

There was no place to bury so many bodies, and September in Maryland was not cool. Trenches were dug and mass burials occurred in this manner; not so much to honor the dead, but to try and protect the health of the living from disease and odor. Just as would happen at the end of the war in Gettysburg, citizens working with the dead would be forced to cover their noses with handkerchiefs soaked in peppermint or vanilla to mask some of the smell of the rotting bodies. This combined essence of spices and putrification would forever leave a sickening smell in the minds of those who had been close-by.

When Teddy entered the area of this battle he began to ask questions at any homestead or village he passed. He would begin by introducing himself and where he was from, and then he would state that his brother was known to have perished in the Battle of Antietam Creek on September 17, 1862, but that the family still did not yet have his remains. He would go on to say that the family had sent him on a quest to bring those bones home if it were possible.

Most of the people he met were kind, but not optimistic that he could acquire anything authentically to have been his brother's. They told him tales of farmers continuing to find weapons, and bones on their land every time they cultivated the fields. They described the long rows of ditches which were dug as mass graves, with little distinction being made as to whom was thrown together within them. They said, in many cases, someone had followed the gravediggers, and recorded the names they would shout out as each man was hurled into the pit, but comprehension, and spelling was rather random. A farmer who had been in the battle suggested that when Teddy's family thought they were getting his brother's remains, they might simply have gotten the corpse of someone who was in the same trench.

Teddy tried not to be disheartened; however, there was nothing uplifting about war, and certainly not a civil war where men were, in many cases, literally fighting their own brothers. Teddy remained committed to the values the Union had fought for, but wished with all his entire soul that there had been an alternative to war itself. He also remained steadfast in his hope that there would be some remnant of his brother on these hallowed grounds, if not an actual notation in some ledger as to where Ben's remains were located.

Teddy's travels took him to historic societies, war museums, libraries and clinics for those soldiers still requiring treatment. He saw his share of graveyards, and if they listed any names he read them carefully. He also took note of any Asian names, though they only infrequently occurred; hoping these names might signal some hint of his brother's division, and this might lead him to the family who actually received Ben's body. But nothing seemed to jump out as even a possibility, anymore than did the thousands of other names.

After weeks of combing the area, and making his name known to every group connected to that battle, Teddy began to consider returning home without much new information. He did learn that some of the trenches had been exhumed to provide individual gravesites for a number of the soldiers, but that had been several years before, and lead him no closer to finding Ben. Before leaving the town of Sharpsburg, where Teddy had been able to take a room for a few nights, he decided to stroll around the town one last time. At the end of a park, in the center of town, were the train depot and a railroad crossing. Several men were congregated close to the tracks with a small open fire blazing near them. Teddy walked over to this cluster, and asked if any of these men had been in the great battle here at Antietam. Slowly they all allowed as they had been in that fight. Teddy said it was astounding that anyone had made it out alive, never mind six!

They grumbled a bit, and said that was probably what brought them together; they wanted to hang about with other lucky bastards. Then Teddy told them about his brother who hadn't been so lucky. After a few minutes one of them suggested he might try over at the old mission. There was an abandoned Catholic mission erected for some Spaniards years back, as he said it, which was now just used by a few squatters, guys who couldn't make it back from the battle, "if you know what I mean" the man said tapping his head. "If you can get their attention, maybe they know something," he added.

So, rather than leave, Teddy headed over to the mission. He could see that someone was living there as wood was stacked, fires had been built, and there was evidence of hunting, and eating with bones and pelts strewn about. He asked in a loud voice if anyone was there and then said his name and that he was seeking information of his brother Benjamin Mills from the fourth division, East Apple, Connecticut. There was no response, but Teddy felt something change in the wind, something he could not explain.

He decided to just lie low and wait to see who might appear. After about an hour he heard a shuffle and saw a figure wrapped entirely in black, including a large hood, walking toward him. No matter how he strained he could not see any of the face within that hood. It was almost like black air was supporting the clothing. It was a very eerie feeling, and he coupled it with the thought that this hooded apparition was almost exactly Ben's height. The black hooded fellow had a limp, but having survived this awful war, nearly every man in the area had a strange gait.

The figure stopped about ten feet from Teddy. When it spoke its voice was absolutely Ben's, but it sounded crippled by emotion. It said, "Please do not come any closer, brother, for there is little left of the man you seek. I know not if I am flesh or spirit, beast or man. What I have done, and seen done, removes any hope of humanness. You must go back to your farm and family. Tell them the body you sought remains untraceable, but that I died with thousands of others fighting for my country. Tell them I am at peace, and do not cry more tears over me. I am gone." Then he disappeared into a small slit in the side of the mission wall.

Teddy remained in the ruins of the mission until he had exhausted all possibilities of finding his brother, or even finding the opening which Ben had appeared to pass through. Hunt as he did to discover Ben, when no options remained of where to look he turned from the building, and reluctantly rode back to the boardinghouse. After a quiet and reflective night weighing all that he had seen the previous day, Teddy rode back through the mission yard. He announced his presence, and paused briefly atop his stallion, but receiving no response he finally turned the animal in the direction of Connecticut.

The long ride home had the benefit of allowing Teddy to ponder what he should say once reunited with his parents and Victoria. His heart beat fast at the thought of again holding Victoria in his arms, and he had barely met his newborn son, but there was a dilemma he must sort out before he could confront the many questions his family would rain down upon him. What would he say about Ben? The most forthright approach would be to simply describe all that he had seen, permitting his wife and parents to draw their own conclusions. But could he accurately represent what he had seen; could he say even now if Ben were alive or a spirit? It was true that there appeared to be hunting and cooking going on at the mission, but how could he be sure that Ben did not live, or walk, among others? Had not the men he met near the railroad tracks described the mission as housing "a few men from the battle"?

So there was no evidence that Ben, specifically, required nourishment the way a mortal man would. Further, how had Ben left their meeting site by simply passing through a wall? Teddy had checked, and rechecked, the area which had been next to Ben, finding nothing moveable. A solid man cannot pass through hardened adobe bricks even though priests had brought them to this site from New Mexico, believing them to be blessed. How did Ben disappear through that wall?

Yet Teddy could argue the opposite perspective. There had been such emotion in Ben's voice and such pain. He was a man who had lost everything, everybody, and suffered each day haunted by the memories of gore and carnage, for that was what this battle had been. He had called Teddy "brother" because he still felt a connection. How could Teddy leave him to suffer alone, and in isolation?

Then there were the spoken words of Ben; words that could not be denied, he wished to handle whatever he was going through alone. If Ben was mortal he could only handle the horrors of his life by living in monk-like isolation. He could not pretend to express love, or caring, or any sensitivity; he was too completely devastated by what he had experienced. It was likely his very survival depended on his separation from those he loved; he could not both accept love, and then manage to deny the depths of the horror he had observed, participated in; war could well destroy even a man whose heart remained beating.

Thus, as he neared his Connecticut farm, Teddy concluded that he must honor his brother's wishes and allow him to remain a spirit. It was Ben's choice. Teddy could make it easier for his parents and wife to permit Ben to rest in peace if he denied the possibility of any other choice. For the sakes of all involved he must report that Ben had been dead since 1862.

Teddy's return home was a momentous occasion. His family had missed him, and he was badly needed to assist with the harvest. It was the first harvest for his friends that would mean the vegetables and meat they put up were really for their own use. Until Teddy had brought them to East Apple, from down south, they had still worked in an environment where they were treated as slaves. They were not given a share of their goods commensurate with the work they had performed. Now, if they filled six quart jars with honey, five of those jars would stay in their kitchen, or could be sold by them for their own profit. Teddy kept approximately a sixth of what they earned. They had all agreed to this arrangement as Teddy and Victoria owned the land that they worked on, and provided the housing in which they lived.

But it also meant that if Teddy had a problem, Abraham's services could be temporarily requested until that problem was resolved. So if Teddy got a wagon stuck in the mud during spring, both men worked until it was freed; and Teddy would do the same for Abraham. It was like a friendship, and so that is what the two families always called it.

After he had been home a few nights, Victoria expressed more curiosity regarding his travel to Maryland. He confessed that what he saw this trip, while seeking his brother's remains, had brought him face to face with the war in a manner he had never expected. When she urged him to tell her more of the things that seemed to be disturbing him at night, he told her about the Confederate soldier in the barn full of corpses.

This was a story repeated by someone from Gettysburg, Teddy thought, but all such tales seemed to run into one another. At any rate, it had occurred after a battle with multiple casualties, in which there was no time to properly sort through the bodies and label them or even, so it seems, be certain that they were dead. One poor man awoke in the midst of a pile of some 300 corpses inside a barn, and devoid of any living contact. The weight of the dead bodies kept him from being able to move. Finally, after several days, his shouting and screams were heard, and he was rescued from this mountain of dead. But by then he had lost his mind so defiled was he with the stench and blood from his compatriots. Not only had he lost his mind but he was never again able to speak.

Victoria, naturally enough, recoiled at this story, the images of which would make any person quake. Then she added that she was grateful that Ben had not been the subject of this story, for this poor man had a fate worse than death itself. Teddy agreed with her, and was about to shut their lantern off when she added, "I know it may seem strange, and this is no discredit to you my dear husband, but there are times when I do still feel Ben's presence. I feel his spirit watching over this house and I think he is happy that we are a family. He approves of all we are doing, and that comforts me."

Teddy said he could believe this, and wished his brother peace and still loved him, maybe more than ever after the information he had learned on his trip south. And so this night seemed to end quietly but all this was to change. By midnight Teddy sat bolt upright, sweat running down his back, and a scream nearly emerging from his throat. He choked it back hoping he had not awakened Victoria, but found she was nursing baby Ben in the chair right across from him.

"You are still very restless and anxious about something", she stated rather than asking. Teddy responded that he had seen too much of what remained from the horrible war, and could almost believe that he too had been one of its participants, rather than simply an observer seeking his brother. What he didn't say to her was that, just as with Grandmother Emily, his own actions left him in torment. He had not kept his promise to Emily, and now he had walked away from his own brother who was clearly in need. Would he have left Ben in that abandoned mission if it were not for the fact that he had married his brother's wife? Was his fear of losing Victoria so strong that he would withdraw from the brother who taught him to ride a horse and to make apple cider? Could he be putting his own needs above those of a war hero? Teddy was a sensitive man, and these possibilities drew him further inside his mind to a place that was terrifying.

During this conversation with Victoria he dismissed the real depth of his worries. He said the recent trip, and her fried peppers, had combined to give him nightmares. This made her laugh, and throw a pillow at him. He believed he had gotten her distracted by saying these things, and they both turned their attention to baby Ben.

Later that afternoon Teddy had an opportunity to come back from the fields, to the house, in order to surprise Victoria with a bouquet of fall flowers. As he was about to entire the farmstead from a side door he saw Victoria standing in front of Ben's portrait. He stood still for a moment not wishing to startle her. What he observed startled him, for Victoria was speaking to the painting, and the picture was answering her back.

15

TORN LOYALTIES

Whatever was going on inside of Victoria's head was a mystery to Teddy, and one for which the possible answer frightened him. How could he be jealous of his late brother, the war hero, who had suffered so much, and yet how could he share his wife with a spirit which would always appear perfect to her? A mortal man cannot hope to compete with an angel, and perhaps the projection of his wife's needs, some of which he could only hope to comprehend.

Teddy came around to the backside of the house, thus giving Victoria more notice of his presence, by the sounds he made walking through the house. When he entered the front parlor, where the portrait hung, Victoria seemed to be having difficulty focusing her eyes, and her steps were slightly shaky as though she had not been used to standing or walking for some time. He wondered how long she had actually been in that room communicating with the portrait. With two wee children in the house it seemed a miracle she had not been bothered by crying but perhaps they now napped on the same schedule; at any rate, there was a decidedly dazed quality to her countenance.

Teddy did not wish to make any accusations, for what had he actually seen? Victoria probably talking to herself as she still suffered grief over the loss of her first husband, but he had heard the low murmur of Ben's voice appearing to come from the picture. Perhaps there was something wrong with his own head. Teddy had awakened many times since his encounter with Ben at the mission, wondering what he should have done, and what the state of Ben's mind and health was truly. Maybe he had imagined this entire episode. Thus he inquired if Victoria was well, and when she said yes, he gave her a quick kiss and the bouquet from the field cautioning that he had to get back to work but would see her at dinner time.

Life was busy but fairly normal following that day, and Teddy put those moments by the portrait out of his head. The only matter which was beginning to be noticeable was the decrease in marital contact between them. Before Teddy had left for the South they had continued to have sexual relations even though it was quite soon after the birth of baby Ben. He would not wish to pressure Victoria while she tended to the small children, but she was frequently the one who turned to him in bed and began to caress him in a manner which always got his attention. That was, she had been, but she had made no such moves lately. Well, he thought, she is still recovering from both childbirth and having been so burdened by chores while I was away. And, as Teddy too was very tired, he let night after night pass without any intimate contact between them.

Then one night he awoke, as often he did, when Victoria had to turn from him to nurse one of the babies. She still allowed Jane to take the breast during the night in order to keep the household quiet, even though Jane was placed on soft foods once her brother was born; so it wasn't unusual for Victoria to be nursing both children in the wee hours of the morning. Teddy glanced over at them, he thought, while she is doing all this, little wonder she is not interested in making more babies. But on this occasion, Teddy noticed that her side of the bed was empty yet both children were deep in sleep.

He silently arose from the bed to see if Victoria was feeling well for there was a chamber pot in their room, and thus little cause to leave the bed chamber. He walked steadily but softly down the bedroom stairs certainly not wishing to disturb the sleeping children and thus cause chaos. When he walked around the backside of the chimney approaching the front parlor he stopped dead in his tracks. There, on the braided rug, in front of the portrait, was his beautiful wife engaged in the sex act, missionary position, with the man he had last seen in the mission! His brother, cloaked in a black cassock, was making love to his wife, and she gave every indication of enjoying it.

He watched spellbound for a few moments. Ben moved from suckling Teddy's babies' milk from his wife's full breasts, to placing his mouth between her legs and then entering her, setting them both into frantic motion as though he might propel her body across the floor and through the wall; yet they remained in the same spot. All during which Victoria was crying out and moaning until Teddy was about to burst wide open as he tried to contain the scream within him. If his mind had not conjured up those beautiful children sleeping in the bedroom above them, he was not sure what he might have done; so intense was his horror and his pain.

Finally, Teddy cried out "Cease and desist! I cannot bear this nor will I have it in our own home!" Victoria looked up suddenly appearing as though she was coming out of a trance and Ben simply disappeared like vapor with a wind shift. Teddy fell to his knees and said in a most anguished voice "Victoria what are you doing?"

She blinked her eyes several times, and looked at him responding "I don't know what I am doing here on the parlor floor. How did I get here?"

Teddy slowly and painfully explained what he had experienced and witnessed. Victoria shook her head vigorously from side to side, protesting and insisting, over and over again, that what Teddy said could not be true. She was crying very hard and appeared to genuinely be unaware of what she and Ben had been doing. She was close to hysterical when first Jane, and then baby Ben began crying.

Teddy then relented, letting his anger go, and his insistence that he had witnessed fornication between his wife and brother. He believed that Victoria must have been the victim of a spirit, and not responsible or even aware of what she had been doing. He held her and comforted her so that she might calm her fear and go upstairs with him to feed, and comfort their babies. After several minutes she was able to speak and seemed unconscious of pulling her nightshirt closed over her bosoms, and straightening out the skirt which was tangled about her. She allowed Teddy to help her stand, and together they mounted the stairs to their bedroom where they both greeted their children with happy voices.

Teddy assisted in the double feeding and rocking of the children. When Jane and the baby fell asleep, Victoria looked very drawn and exhausted, almost as though she had been totally consumed. She shakily reached for the bed and Teddy pulled the quilt up over her. He stood above her for a few moments trying to decide what he should do, and then walked around the bed to his side and carefully lowered himself into the bed beside his sleeping wife and next to their beautiful children.

He wondered if this could have been a dream but felt sure of all he had seen, and wondered what could happen to them next. Was their close and precious relationship to be shattered by this? Did Victoria even know what she had been doing? Did his brother have her under a spell or some sort of demonic trance? How could Teddy break this? After all it was his right as her husband and the father of their two dear children no matter who his brother had been to her during his life.

The next morning Teddy arose early and began the chores even getting the fires started so Victoria would have less work. He rode over to their guest house and saw that Abraham was already awake and moving about. He beckoned Abraham to join him in the yard. Once they were together Teddy told him he had an unusual request. He wanted Abraham to schedule a special wagon trip into Hartford within the next few days. He had something out of the ordinary he thought would sell in one of the city auction houses as a keepsake of the war, and his family really needed to steer away from sad memories, he explained to Abraham.

Further, he informed Abraham, I want you to keep whatever money this portrait brings you, as your reward for selling it. I want the proceeds of this sale to profit you and your family. It would mean a great deal to Victoria, and I to know that picture profited the folks for which that soldier fought and gave his life.

And with that he rode back across the lawn to properly wrap and protect the painting of his brother which was now to change hands.

16

THE PUNISHMENT

Both Teddy and Victoria were drawn and uneasy that next day. Teddy had already been up and had removed Ben's portrait placing it within wooden frames and rough cloth to protect the picture from damage. This wrapped package was now in the rear of an ell attached to their barn, and awaited a day when Abraham would be able to take the long ride into Hartford in search of a dealer who would pay him for this remembrance of the war. Teddy had already spoken to Abraham before either household was fully up and about.

But now Teddy had to bide his time to see how Victoria planned to act following her interlude with his brother. He was willing, even anxious; to do all he could for her, and hope she would go back to her loving, happy ways with him. The children meant the world to them both, and her parents appeared most comfortable being a part of their everyday household with Teddy treated nearly as a son. This life had been everything he had ever wanted, and all he wished for was for that happiness to return and endure. When Victoria arose that morning, he had readily observed the dark circles under her eyes and her manner seemed somewhat subdued. Still this could all be attributed to the lack of solid sleep from the previous night, something they both had experienced. Now the proof would be borne out by how she reacted and spoke to him.

He could detect nothing definitive in the brief time he was able to linger near her before rushing out to perform chores. He decided to concentrate on work and thus provide Victoria space to gather her feelings together. She simultaneously had to care for the children, and cooperate with her mother as they always did, to manage a bit of gardening, egg gathering, washing and butter churning. It would take a committed effort to get through her day, and if Victoria managed it, he thought that would speak well for their marriage.

By evening time, when Teddy was stacking more wood by the shed door, he finally felt prepared to see how the household was running. To his relief and surprise Victoria was wearing one of her prettier dresses and the house was filled with the aroma of roasting meat and baking bread. He entered by declaring that it smelled like a feast in the house, and both women looked up smiling. He went to Victoria and kissed her cheek to which she cooperated fully, no pulling away, and handed him Jane saying they should both wash up for dinner. Of course, Teddy always washed before he entered the house, given the messy nature of his work in the fields, barns and woods, but he happily took Jane out to splash in the wooden bucket which always made her giggle.

Next, he scooted Jane into the house ahead of him, as she was now walking, and Teddy gathered a great armful of wood to burn beside them as they ate. He passed through the parlor only glancing quickly to be certain that his brother's portrait had not magically returned to its previous spot on the wall; and felt a surprising relief to see that it was indeed gone. Had he imagined that it might come back on its own, he wondered. What power could that canvas, wood and oil possess? Obviously it served as some type of medium beyond the one of art and culture, or it could not have housed his brother's spirit as he knew it did.

The meal progressed nicely with Teddy, his mother-in-law, and Victoria all taking various turns to sooth the children as the adults ate. Victoria's father was able to care for himself, but not to manage much else, which they all accepted at this point. He had certainly been an excellent farmer in his time. No one mentioned the empty space on the wall in the next room, and Teddy began to feel encouraged about the future of his family.

85

They passed an uneventful evening primarily focused on getting the children's needs taken care of and putting them up to bed. Teddy played a couple games of checkers with his father-in-law, and discussed the price of grain and feed for the coming months. Victoria and her mother made cocoa and did a little needle work in the parlor by the fireplace, and then Victoria told Teddy she had better go up to bed before baby Ben would wake for his next feeding. Teddy stood up from his last game with her dad, and announced he would be right up after he did a quick look around the barn.

Most evenings it was Teddy's habit, as it had been his father's, to check on the livestock and particularly the chickens, to be certain nothing had disturbed them after dark. While they lived in town, all manner of critters were not afraid of robbing them of eggs or chickens, if they could gain easy access. One deterrent was the scent of humans, so the fact that Teddy went out there every night left a lingering reminder. Still, his best weapon had always been a good old barn-sleeping dog, and he enjoyed checking on the dogs to be sure they were home and on duty. The dogs usually kept the larger predators away, such as the coyotes and, an occasional wolf who, if hungry enough, would try to take a lamb or calf.

Then there was that other predator, men determined to take what wasn't theirs. Teddy knew that a walk through the barn before bedtime had multiple purposes which made it worth him stretching his legs in the evening no matter how busy he had been all day. This night was like all those other nights, with the added task of checking to see if the painting was still in the shed waiting for Abraham to pick it up. To Teddy's delight it was gone. He had arranged with Abraham to come by and collect the art the night before he planned to go into Hartford. When Teddy discovered the painting was missing, it was his duty to hitch up the workhorse to the wagon, and lead it over to Abraham the next morning. So, their plan was now in motion. Just having the commitment made, and the portrait out of the barn, gave Teddy a deep sense of relief.

The primary reason he had asked Abraham to take the art, and sell it, was so he would not know where it had gone. Teddy wanted to be able to tell everyone, especially Victoria and Levy, that he had no idea where it was and, of course, from here on out, that would be true. He also didn't wish to be away from the entire operation of the farm and his wife and kids so soon after returning from his last major excursion. He wanted to be sure Victoria knew he was there, and that she could count on him. He didn't want to fear that another predator, man or spirit, might lay claim to what was his.

Knowing that the portrait was now with Abraham, and that there did not appear to be any vermin about, no matter what their size, Teddy went happily up the stairs to his bedroom where Victoria and the children should be sleeping. He undressed in the dark, to be certain he did not disturb anyone, and he crawled into bed next to his wife. As he eased himself into bed she stirred and rolled towards him, and whispered "I know you have taken the portrait of Ben. That is good, for it was giving me strange nightmares, but will you tell me where it is? I just don't wish to happen upon it by accident." Teddy thought for a moment and then responded, "I did take it down but now I have no idea where it is but you should never see it again so do not be troubled." She replied, "All right." Victoria said nothing further; she simply rolled away from Teddy and appeared to fall asleep. He sighed lightly and then, containing his frustration, rolled the other way also falling into a restless sleep.

Thus, the weeks began to pass with a mixture of joy and sorrow. By day they seemed the same happy, hardworking family that they had been from the beginning of their relationship, but by night they were merely cooperative and friendly, like good natured siblings, but not the passionate man and wife that they had been, and for which Teddy longed.

Teddy could no longer live without physical love. Seeing his beautiful wife each night, feeling her warmth next to him, observing her full breasts as she nursed their children, taking in her scent and yet constrained from reaching out for her by the unspoken 'spirit' between them; he was becoming less of a man in his own eyes, and so he became determined to change this flaw in their marriage.

The following evening he made certain that Victoria knew he had bathed before bedtime hoping this might provide a hint to her of his intentions so that she would prepare herself, if not physically, at least emotionally, for his intended actions. Then, not long after the evening meal, and only shortly after he had completed his walk about the barns, he suggested to Victoria that they might do well to retire early to their bedchamber. She seemed neither pleased, nor displeased, with this suggestion. Victoria rose when Teddy made this request, and they each carried a child, and bid her parents goodnight.

Once in bed Teddy immediately encroached upon Victoria's space. He placed his hand upon her bosom squeezing it both playfully, and yet also rubbing his body against her in a manner that fully disclosed his physical desire for her. She pulled back from his caresses, as much as the small space he had left her permitted; then she spoke clearly into his ear. "I have not had my courses for near two months, so please be gentle least we disturb the babe who is within me."

Teddy nearly jumped out of the bed, and would have, if not constrained by thoughts of disturbing his children. "How is that possible?" he said as quietly as he could manage given the shock of her comment. "We have not had sexual contact since before I left for the south?"

"But, of course we have!" was her reply. "Don't you remember waking up with me on the parlor floor and the bodice of my night dress was pulled wide open, and my insides were wet with your love? My body felt as though we had performed many acts upon that braided rug. Surely, we must have created a child that very night. Then you helped me up to bed as I was most exhausted."

"But," Teddy struggled to continue with thoughts racing through his head; do I deny this child is mine? Do I try to convince Victoria that she has conceived through a most unholy spirit? Or do I play along with her belief that she and I made this baby? If I do, I protect Victoria, and perhaps save my marriage, but what will this child be? Will we have another sweet little babe or a beast from another world?

And so Teddy continued, "But, you think we conceived the child that night?" Teddy said.

"I certainly do," said Victoria. "And why not, when have we ever felt such passion?"

"Yes," stammered Teddy, "When indeed."

Teddy was unable to make love to Victoria that night. The shock of her pregnancy and her certainty that it was his child and not his brother's, or the spirit of his brother, shook Teddy to his core. He had quickly made a decision to stick by Victoria for the good of the family, yet he could not imagine what this child would be like. But of one thing he was sure, he would check with Abraham to be certain that that portrait of Ben was far away from them, never to return. He fell asleep looking forward to learning more from Abraham in the morning.

17

A DARK SKINNED TRAVELER

When Teddy approached Abraham, asking him to explain a bit about the trip into Hartford to sell the Civil War soldier's portrait, Abraham felt anxious. Although he trusted Mr. Teddy, as he insisted on calling him, he wasn't sure how to describe the situation in which he had found himself. He happily left East Apple with the family wagon and the well wrapped box, but soon he was out of his comfort zone. While he traveled in East Apple everyone knew who he was, where he lived, and for whom he worked. But, as he drove down the main road toward Hartford, he began to encounter what he thought of as 'unfriendly stares' from total strangers. As more of these strangers drove past Abraham, he began to see their attention as perhaps even hostile. He greeted each passer-by with a touch to his hat and a friendly "Good morning sir!" but did not hear or observe that these greetings were reciprocated, excepting in one or two cases.

He had only driven into Hartford two other times, and both of these trips were with Mr. Teddy. With a Whiteman in the wagon no one had seemed to question Abraham's behavior or his actions. But, a Black-skinned man, alone in a good wagon with a valuable horse and a package wrapped so that the contents were not readily known, that seemed to provoke too much interest. The more he traveled that morning, and the further he got from home, the worse became Abraham's ability to tolerate the fear. About one third of the way into Hartford, Abraham saw a signpost which read Town of Willington. He was now on a large town green in view of a church, a blacksmith, a general store, a schoolhouse and a chair caner.

Abraham believed he had been very blessed with the masters who had owned him earlier in his life. At a young age, although he had received his share of whippings and still bore the scars, he had also received some education. Initially the mistress had wanted all slaves educated enough to read the Gospel. He and the other slaves were required to attend church on Sundays and expected to sing the hymns from the hymnals. Abraham knew his name came from the bible, and he enjoyed the singing; being required to go to church once a week was a much nicer request, or demand, than he usually had to fulfill, so church represented a treat. When his owners tied learning to read to this requirement, Abraham took it as a blessing. He was fortunate enough that he recognized and remembered the words quite easily making new hymns fun to learn.

When he was sold to his last master, the fact that he could read was used as a way to increase his value, even though most masters did not want their slaves to be literate. These masters believed it would make the slaves less likely to follow rules, and more inclined to start trouble, and demand their rights if they were able to read the propaganda being sent around by groups like the abolitionists. However, the master who purchased Abraham wanted a slave who would help with the business end of the plantation as this master was getting older, and slower, and was in need of someone who could count, add and list the goods coming in and going out. Abraham liked this work. He had started a family during this time, and had not rushed away as soon as it was legal to go, because he had known no other life.

Still, reality was that he was not getting paid for his labor, and that the master could choose to sell his wife, or his children, without ever discussing it with Abraham. So, Abraham became very focused on finding a way to freedom after he knew about the Emancipation Proclamation. It took several years before the church and the Quakers discovered a possibility of moving Abraham East with his family, and guiding him to be sponsored by Teddy's church in East Apple, Connecticut.

Teddy had only wanted to be "a friend" to Abraham, but Abraham was too polite to call this man by his first name, thus the Mr. Teddy. Abraham felt he owed Mr. Teddy a great deal for all his help including the roof over his head; that was why he had readily agreed to take the portrait away and to sell it. It was a surprise bonus that he had been instructed to keep whatever he made from the sale. He had then been very excited about the prospect of the extra cash as it meant that for the first time, they could put aside a little money. He dared to hope that maybe one day his family could own a place of their own, and this would be the start. But now that Mr. Teddy wanted more information about the sale of the portrait, Abraham was not so certain of what was to happen next.

Part of his concern arose because he had decided not to go all the way to Hartford to sell the painting. When he had pulled over in Willington, he went up to the front of the general store and saw a list of the types of business conducted within its walls. One item on the list read 'used furniture'. He wondered if a secondhand portrait would be considered as 'used furniture' so he asked the storekeeper. He was told that depended on the quality of the painting, it could be furnishings, or trash. So, the shopkeeper came out to the wagon, and the two men examined the portrait very carefully. The shopkeeper was visibly impressed by the quality of the art, and the importance, in that area, of a Union uniform on a Civil War soldier.

Abraham explained that his friend had wanted this picture, of his brother, sold as it stirred up too much emotion within the family. "Well," the shopkeeper said, "As long as you didn't steal it, I'll be glad to take it off your hands." Abraham liked the amount they then negotiated for the painting. It also meant he could get back to East Apple relatively quickly, thus avoiding prolonged exposure to the stares of strangers who, all seemed to be considering him as a thief.

Since the money was his to keep, and as it meant he could then put more time in at the farm, Abraham had thought the sale of the portrait had been handled well. But now that he would have to explain this to Mr. Teddy, he felt a bit less sure of the decision to sell it in Willington rather than going all the way into Hartford.

Abraham began his report on the sale of the painting by explaining how difficult it was for a Blackman to travel without attracting the wrong kind of attention. Teddy acknowledged that he had not fully appreciated the situation when he asked Abraham to do the job and apologized for the worry it must have caused Abraham. Then Teddy encouraged Abraham to go on with the story.

Abraham explained his good fortune in stopping in the Town of Willington just to see what that town had to offer. He was pleased that the General Store shopkeeper had been reasonably friendly and most helpful once he saw the portrait. He stated that to avoid more unwanted exposure, and to have more time to work, he had taken this offer and left the painting with that man.

Teddy had mixed feelings. First, he was grateful to Abraham for the help, and next, he did admire Abraham's resourcefulness in finding a good solution to his difficulties in traveling to Hartford. The third reaction was one of which he planned to keep mostly to himself. He was disappointed that the portrait had not made it further away from East Apple before it was sold. He wanted to ensure that neither his mother nor Victoria would happen upon it in someone's home, or be told that a friend had seen the portrait on display at a mutual friends' house. Teddy wanted the painting gone and far away from them.

Teddy told Abraham that he did not want the painting to be close enough to stir up emotions again for his mother or wife if they happened upon it, but he reassured Abraham that there was now little chance of that happening. Then he changed the focus of the conversation so that the poor man would not feel punished for doing a good thing for him. They spoke of selling milk at the Friday market near the church and how much they should bring. Teddy realized it would be best to put this worry out of his mind, but he did wish to get a chair caned for Victoria. He would take the chair to Willington early the next week and see if he could learn more about the location of the portrait.

When he reached Willington a few days later he went to the caner's first. He had arrived with the chair strapped across his horse and tied to the saddle. This kept him from having to take the wagon and follow a more arduous route to this neighboring town. Once he left the chair for its repairs, he journeyed into the General Store. Initially he roamed the store hoping not to see his brother hanging on a wall and staring back at him.

When Teddy felt certain that the portrait was not on display, he took the shopkeeper into his confidence just to inquire about the whereabouts of the painting. He was told that a 'dealer' had come through the store on Saturday, and had been quite interested in the craftsmanship of this work of art. He had immediately purchased it, and as far as the Willington shopkeeper knew, the painting was now nestled somewhere in Massachusetts. Teddy backed down on his interest saying only "If it had lingered for some time, we might have wanted it back but, I am relieved that it has found another home."

He left Willington feeling satisfied that Ben's portrait had left the state.

When he arrived home for the evening meal, he discovered Victoria was pacing the floors and her mother was caring for the children. Victoria told him that she had gone into labor and that the pains were already hard. "But", Teddy tried to protest, "Is this not extremely early for delivery?"

Victoria pulled aside her apron and bid Teddy to touch her abdomen. Upon doing so he found her both large, and distended, and could feel her body quiver as another contraction hit her. Stammering that this seemed nearly impossible to believe, Teddy asked if he should go get the midwife. Victoria said "Yes, dear, and perhaps you need to make all haste." With that declaration Teddy nearly flew down the street to capture the needed help.

By the time he returned, Victoria had made her way to the birthing room, but was writhing in agony and clutching the sheets with all her might. When the midwife and Teddy attempted to render assistance, Victoria became nearly hysterical. She was fighting for air yet screaming out any air which she managed to take in. Her face was extremely red but her arms and legs were white and cold, and she was shaking badly. "I think she is in trouble" the midwife offered. "Perhaps you had best go for the doctor right away!" Teddy was trying very hard to cope with this emergency which had suddenly beset them. He could not believe that Victoria was giving birth so early in the pregnancy. He was further astounded by the incredible pain which accompanied each contraction even though these were all early on in a typical birth. And further, he recalled just how easily she had birthed baby Ben. He wondered why this baby, presumably smaller than full term Ben, was causing such extreme difficulty.

Bewilderedly, he led the doctor into the house. They arrived upon a shocking scene for; there was a great deal of blood not only on Victoria and the bedding but also covering the midwife, and the walls of the room. Teddy had to quickly sit down before he fainted. Yet the doctor barked orders at him to bring boiling water and towels immediately. Fortunately, his mother-in-law had the foresight to prepare these items and still care for the little ones, so Teddy managed this much. But his fear level was quickly cresting beyond anything he had ever experienced. He did not want to lose his dear Victoria.

As he paced the parlor floor, he wondered why his brother had hated them so much that he did this to them? What had his brother learned of death or life that would lead to this horrible situation? Would Victoria survive this child's birth, and what would become of the baby? Was it to be a monster and the murderer of its mother? He was so distraught that a most bizarre remedy entered his head. Perhaps if he begged Ben's forgiveness for ridding the house of his Ben's portrait, Ben would allow Victoria to live. Could he appease his angry brother and even beg to have the child spared, or was this all too much and too late?

And so Teddy fell to his knees in the parlor and begged Ben to save his family.

18

ANSWERED PRAYERS

Although one would think that Victoria was doing all of the hard work in this baby producing effort, Teddy's anxiety had worn him out. While he was on his knees praying, calm had come over him, and he must have fallen asleep, or passed out, from exhaustion. It was obviously many hours later when he awoke and discovered himself on the parlor floor. Suddenly, recalling what was transpiring in the house, he stumbled to his feet and rushed down a corridor and into the birthing room.

He could not have been more surprised, or pleased, with the scene before his eyes. There sat Victoria in a clean nightdress and propped up on snow white pillows. Her face had a radiant glow, and her hair looked freshly washed and full around her face. She was stunning and sweet. In one arm she held baby Ben, who appeared rather large by contrast, to the newborn in her other arm. Both babies were suckling, and both seemed dreamy and content.

The walls no longer bore blood or even a hint of stain. In the chairs at the foot of the bed were two sleeping women: one was Victoria's mother, and the other was the midwife. There was no longer any sign of the doctor, nor did he appear to be needed. Victoria looked up and greeted Teddy's gaze with a smile. He moved toward her asking if she was alright, and was the babe also fine. She told him "Yes, all is well, and you have another daughter."

Teddy then ventured further into the room, explaining that when last he had seen her, she had been in great distress, and he had feared for both her life, and that of the child. "Fear not," was Victoria's reply. "Right after the doctor's arrival it was as though a golden light had entered this room. My pain ceased, and the baby came without further urging. She was large and strong, and seemed to breathe life back into us all. Mother held her and bathed her, then lay her in a basket; and while she slept I was bathed and the bedding changed. After speaking to the midwife, the doctor left, wishing us all well. The midwife borrowed a frock from mother so she too could bathe, and then used her petticoat to wipe down the walls. I was surprised by this, but she said they were old clothes and she needed to clean the mess."

Teddy leaned over the bed and kissed Victoria with real passion. He said, "I have never been so happy to see anyone in my life," to which she simply smiled contentedly. "Soon" he added, "I will have to find the doctor and thank him for saving my family for certainly there was a miracle here last night." Then he said he thought it best if she took some broth, as liquids would leave a woman quickly after blood loss, and while nursing two babies at once. She smiled and agreed soup would be grand.

Teddy reheated some chicken stock he knew his mother-in-law had made for Victoria. He took the babies, and placed baby Ben in a cradle, and the new child in a box stuffed with a pillow. Then he headed for the staircase to look in at Jane, who must be in her crib in their bedroom. As Teddy passed through the parlor, he was startled by a large dark and oval shape hanging on the wall, his brother's portrait had returned.

The sight caused him to stagger, but he recovered his footing and ran up the staircase in a burst. It suddenly seemed urgent to make certain that Jane was alright. His heart quickened as he be held her sweet face. He gently touched the back of his hand to her cheek rejoicing that she felt warm and well. Then, without disturbing her, he walked quietly down the stairs and into the parlor. He thought he had better check on Victoria again, but something held his feet in place in front of the portrait. There must be words that would come to him, a comment he could make, or a question he could ask. But all that came out was "Thank you Ben for saving Victoria, she is my life."

He thought he caught a fleeting smile around the corners of his brother's mouth, but just as quickly as it appeared, it also disappeared, and the lips were as composed and neutral as that of a gambler not wishing to have his face read. "I will thank you again, and then I must go care for my family. I think it would be best if we do communicate directly at some point. I must understand your needs and your place in this family." With that statement, Teddy headed for the birthing room to do anything he could for his family.

That afternoon Teddy met with Abraham to mend some fences out toward the back of the property. While they worked, Teddy decided to tell Abraham that he had thought it better not to let the portrait go and, at Victoria's urging, he had recovered it from a dealer in Massachusetts. Abraham instantly stated he would return Mr. Teddy's money to him for the amount of the sale, but Teddy insisted that there had been no charge for its return. Shaking his head and sounding a bit bewildered, Abraham reluctantly agreed to keep the money if Mr. Teddy was certain that was fair. With no further mention of the matter the men resumed their work.

Back in their bed that evening, Victoria confided she had a tale to tell Teddy. She said "I truly felt I was dying yesterday, when the labor pains started, and the blood commenced to flowing as though I was a bursting cloud rather than a woman having a baby. The pain would not allow me to think, and the blood was taking me away. I felt I was in rushing water with you, Jane, baby Ben and even my mother trying to call me back. But your voices were getting further and further away as I was rapidly pulled downstream by the water. Then I crested at a great waterfall and was just about to crash over this wall of rock and water, when I was gripped by a spirit and pulled back to my family. A black cocoon was all around me and I knew I was safe."

"I felt at peace, although I could not be certain to where I was now being propelled, or to whom, and then I awoke to a warm bath with my mother and the midwife telling me I had done a wonderful job, and delivered a beautiful baby girl. I was truly astounded, but so relieved and grateful. I wanted to tell you but could not see you in the room."

"After a time, the others finished with their cleaning and the doctor came and went. I found myself alone with my two youngest babies, and it felt like a beautiful dream. It seemed I could ask for anything and it would be given to me, but all I really wanted was you and the children." At that she paused and added, "Or perhaps, in some strange way, I wanted Ben as well. He and I had shared such dreams before he went into the Union Army, and I believed he would return to me and make them come true."

Teddy thought long and hard upon hearing these words. He held Victoria for a moment and then said, "You know his portrait is back don't you." And she responded, "Teddy, I think I asked him to return just before the pain and bleeding stopped. I felt somehow he would be able to help me, when I might be beyond help. He is dead, and I was about to be. We made a connection through a hazy gate between our two worlds."

Teddy responded, "And at almost that same moment I was on my knees in the parlor begging him to save you and the baby. I was trying to pull him back here to keep you from oblivion for I could not bear to lose you. Perhaps, we shall have to share what we can of life with a man who is neither dead, nor alive, but loves and sometimes hates us all."

"He tried to explain it all to me." Victoria added. "When he surrounded me as I was rushing away in the water, and as he was pulling me back, he said I should not fear for he was now a portal between the two worlds: of the living, and of the dead. While his life as a man was over, and with that, both joy and love were gone; still he could serve to protect or punish those in the world around him. Those, whom he had loved or had reason to care for, would always be able to reach him, but he would be alert to any who tried to misuse this access, and that misuse could lead to rather dire consequences."

19

RAISING OUR SPIRIT

It was not long after her birth, that Teddy and Victoria became consumed by the idea of naming their new baby girl, Grace. It seemed to all who knew the story of her extraordinary birth, and to all who met her, that this was a special baby. The couple didn't know what Ben thought of the name, for they didn't feel it appropriate to put so simple a question into the portal for a response; this much they felt they should be able to manage on their own. "Grace" not only had a lovely sound to it; but described the blessing they experienced by her having been saved, along with her mother, on that near tragic night.

Life had then calmed down with only the ordinary ups and downs, such as too much rain one year, and too little the next. Weather plays a major role in farming, but none of it was so extreme that the residents of East Apple had to go without food. Some years the menu might have been limited, but all managed to survive. A smart farmer had an extra cow or goat that could be sacrificed in order to prevent starvation, so long as the following year brought better luck and richer crop production.

Teddy returned to normal relations with Victoria, save that he was extremely careful to block conception, for he could not bear to see her go through another delivery. Victoria understood his wishes, as she too had been traumatized by a good part of that last experience in which Grace came into the world. Jane was always peppy and fun, baby Ben enjoyed teasing his sisters as the only male sibling will do, but Grace was a bit less predictable. As the years went by, Teddy and Victoria continued to observe more disquieting behavior from her.

When her grandfather was struggling to walk, even a few feet, she would simply stare at him. Never did she offer him a hand, or ask if she could bring something to him, or chat with him about anything that might entertain him. She appeared quite disconnected from the poor old fellow. He, on the other hand, was amazed by her beauty and agility. She was the only blonde of his three grandchildren, and that appeared to bewitch him into thinking that she was somehow angelic. She could also climb any tree, or even show up at the peak of the barn, and report as to how many bats were sleeping in the cupola. Extraordinary, he would always say, extraordinary.

For his part, Teddy was simply relieved that, as Ben and he had looked so much alike, no one questioned Grace's paternity. Teddy did not want any shame or superstitious mumbo jumbo connected to her. Nor did he want any dispersion cast upon his beautiful Victoria whom he held to be utterly innocent of this last pregnancy's occurrence. Although, Teddy had witnessed his wife in the sex act with his late brother he knew she was in a trance-like state, a fugue, and had no recollection of what had transpired.

It must be added that Grace's odd behavior, if we may call it that, did not dissipate as she grew, but became most profoundly objectionable. One of their barn dogs had a litter of six brown and white puppies. The dogs were living in the barn and nursing from the bitch a good part of each day. All three of the children made frequent trips to that area to watch the babies nurse and to pet them. Teddy encouraged that petting as it helped ensure the pups would be more manageable as they grew older. The dogs needed to have human contact if they were to be friendly with people, and to take orders from their masters. Without that human contact the animals would be wild acting and often snappish.

One evening, after Teddy had made his rounds of the premises, Grace announced she wanted to go into the barn one last time too, like her dad did. Having just been out there, Teddy felt no concern for the child to be just a few paces from the house in an area he knew was empty of trouble. After about ten minutes, Grace returned, and simply announced she would go up to bed early.

First light the next day, Teddy and one of their hands, for they were now prosperous enough to hire help, met in the barn for milking. There, they saw the bitch on her side nursing four pups, with two dead ones under her head. All the pups had previously been named and spoken for by the kids, and their friends. The two dead pups were ones which had been chosen by Jane and Benny as their own pets. This observation sickened Teddy, and he wondered how he could make this okay with the family.

He and Victoria had an intense discussion with Grace that night while her brother and sister were crying in their rooms. As was her nature, Grace steadfastly denied any knowledge of what could have happened to these pups and swore on a stack of bibles that they had been fine when she last saw them. Grace even concluded the discussion by bursting into tears, and saying how dear those poor little dead doggies were. Her parents had to let the matter go for the night, but they were very unnerved by it.

Six months later, her grandfather died while ten-year-old Grace had the responsibility of making certain grandfather had everything he needed, and to check on him every thirty minutes. The rest of the family was involved in a church pageant for which Grace held no regard. Grandfather could no longer do for himself, so he needed her there in any case. When the grownups returned, the child was ashen, and again swore that he had not called out for her. She threw herself into mourning him as though they had been closely bonded. She begged to be given a locket of his hair, and swore her never ending love to her grandmother; that she would never allow her grandmother to be lonely. She would stick by grandmother's side as a tribute to this great man who had just died. They all knew this later would not be the case, but grandmother insisted that Grace not be punished as she was just a little girl.

A week later, when Victoria found Grace speaking to the portrait, she knew something was truly awry. She observed that not only did Grace seem familiar with the spirit through the portal of this painting, but she called him "father". This term, directed at Ben, made Victoria wish to remove the eyes of portrait, and to beat her daughter; something she had not done heretofore. When she approached Grace with anger, and demanded to know what Grace thought she was doing, Grace responded with her usual denial. "Nothing mother, what is the matter with you? I was simply thinking out loud as to how much Uncle Ben looks like my father," was her clever reply. But Victoria knew what she had seen, and also knew what and how her ears had taken in.

That night, when they were alone, she repeated the scene to Teddy. More and more of their private time seemed to be devoted to trying to convince themselves that nothing was really strange about Grace; while at the same time they always wished to have a backup plan for her, should one be needed.

Even Grace's grandparents on Teddy's side, who did not see Grace often, made guarded inquiries with respect to her emotional stability. They too had seen something that was not proper, or normal, in this girl's behavior they too were worried. And naturally, in a small town where your own sister is a neighbor, Teddy's aunt and cousins on Rattlesnake Hill were equally concerned. How could such a beautiful girl be so oblivious to the needs and safety of others, whether they were people or animals?

Aunt Esther and Teddy's cousins wished to become part of the solution. They sought to have Grace come work at their farm, just to provide her with new experiences, and so, they stated frankly, that they might keep an eye on her. Victoria wasn't certain what they had in mind, but she certainly did not find their help objectionable as she could use a respite from the demands of so unusual a daughter. Thus, Grace commenced working at the Farmhouse on Rattlesnake Hill Road, every Wednesday.

It was Grace's custom to walk home on Wednesday, late afternoon, in time to help finish with dinner preparations. Some Wednesdays she wasn't particularly prompt saying she had been distracted by someone's flower bed, or children flying a kite. One evening she had difficulty walking through their barnyard as their own dogs had threatened her, baring teeth and snarling, until her dad had happened by. Somehow those critters had no love for Grace. Then one Wednesday she didn't arrive at all. Her father and Abraham set off with torches to be certain she could find her way in the dark.

When they got all the way to Aunt Esther's house, they caught sight of Grace just skipping out the door. Teddy grabbed hold of her arm, perhaps a bit more roughly than he meant to, but he was angry. It was rare for sweet, mild mannered Teddy to be angry, but he let her know that she had worried them all, upset her grandmother who was counting on her to help with dinner, and now both he and Mr. Perkins, as she was taught to call Abraham, had lost time too.

At Teddy's words she blew-up like a wild creature, yanking her arm back from his hand, curling her lips and flaring her nostrils. Then she commenced to cursing Teddy ending with the phrase, "What the hell do you care anyway, you are not my father!" Teddy stopped by the side of the road and lifted her up tucking her under his right arm in a hold that allowed her no purchase for a counter attack upon him. Grace continued to rant and rave but Teddy, used to heavy farm work as he was, paid her no attention. He continued to walk back home maintaining small talk with Abraham who initially appeared shocked at the girl's behavior, but seemed rather amused at the manner in which Mr. Teddy handled her.

When they reached their farm, Teddy apologized to Abraham for wasting his time that evening, and bid him farewell. As Ted entered the house, Grace was not as confident as she usually appeared. Fortunately for her she thought to apologize to Teddy as he was quietly fuming. She was sent to bed with no supper and seemed relieved to get away from her father.

The following week, after repeated cautions, Grace again did not get home from Aunt Esther's in a timely manner; in fact she did not appear for supper. Teddy decided to let her find her own way home as he was again angered by this behavior. However, when he was about to make his final rounds of the barnyard, he relented, and walked the distance to Aunt Esther's farmhouse. His cousins seemed happy to see him, and cordially invited him in, as though nothing was amiss. And so they thought, until Teddy asked where Grace was. They were surprised to have to tell him she had left hours before.

20

LOST IN THE DARK

Thus a hunt began that is a parent's worst nightmare; a little girl was missing in the dark, and no one knew where she might be. Teddy asked his cousins and Uncle John to join in a search. He then walked home at a rapid pace calling Grace's name every few paces. When he arrived at his farm, he told young Ben and Jane to dress in warm clothing, to stick together, and assigned them a portion of the town in which to hunt for their sister. He woke the hired hand, and together they went to Abraham's home. Whether they were on the road, or cutting through farmland, they continually called Grace's name. Once at Abraham's, they commandeered him, as well as three of his children, to assist in the search. All took up torches and followed the parameters Teddy outlined on paper, to be certain no quadrant of the area was missed.

Teddy went back to his farm, and searched once in the house, just on the off chance that Grace was playing some sort of game, but to no avail. She was not there. Victoria then insisted on joining Teddy saying she could not remain at home with nothing to do but worry. Then the two of them hustled throughout the central village which the others were skirting. They went by the church and Grandmother Emily's secret gravesite. Teddy told Victoria he wished Emily was now there to help him, for he felt so lost having ignored the fact that Grace was actually missing for as long as he had.

Victoria responded that Grace's behavior had prompted many hard feelings, and it was difficult not to suspect her of enjoying their current suffering. They continued to travel, calling her name and listening for all they were worth, but no reply came in response. Finally, as sunrise neared, they had to consider all the people who had lost a night's sleep and who had chores beginning at daybreak. Teddy walked Victoria home and then went about the task of checking in with the entire search party to get a sense of any possible progress; Teddy also released the others from their commitment to help them. Their animals all needed to be fed and milked, even if they could go without sleep.

Eventually, Teddy arrived back at Aunt Esther's kitchen, and sat with his Uncle John and cousins to review how Grace had behaved that day, prior to the disappearance, of course. His cousins seemed to think Grace had been in a good mood and did not display any hostility. But then it was mentioned that, shortly before she was to leave for home, Grace had spent an inordinate amount of time in the cellar. "In the cellar?" gasped Teddy. "Pray tell, what was she doing down there?"

"We don't really know," stated his cousin Martha, "although I asked her what she always seemed to find so interesting down there, for she went in the cellar upon every visit. She just said there was a little mystery to the place, and she had interesting feelings while she was down there. Once she even joked that it helped her to communicate with the dead, even her own father. Then we laughed and said, 'But Teddy is the liveliest person we know. Just go home and have a good chat.' To which she shrugged and said we simply didn't understand."

Teddy thanked them all for their help; and apologized again for taking up their entire night. Also, he expressed gratitude for this last information regarding Grace's tendency to spend time in the cellar. He said it might help him to better understand her state of mind. Then he excused himself to hurry home to Victoria, whom he knew would be extremely worried.

When they had gotten Jane and Ben settled down, and their grandmother was finally resting, Teddy told Victoria what cousin Martha had said about Grace spending time in the cellar. The look of horror on Victoria's face reminded Teddy of seeing a man once wakeup from camping on the ground, only to realize his bedroll was filled with rattlesnakes; there was a painful look mixed with a sense of doom and terror. Teddy continued, saying that he would have to approach the widow again to see what she knew regarding Grace. Victoria began shaking her head and said that suggestion sounded too dangerous, and perhaps there was an easier way.

"The portal," Victoria uttered, "I think your brother Ben may be able to tell us where Grace has gone off to, given her comments about 'communicating with her father'." Then Teddy knew two things: first, that they both realized Grace might no longer be in 'their world', and second, that Victoria knew full well who Grace's father was. Both realizations sickened Teddy, but he knew this was no time to worry about his own feelings; this was the time to locate a girl named Grace.

He explained to Victoria that he must help the hired man and Abraham to complete the most necessary chores for that day, then that he needed a two-hour nap to help collect his thoughts. After that time, the family should gather for dinner, and if there was no news on Grace, he would attempt to reach his brother for assistance in locating their child. Victoria, with her head held low, agreed to this plan.

When their duties were completed, and the rest of the family was in bed, or busy within their own rooms, Teddy and Victoria approached Ben's portrait. Teddy took a deep breath and began: "We hate to disturb you, Ben, as we know not what efforts it takes for you to connect with us, but we are most concerned about the disappearance of Grace. Her behavior isn't always easy to deal with, but we love her and are forlorn that she is missing. Could you tell us anything to assist us in our search for Grace, please?" Then Teddy held Victoria's hand and they waited.

After as much as ten minutes had passed, Teddy turned toward Victoria and said, "It does not appear that he will respond." Victoria replied that she would like to try contacting him. Teddy hesitated with all manner of emotions flooding his head: competitive and jealous thoughts toward his late brother, fear of losing face as weak in front of Victoria, and desperation in seeking to find Grace. The desperation won out, and he encouraged Victoria to go ahead and try to reach Ben.

Victoria cleared her throat, as emotion was making it difficult for her to speak. She then spoke clearly to Ben: "My dear," she began with, for he would always be her late husband, "We are in extreme despair trying to find Grace, who is, after all, still a child. She does many mischievous things which we must continue to guard against, but we wish to have her with us at home, to guide, and to love her. Can you search through your mysterious ways and tell us where she may be? How may we find her? We have tried every possible road we can think of to determine her whereabouts, but with no success. Please tell us what we must do."

Again they waited, but only about thirty seconds. The eyes in the painting took on a true three dimensional shape and Ben's voice emanated from the portrait. "Do not ask me where she is" he stated harshly.

"But we must," insisted Victoria.

"Then you will be burdened by my response," came an equally harsh reply. "For I have taken her from you and should have done so long before this. She is not simply a naughty girl or a mischievous one; she is not even within the realm of a mean child or a cruel one – her repugnant behavior goes beyond what you could imagine and will destroy you all if I should leave her with you longer."

"Yes, she killed those puppies in the barn, and only because they made her sister and brother happy. She has often made food go bad or eaten more than was her share of anything she wanted whether at home, at Abraham's home or at Aunt Esther's. She cares nothing for other people. She does not see them as having feelings. They are shells to her, put on this earth, she believes, as puppets to simply play in the background of her life."

"She has spent much time talking to that widow in her Auntie's cellar, and was fascinated by the dead as described by the widow. She thought about killing herself just to see 'what the other side was like' but was concerned that she wouldn't want to live as skinless and walk around as bones. So, I am sorry to say Victoria, she hastened your father's demise just to see if she could feel the life slip from him into the dark. And she enjoyed it, relished it."

"Some time passed but she was not content without feeling the exhilaration of such life-to-death power again. Now she began plotting to kill many people within a short period of time. She knew about the effects of the arsenic from the graveyard at the top of Rattlesnake Hill Road. She believed she could find the poison and replicate the disaster making it happen on your land, including destroying Abraham's family. She then planned to live with her Aunt Esther so that she could stay in communication with the widow."

"If you will both sit down and close your eyes, I will show you how she planned to complete her orgy of death." Victoria and Teddy looked at each other and decided they must do as Ben suggested. They sat upon the parlor floor with closed eyes as Ben began to speak again. "Grace returns to your house after a long time at her Aunts. She seems a changed child, sweet, compliant, affectionate; even the dogs appear to almost trust her. She is especially happy to see her siblings and they seem close for the first time in years."

"Several nights go by; your hearts are filled with joy to have this beautiful girl back among you. You all begin to relax. One night she wants to stay up later than everyone else to prepare a treat for breakfast. That sounds good to all, and Teddy is the last one up with her as he does his rounds outside. She moves to him and hugs him and says 'I love you father'. He returns her words with an "I love you too Grace," and with a smile on his face he goes up to bed."

"Grace listens for about ten minutes and when all is quiet; she goes out to the barn and removes some slabs of wood she had stacked in a corner. Behind the wood, two jugs of kerosene are revealed. She carries the jugs toward the farmhouse resting them near the backdoor before she again enters the house. She slips quietly into the parlor and removes my portrait commenting 'Don't worry father, I know to protect my own,' and she carries my portrait to safety in the milk shed. Next, she sloshes the oil all around the house but starts first at the staircase to the bedrooms making certain that no one can escape down those stairs. Then she returns to the outside where she plans to light a match and walk away."

"Knowing all this I had no choice." Teddy forces his eyes open, turns toward Ben and utters "No choice but what?" To which Ben replies, "Knowing she was going to do all this I had no choice but to break her neck and take her spirit with me back to the mission. I never should have thought it would be possible for someone from my world to leave a child here."

With that, the portrait lost all animation and ceased to speak. Victoria was overcome with grief and sobs, and Teddy held her; but once more he was grateful to his brother.

PART TWO

FINDING PEOPLE
2020 - 2021

2.1

PANDEMIC DAYS

E lena Maria awoke being kicked from inside her body. The baby seemed to be an active little fellow, which she knew was a good sign, just a bit troublesome when she wanted to keep the world shut-out a little longer. Full consciousness brought the impact of her grief down all around her. Her beautiful, energetic mother had given her own life to save this baby as the hideous, skeletal-creature that still lay buried in their cellar would have gladly snatched him from her womb. And Elena Maria might have let this happen if her mother had not insisted on sacrificing herself to save this child. It all happened so quickly that there was no time for discussion; with a flash of light her mother was taken.

The police investigation was completed and rendered an "inconclusive" finding. No one knew where Elena Maria's mother was, but the officials would not accept Elena Maria's statement that her mother had disappeared in some burst of fire, never to be seen again. No charges were filed against anyone, yet the case remained open. Making the entire situation worse was the very 'unreal' reality of the COVID-19 epidemic. Elena Maria could not freely move about the community attempting to investigate any aspect of this case. She was trapped in her house.

Both she and her husband, Matt, a university professor, wanted to sell this house but it was not recommended to allow prospects inside due to the Pandemic. They had not had the energy to set-up

115

a virtual tour. Further, there had been considerable publicity regarding the supernatural aspects of this case, and it did not make the property more desirable to associate death and destruction with it. Who wants to purchase a property, no matter how lovely, when the owners have publicly described the haunting of said house by a centuries' old enraged skeleton that arises from her grave without predictable provocation?

So Matt and Elena Maria had resigned themselves to living in this home that they had once dreamed of owning, and had worked so hard to restore. 'Resigned' because it was not an enjoyable decision to live there but one reached out of necessity. They would make the best of it because there was no alternative even though the urge to flee was strong. Knowing what lay beneath them in that cellar and knowing the power that existed here had destroyed her mother, made remaining in the house a task. Yet they must stay if they wanted to keep their baby safe from Covid.

When Matt was engaged in his research or on-line teaching, Elena Maria simply fantasized about how she might look for her mother; first through the internet if libraries were closed, or via old archives in basement offices housing historical records. She did not think it possible that her mother was somehow located on the premises but could not accept that her mother was really and completely gone.

How would old records find her mother? Well, she thought that whatever struck her mother down, or the problems of the angry remains which had challenged her mother, might have been recorded somewhere at a previous time within the town's history. She had to look to see if this was possible.

After many failed attempts to view local archival materials via the internet, Elena Maria resigned herself to the fact that the Town of East Apple simply had not gone back to digitize it's most historic records; if these records were to be reviewed she would need to sort through the ancient files on her own; by hand. Perhaps the town would permit her access to the archives as long as no one else needed to work in this area when she did, and, of course, she would wear a mask. Her first step would now be to make an appointment for this search.

Elena Maria also wondered just how she would describe the purpose of her search if asked by the town officials. How would she explain that she wished to know what an angry 250 year-old skeleton was doing in her cellar, and how and why had it sought to destroy her mother? She decided to say that she was trying to write a history of previous inhabitants of her historic home going back to its days of origin. Everyone seemed to enjoy the histories of their own towns.

And so she began with a phone call to the town clerk. The town's answering machine informed her that the office was on severely restricted hours due to Covid but if she would leave a message explaining the necessity or requirements of her needs, her call would be returned and arrangements made. It even sounded as though preference might be given to those who required the least assistance. Fine, thought Elena Maria, just point me at the material and leave me in peace! Thus, she left a message to see when her explorations might begin. Two days later, loaded with a flashlight, a magnifying glass, her cell phone and a notebook, she entered the town hall prepared for a lengthy time of solitude and research.

If she could learn anything about the evil remains in their cellar, or the reason for the attack on her mother, she would be comforted. It appeared that the records she wanted did exist but there were layers of dust on these files and most of the material was handwritten. Between unearthing the correct containers and cleaning them sufficiently to believe she would not contaminate her lungs, Elena Maria lost several hours before she could actually begin to read through the documents. When the reading began she was surprised to see that the file about the widow contained what appeared to be a newspaper account. She had never suspected that the Town of East Apple actually had once supported a paper. Cleverly, it was called the Cider Press.

Elena Maria marked the areas wherein she would begin her review the following day as her scheduled time in the Archives was about to run out. She also felt constrained by her bladder and her need to feed the dog on schedule. Having pets during these days of isolation was a tremendous comfort and she wanted to be certain Scruffy and Sybil were happy.

She was excited about returning in the morning. It wasn't that she anticipated being able to find a direct lead to her mother, but she did hope that, as she learned more about the widow, she would unearth some gem that might provide a clue as to what would entice this creature to release her mother from the darker side of the world. At this point all she could do was try.

2.2

PANDEMIC UNIVERSALLY ACCEPTED

Initially the pandemic had only created fear, and some panic in the minds of well educated scientists, as they could foretell the terrible future tragedies this novel virus would cause. But by late March, 2020, it was now obvious to all intelligent people that there was a plague unleashed on the world causing grave illness and even death. It was spread invisibly through exposure to virus in the air when it met the mucus membranes of the eyes, nose or throat. The carrier of the virus might appear healthy but could still contaminate others. The only way to be relatively safe was to wear a mask, avoid others and to maintain a safe distance, plus to wash hands thoroughly whenever exposed to something outside of one's own environment.

Because East Apple was the home of a research university, this Corona Virus had been recognized more quickly for the problem that it was; many parts of the country took longer to accept the harsh reality. Added to that was Elena Maria's frequent communication with her family in Italy. Italy had an alarmingly high number of victims of the virus; they were hit more heavily than had been many other countries. Perhaps the Italian culture with its family closeness, and multiple kisses upon greeting, was set up for failure to avoid the virus. In any case, poor Italy had to be closed down early and the hospitals and morgues were not able to keep up with the numbers of victims. As her cousins explained all this to Elena Maria, she and

Matt recognized early-on that this was no ordinary flu to which they might be exposed. East Apple caught on to the entire pandemic well before the President of the United States had issued warnings to the public. Although this allowed them to protect themselves and their future baby, it added to the length of time for which they were restricted as others continued to spread the virus.

The second morning Elena Maria was to do her archival research, she awoke with a bit of excitement and a sense of purpose; much more positively than she had been rising since the loss of her dear mother. The chief reason for this change was that she was feeling hope again, hope for better days to come and a deep sense that her mother was not truly gone forever. This hope helped her to believe that her mother might be able to resume life among them on this earth again. Elena Maria just had to find the steps that must be taken and they seemed to involve that horrible skeleton referred to as "The Widow". She had her mission and she had a sense of direction. She just prayed that what she would try would work, and before she would give birth to their son. Somehow having her mother with her when the baby would be born gave her back the sense of security that her mother's shocking death had eliminated.

She returned to the basement of the town hall wearing a mask, gloves, and carrying her cell phone and a notebook. She had an appointment so she was waved on down to the archives by a masked clerk. Her first order of business was to relocate the bins she had discovered the day before. They were there and a cursory review indicated that the further back she went on the history of her house, the better was the order of the material. This might simply be due to the early days having had less material to store, but somehow Elena Maria kept sensing that someone else had gone through these records and put them in order. Of course, they could have been reorganized many times having sat here for so many decades. Still she felt the touch of a kindred spirit.

Once Elena Maria reached the earliest days, when the judge had first built the farmhouse, she recognized that the house had no street number and was called Rattlesnake Hill Road instead of Cemetery Hill Road, all information she knew but was pleased to see verified. For several of the years she reviewed she only gleaned very straight forward facts concerning material costs, a small loan and what seemed like extraordinarily low taxes. Then, towards the end of the judge's time in the house, very fragile newspaper clippings had been added to the file. They were from The East Apple Cider Press as she had observed while reviewing the box on the previous day.

These were written by a reporter named William Edwards and initially covered an apparently notorious proceeding conducted by Judge Alexander Rider in Elena Maria's very house. Pointedly, they contained the outline of what was to become the curse her home still bore due to interactions with the Widow Loudon. Elena Maria had learned of these sometime ago but her original information had not come from the newspaper. Now she read that there was a portion of the story in the reporter's unpublished notes. He told of witnesses believing that the judge had become so enraged with the widow's behavior that he had ended up engaged in hand-to-hand combat with her. The passion and aggression which this unleashed pushed the judge out of his boundary of sanity and he reportedly actually raped and murdered the widow before he could get himself back under control. No one was permitted to speak of this or bear witness to it.

The judge then conspired with the sheriff to completely cover-up his wrong doings. Both men would forever swear that the accused woman was sent off to a poor farm where she could work to cover her own keep so the Town Of East Apple would receive no bills on her behalf. But, her body was actually interred in the dirt cellar of the judge's home, making it nearly impossible for someone to happen upon it, and the judge quickly moved away selling the farmhouse to Emily Harrington's family.

Added to all this was the fact that the kind-hearted reporter and his wife had stepped forward to adopt the widow's two little girls, and the judge thought he was home free. In his reality, the judge was free, although one may only hope that he suffered some form of guilt for his rash behavior. Nightmares were none too good for him, or perhaps all this drove a wedge between him and his wife. In any case the judge was gone and poor Widow Loudon rotted in the ground never to be with her children again.

121

Elena Maria noticed that part of what she was reading was in handwritten notes as an addendum to the actual files. It was not annotated by the town clerk nor worded as though composed by the journalist. It appeared, while not recent, to have been added sometime after the incidents had long been over. It rather appeared as though someone had been reading these files and jotted down the information she now discovered, quite separately from the actual record. In fact, in one place there was a small signature and a date: "Victoria Mills 1871".

How very interesting thought Elena Maria; Theodore Mills had been Emily's grandson who had moved in with her and Reverend Benjamin Wilbur, perhaps they are kin. That would be worth looking into.

The following morning Elena Maria contacted a librarian at the State Library to see if he could track Victoria Mills through his genealogical records. Given Elena Maria had a date as well as a name with which to work, and the town name, it did not take the librarian long to gather the requested information.

He said the woman in question was Victoria Chase and that Mills was her married name, apparently twice. That is, as a teenager she had married a Benjamin Mills shortly before he was lost in the Civil War. A number of years later she had remarried and this time it was to his younger brother, Theodore (Teddy) Mills. They took over the Chase family farm, had three children, the youngest of whom, a girl Grace, had died or disappeared at an early age. They had been active in his grandfather's former church helping to support newly emancipated slaves, and had owned considerable land in several locations. Certainly she would have been a guest at the home of her husband's aunt so she might well have developed an interest in Elena Maria's current home then on Rattlesnake Hill Road.

This was a treasure-trove of information raising several possible avenues which Elena Maria might pursue in hunting for clues that could lead to her mother.

2.3

LIFE IN THE CELLAR

Elena Maria was discussing her quest with Matt over breakfast the next day. She began with an inventory of who they firmly believed was buried in their cellar. Based on everything Emily had written in her diary they knew that her son Will had been placed in a coffin and interred in that ground. Just prior to this an entire colony of Goliath Bird Eating Spiders had also scurried into that soil, many killed as they hurried to get away, but many surviving and adapting to this new environment. Prior to Will being laid to rest, there had been the horrible murder of the "widow" by the judge who had built the house, and her body had been hastily hidden in that soil. Apparently, the widow raised no alarms when the Reverend Wilbur and Emily Harrison buried Will near her but many years later she refused to permit Emily to join her son within this same area. Emily was buried in some other, unknown, location. The "widow" had said Emily's grandson had buried her near the church but that didn't sound convincing, and certainly lacked detail.

It was not until very recent times that Elena Maria had witnessed her crazed neighbor from the woods being dragged screaming into the ground by the angry skeleton of the widow. That had convinced her that he was in the cellar; but was he still? She and her mother had exhumed them all with the intention of transplanting them far away, but the next morning the cellar appeared to be returned to its cemetery-like original configuration and no one knew which bodies were there. Plus, there was still uncertainty as to whether or not all missing parties were actually deceased. In short, neither Elena Maria nor Matt could say who, if anyone was still lying dead in the basement of their home. But Elena Maria strongly believed that in order to ensure the return of her mother she had better find a way to appease the "widow" and the chance was greatest that "the widow" still lurked in their cellar.

Matt suggested they concentrate on other matters for a while. Prepare the nursery, order some things for the baby on-line. He wanted Elena Maria to distract herself from this morbid quest which was likely to end in more disappointment. He encouraged her to order maternity clothing and books they would want to read to their son, but she remained fixated on knowing where her dear mother was and if she could get her back. Matt was worried.

A few days later Elena Maria noticed she had an email from the state librarian who had assisted her with tracing the genealogy of Victoria Chase Mills. He wondered if she would be interested in knowing that Victoria Mills had published a small history of the Chase-Mills Family which included several references to Emily and Reverend Benjamin and to Elena Maria's home. Her response was immediate, she was most interested!

Due to the Pandemic she could not simply drive into Hartford and read this manuscript at the State Library where it was archived. In an ordinary time she would have driven in, been seated at a table and asked to wear gloves to protect the aged document from oils on her hands. She also would have been asked to keep all pens away from any possibility of marking the family history, but she would have been permitted to make notes in her own notebook. Instead she now had to beg the librarian to make a copy of the document so that she might borrow the copy and not wait for access until the Pandemic was over. There was a certain reluctance to subject the original to the lights of a copy machine for fear of damage, but reluctantly the librarian agreed to make a copy that was actually a scan so that it could be stored electronically. This seemed like the safest way to save the history for posterity and make it possible for unlimited viewing. They assured Elena Maria that she could find it by the end of the week and she insisted that she was mailing in a donation later that day to support all of the library's good works.

And thus, at week's end, she was able to open a copy of The Chase-Mills Family History by Victoria Chase Mills on her home computer. She was very excited to receive this document. From the moment she had read Victoria's signature while she searched through records in the basement of the town clerk's office, she had felt drawn towards her. It was almost as though Victoria was an old friend. Perhaps some of her Italian intuition was maturing and finding an important connection; perhaps her pregnancy was helping her insights to "ripen" in some way. At any rate, she could not wait to see what Victoria had to tell her.

She began reading and found the information logically set-up. It began rather like a family tree with Victoria's children, Jane, Benjamin and Grace, at the bottom. Above them she had listed herself and her second husband Theodore along a line with his two brothers. Victoria was apparently an only child. The brother, Ben, was listed as deceased but she mentioned his marriage to her and the other brother's children. Then she spread the names of Theodore's parents along a line with her own parents. She gave the names of their parents but did not seem to have all names, and she traced some of their ancestors back to England.

Then she did something very interesting; she told stories taken from each family history, about their time in the East Apple area or what had brought them to East Apple.

One particularly interesting inclusion in this document was her attention to detail regarding her late husband, Ben Mills. She might have felt guilty that he had given his life in the Civil War, in a horrible bloody battle, and now she was his brother's wife with three children and apparently a great deal of land. The contrast with his early death could not have escaped her as she lived in relative comfort, although the life of a farmer's wife was never easy.

Then suddenly, Elena Maria saw something so shocking that she nearly fell off of her computer chair. There was a photo of Ben in his uniform which was the replication of a portrait his mother had commissioned when he went off to war. Elena Maria and Matt owned that portrait! They had bought it not long ago from Priscilla, the antique dealer, who thought it would look good in their home. It was unsigned but unmistakably the same painting.

Elena Maria ran around the corner to her front parlor where they had hung the portrait of an unknown Civil War soldier. He was quite handsome and remarkably identical to the likeness in Victoria Mills' family history. She was looking at the grandson of the Reverend Benjamin Wilbur; this man was also the brother of Teddy Mills and the first husband of Victoria. She owned and had hung this portrait very early on in their ownership of this home. What an amazing coincidence, and to think she had initially been disappointed with this purchase!

Victoria further noted that there was an addendum to the information on this soldier. It was placed at the back of the history so as not to distract from the order of the manuscript but because it was important family history to note. Elena Maria's curiosity was strong; she could not wait to reach this section.

Perhaps because she was alerted to this addition about the soldier, Elena Maria paid careful attention to the history each time Ben Mills was mentioned. She was somewhat horrified to see that following his death his body had been difficult to recover. But it had to be noted that the brutality of the Civil War left many bodies unidentifiable. Then, when his remains were discovered, a fee was paid for its embalming and return to Connecticut. It was eventually discovered that the embalming fluid, and that of many soldiers, was emitting arsenic and contaminating wells as the bodies decomposed. In Ben's case this led to a shocking exhumation which revealed that the body in Ben's grave actually belonged to some other poor soldier. Many twists in this story kept his family anxious and grieving for Ben to rest in peace.

Teddy wanted more information about Ben's actual death and he hoped to at last retrieve the actual body. His mother also prayed that some miracle would still bring her lost son's body home to them. Teddy embarked on a lengthy trip to Maryland where he searched for his brother and made many inquiries. Finally he ended up at an abandoned mission which appeared to be occupied by a homeless man or two, one dressed as a monk. As Teddy unfolded his tale of this trip to Victoria he eventually had to admit that he believed the monk to be Ben, but he did not know if Ben was dead or alive.

Elena Maria felt a chill go down her spine when she read these words. She decided to read out of order and skipped to the addendum which Victoria had placed at the back of the history.

2.4

ALIVE OR DEAD

The addendum began with almost an apology. Victoria believed future generations should know what she and Theodore Mills knew regarding his brother Benjamin Mills, and perhaps even about Ben's portrait. But she was adding this addendum in such a way that it would only be unsealed 50 years after she and Teddy were both gone. Presumably, this would ensure not only that their parents never read this material but also that their children were unlikely to read it. This peaked Elena Maria's interest even further as she tried to imagine what on earth this information could be. Of course, it would eventually be known that the hidden issues were NOT necessarily of this earth.

Victoria continued by describing a strange aura she experienced each time she passed by the portrait of her late husband which hung in the parlor of her home with Teddy. She said there were times when she could not break away from the painting but would stand "as though transfixed" in front of it simply gazing into Ben's beautiful eyes. She had to admit, although she loved her husband, that the face of her late husband still brought out a consuming feeling of love and even a sense of passion. She was truly disturbed by these moments for she would then experience guilt as though she had been disloyal to her dear Teddy.

Initially, she tried to cope with these feelings by hurrying past the painting and making it her business to rush into the next room.

She thought she had found the correct solution until one night when she awoke on the parlor floor, and Teddy was trying to help her up and cover her body at the same time. She was dazed. All she could recall was a passionate lovemaking scene with Ben, who was of course dead, but here, was Teddy trying to help her up and back to bed. She was most confused, and by morning the memory was all but completely blocked. She was grateful to Teddy for not raising questions about that night, although shortly thereafter, Ben's portrait had disappeared from their home.

The most important aspect of all this, from a genealogical perspective, was that within a few months Victoria knew that she was pregnant with their third child. Only she had not had sexual relations with her husband during the time period which would have been required for him to be the father. In point of fact, she had not had sexual contact with anyone, save within her dream regarding the portrait of her late husband. Yet, she knew herself to surely be with child. Her rational side kicked in and she decided that she must have been having intercourse with Teddy whilst she dreamed of Ben. Teddy might be thrilled to know that they were having another babe.

Yet, such did not seem to be the case, as Teddy challenged her until she had to insist that of course he was the father. Teddy saw that there would be no other way to describe this pregnancy to others, and he certainly did not wish dispersions to be cast upon his wife, so he relented and acquiesced to Victoria's memory. She seemed greatly relieved and most grateful to him.

The birth of this baby was horrendous, apparently even by old time standards which had few of the conveniences of modern medicine. In fact, Teddy was frightened nearly out of his mind that he would lose the baby and Victoria, so great was the blood loss. He ended up turning to his brother's portrait which had only recently reappeared in their home, and begging for the lives of his wife and baby. When he reentered the birthing room all was well; there had been a near miracle. Victoria was fine and so was the baby. The bleeding had stopped and no ill effects remained. His mother-in-law, the midwife, and the doctor all proclaimed it incredible. Teddy felt certain he owed his brother for this event.

He and Victoria named the baby Grace, in keeping with the miracle theme, and rejoiced in holding their third child. If the contact with Ben could have stopped there all might have been well; and for a time it was, but Grace was as difficult as a child, apparently, as she had been to birth. What followed were years of troubles with the girl's behavior escalating from challenging, to exceedingly difficult, until the point where Grace disappeared.

When she could not be found, after being on her way home from her aunt's, Teddy and Victoria were overwhelmed with sorrow and grief and driven almost to the point of madness. The entire community helped with the search. Then, they once again turned to the portrait of Ben, which they had come to realize was a portal into another world, to seek help in finding the missing child.

The news which Teddy received from this interaction with his brother was that Grace was indeed born from a half-dead man and a living woman and that the mixture was apparently toxic. Grace is not capable of behaving as a normal human being. Grace was plotting to commit horrible crimes possibly even to erase her living family. It is Ben, concerned for all his actions in creating her, who acts to remove her from the living.

According to the addendum, Victoria and Teddy never find out if Ben has taken her away to somehow reside with him in a half-world, or if she is dead and gone. At this point the portrait ceases to work between the two worlds and becomes mute, never reacting to the family again. Ben and Victoria are left to mourn Grace and to pick up the pieces of their lives enjoying the two children that are naturally theirs. These children have presumably had their lives spared through the actions of their late Uncle Ben. If he had allowed Grace to live with them longer it might have proved catastrophic for all.

Victoria has the hardest time with this situation, for in any case, Grace is her daughter and she has lost her only child with Ben. This addendum seems to be somewhat of a testament to him and their love at the same time she professes to love Teddy. A sad situation to which Victoria appears to slowly reconcile herself as time goes by, and her children, Jane and Ben, seem to flourish according to the rest of the family history.

Elena Maria is fascinated by this information and wonders which details might have been altered and which are as true as the writer, Victoria, knew them to be. She cannot help but think that something is missing. She jokes to herself that the only way she will ever know the real account is if the portrait of Ben decides to converse with her someday. With that thought in mind she goes back out to the parlor and looks the portrait over very carefully. She sees a handsome officer in a black dress uniform. "Are you likely to have wild and passionate sex with me some evening my handsome officer?" she addresses to the painting. Then she answers herself by saying "Probably not given that I am already pregnant with a son. But the day may come when you will find me more attractive." She stops then and almost nonchalantly walks away from the portrait.

She tells most of this story to Matt that evening wanting his take on the theme of a "portal into another world". His reaction surprises her since she has always thought him to be a very concrete, evidence based scientist. When she says this to him he reminds her how his own work, on multiple personality disorders, is on the fringe of science according to many. That he has left his mind open to possibilities that others have shunned because they could not see them under a microscope. Then he continues with the science he wishes Elena Maria to consider.

He tells her that a physicist connected to Harvard University believes that there are layers of dimensions. That means he continues, that realities we cannot see or access may yet be very close at hand. Some indications of this occur by weaknesses in gravity in certain areas, with no apparent explanation. And further there is a dark matter around some entities that thus far defies explanation but that physicists are strategizing to capture. They are, as of 2020, attempting to build equipment to measure these changes in matter and gravity.

"So you see" Matt concluded, "I am fully open to the possibility that there is a portal through time and that this very house might be a location in which this phenomenon may occur."

2.5

FINDING A PORTAL

Matt believed that portals to another dimension might be possible, and Victoria Mills wrote as though she had personally experienced interacting through a portal. In addition to this, Victoria described how her husband had actually made requests from his brother via a portal. What this did for Elena Maria was to give her hope. She had felt little but loss since her mother had disappeared in a flash of light while protecting Elena Maria's unborn child. She had no way of knowing how or if contact could be reestablished with her mother, or some entity that might reach her mom. This talk of portals existing on their very property, and the potential that the portrait of Benjamin Mills was actually such a vehicle to another world, was the first hope Elena Maria had found.

She got up quickly the next morning, dressed hastily and hurried through her breakfast rushing to get to her computer screen. She barely had time to greet her husband who was amazed to see this spark of energy in his often morose wife. Once seated at her desk she began to search for stories or evidence regarding portals to other dimensions. She soon discovered that Harvard was far from the only institution conducting such research. Physicists all over the country, and actually, all over the world, had at least part of a faculty member's time devoted to attempting to discover how to contact another dimension, verify its existence, or to travel through time and make contact.

Perhaps it was only slightly more farfetched than was the notion of a telephone or faxing at different periods of history. If one could transport words, pictures and videos through the air then why not an entire person someday? Certainly scientists had to look at this possibility in order for there to be hope of discovery.

Some of the calculations for this work began with the ancient Incas and relied on the alignment of sun and stars at key times of the year. Other information seemed more religious in tone, coming through hieroglyphics within early Egyptian tombs, and some were based purely on speculation that finding black holes would lead to other dimensions which existed simultaneously with our own. There were credible people, not simply charlatans, who believed in these alternative worlds and dedicated their lives to seeking them.

But the one thing Elena Maria could not find was a suggestion as to how she might approach one of these dimensions or be let in on its secrets. She wanted her mother back. She did not know what stress this alternative state might put her mother through; she also wanted her back soon as her due-date loomed increasingly nearer. If the evil widow was in her cellar, she wanted her mother with her for every step of labor. This added pressure to Elena Maria leading her to formulate bold plans for how she might again approach the officer in the portrait.

Since the beginning of her pregnancy, Elena Maria frequently enjoyed afternoon naps. On this afternoon she fell asleep in the parlor on a couch which rested just below the spot above which hung the painting. She fell asleep while mulling over how she might get through this portal. In her dream she was in an unknown location, perhaps in the South, for it felt like a warm, humid climate. And something was compelling her to walk down a sandy path between tall grasses as though headed toward the ocean.

When the grasses gave way to a house it was an enormous building which appeared to be a boarding house or, she thought, perhaps an orphanage. The building had an old feeling to it, but there were signs of habitation with clothing hung on a line strung across one side of a wraparound porch and some dishes set out on the floor near a side door, apparently for pets. Also, the glass was intact and most of the second and third story windows were wide open with their curtains flapping in the sea breeze.

Elena Marie followed the path between the grass and up a slight incline headed over a sand dune. There were several pairs of shoes abandoned here, along with long stockings. The shoes were most curious as they were leather and cloth designed to go far up the ankle and were held in place with laces, holes and hooks. Elena Maria immediately thought she had only seen such shoes in museums or movies. Then she reached the top of the dune and beheld a lovely ocean view complete with a blanket holding a picnic, female children running around barefoot but in long costumes, and three adult women holding umbrellas. As she looked more closely she observed that the women were also dressed in old-time garb with flowing skirts, puffy sleeves and bustles.

Slowly, Elena Maria began to suspect that she was somewhere back-in-time seeing people who might no longer exist. Was she in the South or the Eastern Mid-Atlantic, and why had her mind, for she knew she must be dreaming, wanted her to see this scene? Perhaps these people could not see her for no one had looked up or given any indication of observing her. Still, Elena Maria decided to crouch down in the grass and just keep her eyes open.

The children were playing a game and the adults were simply making sure they did not go out too far in the water. The girls would squeal and splash each other with the exception of one girl who appeared to want to knock her friends down into the big waves. It appeared harmless enough until one of the adults called out "What have we told you about playing too rough, Grace? Now settle down or we have to take you back inside." At this point the girl of about ten or eleven looked a bit dejected and walked away from the others. She made her way down the beach a short distance kicking every rock or shell within her reach. She used great force on these objects, and her intention appeared to be venting anger. The others ignored her.

"Grace" reverberated in her head. What a coincidence that I should happen upon a girl named the same as was Benjamin and Victoria's disappeared daughter. Then she thought, of course the actual Grace would be much older than this child by now. But the thought replayed itself; or would she be just this age, for Elena Maria had no idea what year she was in or in what town. Was she here to get a look at the obstinate Grace who now flourished in a new area? And was Grace actually under her father's care or was he simply a spirit who arranged her care?

With these questions in her head she half crouched, half walked back to the house. Here she knocked on the door and when no one responded she entered and continued to call out "Hello, hello". There was a desk near the back of the room she had entered and she went directly there to have a quick look around. On it sat a newspaper dated 1889, Maryland Gazette. So she was in Maryland, the last known state in which Benjamin was alive, and the place where he likely died! Was she seeing where he had taken Grace when she had to be removed from East Apple? Was she being teleported back to the time of Victoria's history or was this history repeating itself while she was alive in 2020? How unusual these questions seemed.

Then she woke-up in her own parlor on her own couch just below the portrait of Benjamin Mills. It was 2020 and she was pregnant and missing her mother. But finding herself in East Apple was comforting after the strange environment which she had just left. She arose and straightened the couch. When she stood up straight she was looking directly into Benjamin's eyes. Did he see her she wondered?

Without thinking it through she now blurted out, "I suppose you know I have just been with your daughter Grace in Maryland?" She stood there half expecting a response but of course nothing happened. She looked down and wedged her feet into her slippers. When she looked up again she saw one tear drop fall from Benjamin's left eye. She quickly reached a hand toward it but it had gone; evaporated, fallen to the floor, or was never really there.

She turned away feeling both sad and confused. Then she hesitated and said: "I may need to ask you for help. I hope you will consider speaking to me soon." And she walked into the kitchen to begin preparing dinner. She wasn't sure what Matt would think of all this, but he had given her theory of there being a portal here, to other dimensions, at least a little encouragement. And he knew how badly she missed her mother. Maybe he could help her to reach through this portal.

2.6

MATT'S SURPRISE

Elena Maria set the table in the dining room within view of a lit fire. She took out some of their better dishes, and she prepared chicken al la cacciatore knowing how much Matt enjoyed that meal. She also made fresh Italian dressing for their salads and opened a good bottle of red to breathe before they would drink it. Since she was pregnant she allowed herself one inch of wine with water added, one time per week and that was all. It really didn't taste much like wine this way, but it allowed her to feel festive and make good use of their stemware.

When Matt washed and joined her at the table he seemed quite willing to discuss her thoughts again regarding the possibility of portal theories. Within just moments he announced that he had a story to tell her which he had only recalled on his way home this evening. He said for years it was one of his mother's favorite stories, but she had not told it much lately. It happened to her, he explained, when she was a college senior at the University of New Hampshire. She was a social service major intern and had been sent to the New Hampshire Division of Social Services Office in Portsmouth.

Matt's mother enjoyed her training although the poverty around the seacoast area in the late 1960's was naturally difficult and painful to observe. There were a great number of elderly people living in isolation and some did not have adequate housing, or plumbing or electricity. On the other side of this story were a large number of children who needed support from the State of New Hampshire for adequate food and care. Matt's mom, Linda, worked predominantly with the elderly often being sent out to find them for wellness evaluations when they had not been seen in years.

She found the staff of social workers very helpful, friendly and dedicated. They were people that she could easily emulate. Among them was a woman named Betty Hill. One of the more gossipy of the group whispered in her ear that Betty had quite an interesting story to tell if she were encouraged to do so. Matt's mom, took this as a challenge, and over a brownbag lunch one day asked Betty if it were true that she had a special story to tell. Betty gave her a look that lingered but responded in a friendly way that she was willing to share it with those who asked. She also said that she trusted Linda not to ridicule her if she found it impossible to believe. Linda's curiosity was certainly peaked and she sincerely assured Betty that she would be respectful of the story.

Betty began by saying she imagined that Linda was too young, at twenty-one to have been reading the newspapers eight years ago, back in 1961, when all this had repeatedly made the news. And, naturally, she was correct about this. She said that she and her husband Barney, who lived in a rural part of New Hampshire in an old farmhouse, had been awakened one night by lights hovering in their field. These lights were extremely bright. The Hills threw on their robes and immediately went outside to investigate.

"This", she said, "is when it gets weird, but honest to gosh, it looked like you would imagine a flying saucer would look with lights on top and a large spinning base. We were taken inside and gently but firmly, placed on examining tables and this aircraft went into the sky. We were examined for what seemed like several hours and then we were brought back to our field and released."

"We asked each other if we were okay, and we both felt shaken but unharmed. Then we decided to call Pease Air Force Base, as they are close by, and report what happened. Pease said they would send someone out in a few hours and then we thought it best that the community be alerted, so we also called the State Police and the newspapers. We weren't seeking publicity, but because we had been frightened we wanted to know what others might have seen and to warn our area," Betty concluded.

Linda was spellbound. She asked what happened after that. Betty said that "she and Barney had their pictures taken and it was all over the news for several weeks. The Air Force would not deny their story was true but would not corroborate it either. Then the hate-mail started. Some religious groups thought it anti-Christian, but most of the hate-mail was racial in nature. You see," she added, "The photograph revealed that I was a white woman, and Barney is an African-American, so lily-white New Hampshire in 1961, didn't have much respect for us."

She went on, "Our story didn't die there, but it was taken more seriously in other parts of the country. Books were written, and there was talk of a movie. Then in 1965 something truly amazing happened. Very near-by, close to Exeter, New Hampshire, a "credible white man" and two police officers saw a spacecraft that could have been the same aircraft we had described. At first the Air Force had an explanation for it, and then they pulled their explanation back, but there were a number of other witnesses, describing the same things, in the same location, who came forward."

"No one declared that this was a definitive UFO, but many firmly believed that to be the case. The book that was written this time was titled **Incident at Exeter**, and it was a best seller, and a movie was made."

Matt hesitated, and then added, "I can provide so much detail because when we were kids my mother still believed this woman and wanted us to have open minds about UFOs and other mysterious entities. She told us this story many times."

Elena Maria said, "I think I now get why you are so open to the possibility of a portal. If one can go forward in time, like outer-space seems to be, then why not go back in time which appears even more at hand. I'm looking forward to getting your mother to repeat all this for me just to see if it still excites her."

"I'm sure she'll be happy to," Matt responded. "Now may I fill my plate?"

"Yes," laughed Elena Maria, "you have more than earned this meal, and I feel encouraged."

They spent a pleasant night discussing the endless possibilities if one does not limit their thinking to the here-and-now. As they started up to their bedroom Elena Maria took Matt's hand, "I wonder if the portal will take me on another trip this evening as it did during my afternoon nap? It gives me a mixed feeling about falling asleep. I do enjoy the rest, but I'm unsure if I'm comfortable traveling to such unknown places and having to figure so much out."

With that comment they entered their bedroom and prepared for sleep. Matt continued to hold Elena Maria's hand so that she could feel safe and anchored to this world. But he could not hold her mind in place. As soon as she fell asleep she was transported back to Maryland. She could hear the roar of the ocean, and she could feel the change in climate. She was on the wraparound porch and she tried to enter the building but the door was locked. It was dark out and the lights were no longer on inside the house.

Elena Maria sat on a couch that was part of the porch furniture. She knew she was waiting for someone or something, but she wasn't sure who or what that would be. At one point she heard a rustling in the long grass close to the porch, but it stopped. A bit later she believed there was a noise coming from the upstairs window. It sounded at first like a sigh and then a low moan as of regret, but she could not define it and it abruptly ended.

Just as she was thinking it might be best to try and look around the property, perhaps search the inside of a shed, she saw a faint light in the upstairs approximately from where the moan had emanated. Then it disappeared only to reappear at the door nearest to her. The person held a candle up trying to see out into the yard; probably wondering who was out there. As the individual moved Elena Maria caught a glimpse of the face and it was unmistakably that of Grace. She looked amused at something but there was an aggressive look to her eyes.

Elena Maria was not sure whether to wait or to run for cover; with Grace holding a light in the window it was probably too late to try and hide.

2.7

A SMALL OPENING

Grace unbolted the door lock and pushed the door open holding the candle well in front of her. Her face appeared angry with flared nostrils, downturned lips and eyes squinting. Elena Maria made a hasty decision to avoid looking frightened or like she was spying or lurking about. She spoke right up aiming her words at Grace and said "I'm wondering if you can see and hear me?" The response came right back at her: "Course I can."

"Well that's wonderful, Grace, as I wanted to see how you are."

"Well" said Grace, "Just who are you, and how do you know me? I've never seen anyone who looks a bit like you;" and the anger was certainly in her voice.

"I'm sure this is perplexing" said Elena Maria. "I come from the part of the world that you were born in, I even live in a house I know you have visited, but the timing of my life is not in sequence with yours."

"What are you talking about?" screeched the girl while she took an aggressive step forward; clearly she was impatient with this unknown person and wanted control of the situation.

"I'm trying to tell you that I'm from East Apple, Connecticut and live in the village in which you were born." Then Elena Maria hesitated a moment and added; "I have a beautiful picture of your father hanging in my parlor so I look at him every day."

"My father in a Civil War uniform?" she inquired."

"Yes," replied Elena Maria.

"And does he talk to you?" she asked, as though that would be a normal thing.

"No, not yet," was the reply. "But I hope he will soon as I need to ask him for some help."

"Well," interjected Grace, "You had better be careful because if he doesn't like you, he may do what he did to me."

"And what was that?" Elena Maria asked of Grace.

"He snapped my neck and then brought me here to half a life with all these hollow people. I really have no life, no freedom and no growth," she added.

"Are you certain that he intentionally broke your neck?" asked Elena Maria in amazement.

"Oh yes, I was there at the time, but he had no other way to take me with him," said Grace.

Then tears ran down Elena Maria's face and she said, "I am sorry you have known so much pain and at such a young age. Please take care of yourself." And as she spoke these words, an alarm continued to ring until Elena Maria jumped out of bed to begin her day back in 2020.

She tried to explain this last dream to Matt, but he was rushing to campus for a large screen Zoom meeting taking place with several institutions; he didn't really note the dream as significant. So Elena Maria took her shower, and brought a cup of tea with her into the parlor, where she turned a chair to face the portrait. Initially she just stared at him and then said "Grace seems to understand why you broke her neck even if I cannot. Whatever that was all about, I cannot hope to know, but I would appreciate a chance to discuss my problem with you. The solution I seek will probably go back in time, to a place you may be able to reach."

The portrait did not blink or waver from its inanimate state. It simply hung there like a painting on a wall; no life shone in the eyes, no warmth was reflected in its skin, and no inkling of emotion was demonstrated in even the least way. It wasn't until Elena Maria walked into the kitchen, from the parlor, and headed for her backdoor that there was the sound of a most profoundly sad sigh coming from that painting on the wall.

As she entered the outside air, Elena Maria was herself sighing, for she believed the portrait, as a portal, might well be a dead end, no pun intended. She did not know if she could ever move this Civil War soldier to a place where his heart would open up to her needs. How could she prevail upon him so that he would offer help in crossing dimensions to find her mother? Her anxiety was only increasing as she thought more and more about how much she wished to be with her mother again. What would it take to get this man to help her? If her discussion with his little daughter did not move him to be kindly disposed toward Elena Maria, then perhaps nothing would get him to take action. She decided that the only reasonable way to manage a chance to get word through the portal was to find another source. Maybe she would have to approach the detested widow after all. This dreaded creature, who had taken her mother away, might be the only one who could give her mother back. She decided to take a walk and think about the problem from this new vantage point; perhaps something would come to her.

She also reminded herself that no matter what, the widow could not have her son. And there lay the problem. To go anywhere near the widow held risk. On the surface, the widow was a skeleton in some state of death or sleep lying buried in their cellar; but in reality she was capable of cursing, killing and weaving plots against all she believed had wronged her. She appeared to have no "soft spots" or moments of sympathy for anyone. She did not seem to realize that the world continued on and had moved beyond the time she was so wronged. The judge who victimized her was now himself long departed, yet she ached for revenge upon this man and his friend, the sheriff. And, so deep was her hatred, that she thought anyone who did not join her in wishing to destroy the judge, should themselves be destroyed.

Elena Maria had proof of this in the family history which Victoria had written where the widow had come through the chimney, from cellar to fireplace, attempting to burn members of Teddy's family because of her own unhappiness. Victoria recorded the many things

Teddy had tried in an attempt to deter the widow from causing harm to his aunts and cousins who had once lived here in Elena Maria's house. They had been the ones to board up the fireplaces and drop hearth stones into the cellar, as well as to remove mantels so that Franklin stoves could be used. These stoves contained the fire within them so there were no flare-ups to injure the cook or terrorize the household.

Almost with a start, Elena Maria realized that she and Fred her carpenter had restored several of these fireplaces, the main one being in the kitchen with the beehive oven attached. Had this reopening, complete with hearthstones brought back up and new mantles painted as they had been nearly 250 years ago, been enough to stimulate the return of the widow's rage? Did this give her new access to the household? Or had she ever eased off? After all, it was the widow, who had placed the curse on all male children born in this house, and then Elena Maria's mother who had taken the curse away with her sacrifice.

If, somehow, Elena Maria got her mother returned through dealings with the portal, would this bring the curse back with her? Elena Maria was so overwhelmed with a need to see her momma that she dismissed the risk and simply thought "I'll worry about that if it happens." So in a few hours she had come full circle. First, she would do anything to get Captain Benjamin Mills to work with her and bring her mother back and as soon as possible; then she believed that the soldier would never cooperate with her and she had wracked her brain for information on the widow that might lead to access for her mother's return. Now she again felt certain that the portal Ben occupied was her one true chance for access.

She was willing to venture into Grace's world again and again if it meant she could have her mother back as a sane, normal lady, and not one of these tragic, half-dead, zombie like creatures such as Grace. It seemed anything she thought of came with risks. But, to Elena Maria, the biggest risk of all was if she did nothing and simply let her mother remain dead, or missing, in the wrong dimension. And so, she was now determined to redouble her efforts, and to find a way to get through to Benjamin Mills no matter what it took.

These thoughts gave her courage and a sense of optimism that she had not felt since her mother's death. In fact, she felt so good that she went into her mother's bedroom and began to take some of her things out of drawers so that they would smell fresh for her mother's return.

2.8

NO DNA TESTING

Elena Maria felt very well when she awakened the next morning, and had a sense of well being bordering on joy. This was the happiest she had felt since losing her mother. Yet she was somewhat dismayed that she had not dreamt of Grace during the night. In fact, she had no memory of any dreaming and had so hoped for some signal from the portal, or Grace, which she might use to break into Benjamin Mills' good graces. Well, she thought, this is going to work; I just have to figure out an opening, I know that portal is close-by.

She recalled that yesterday she had felt invigorated and positive after a walk, so she grabbed her jacket and headed out the door. Once she started walking, the beauty of this old historic area absorbed her attention. She admired the structures on either side of her; the twelve over twelve window panes, the hardware on front doors, and the stone walls which separated most properties. Even the fields held charm as they too were separated by stone work and usually had an old barn or sheds near an opening in the stones. Although horror had happened in their home, she still felt privileged to live here.

The walk took over for her brain in that she stopped thinking about where she was going and only followed her feet. Before long she looked up and realized she was at the church, a trip she generally made by car. As she looked toward that building she noted that there was some sort of crowd gathering there. Typically, a large group at church meant it was a holiday, a wedding, or a funeral, but she had not recalled seeing any events announced in this week's Sunday bulletin. Everything was so altered due to the Pandemic. Then she noticed a hearse pulling in and figured someone may have passed away whose family requested a hasty burial without time for an announcement.

Elena Maria had joined this church after all the help the pastor had been to her. She still observed many Catholic customs and rituals but she and Matt were both at home here, so she thought nothing of going over to the gathering and simply inquiring as to who had passed away. However, as things turned out, this inquiry was far from simple. It seems that earlier that very morning, when most of East Apple was fast asleep, a paperboy had ridden his bike across the church lawn and discovered a deep area of erosion where the lamppost stood. The weather, of late, had alternated between warm and freezing, followed by a sudden heavy rainstorm last evening.

When the paperboy rode over the church green he saw a skeletal hand sticking up out of the crystallized earth. The change in weather and the heavy rain had revealed a body. The problem was that this was not, nor to anyone's knowledge had it ever been, a burial ground. Apparently, someone had donated a body to the church, and this had occurred quite some time ago. The local constable was there along with a State Policeman. They were still making notes, taking pictures, and interviewing neighbors and the pastor. They were just getting to the stage where they would exhume the remains and take whatever they found to the State Laboratory for forensic examination.

This stopped Elena Maria dead in her tracks, although she did not want to draw any attention to herself. But the thoughts she was having were that this might be where Emily had ended up. Emily had wished to be in her own cellar next to her son, Will. She had gone to extraordinary lengths to make plans so that Teddy Mills would hide her body and bury her there when others thought she had disappeared. Yet there was no evidence that she had been buried there. Elena Maria and her mother had found Will there and they had mistaken the bones of the horrid widow to be those of Emily, but the widow had declared that Emily was NOT there. In point of fact, the widow had stated that Emily's grandson had buried her at the church, and that was precisely where they were!

Elena Maria would have to consider well any statements she might make regarding this corpse. And then she reasoned it was best to say nothing because this might not even turn out to be a female. She simply commented to someone at hand "How strange to find it in front of the church." Then she continued her walk, although her mind stayed behind in the lawn. She also wondered if poor Emily had any idea where she had ended up and why she wasn't in the cellar of the farmhouse.

Had Victoria's family history mentioned some mystery about Emily? Elena Maria would have to read it again and see what she found. She would also pay careful attention to the newspaper over the next few days to see what she might learn about this finding at the church. If it is not Emily then who else went missing back then? Or maybe the skeleton wasn't as old as it appeared. Certainly no one living would know anything about this finding.

Later that day Emily reread parts of Victoria's family history. There was a brief story in there, having occurred before Victoria married Teddy, about Teddy and the entire Farmer family, his aunt's people, searching for Emily for days after she had wandered off. It seems she had grown increasingly confused and simply disappeared one evening. The family conducted a lengthy search for her and all were amazed that she had gotten far enough from home to escape detection from the searchers, but she was never found. The final resting place of her body remained a mystery. Until today, Elena Maria thought, until today.

Still, it was with a mixture of both relief and shock, that Elena Maria read the coroner's report, as published in the paper, stating that the body was that of an extremely elderly woman who had been dead for approximately one hundred and fifty years. A review of news stories from that era revealed the likely identity of the woman to be Emily Wilbur, who had gone missing from her home at around that time, and whose remains had never been recovered. It made even more sense given that she was the second wife of Reverend

Benjamin Wilbur and that she had served as secretary at the church for several decades. The church was a place toward which such a person might gravitate.

But the next day the same newspaper introduced a suggestion that perhaps this incident involved foul play. After all, the reporter wrote, who can believe that a woman of nearly 100 years of age dug her own grave in the dark of night and then rolled up in a tarp and pulled two feet of dirt down around her? That struck a note of confusion amongst the town folk and especially members of that church. Although the death was too old to even qualify as a cold case, it did stimulate a great deal of curiosity.

Elena Maria knew what had most likely happened from reading volumes of Emily Harrison Wilbur's diaries. Before bloodhounds were brought out and the front lawn of the church could be sifted for clues, she and Matt agreed it was her duty to explain to the local constable what she had read. The constable in turn requested that she repeat her story for the State Police. After she had done this she simply refused any interviews with newspapers or magazines, and several amateur sleuths, and the story died down.

She had told the authorities about Emily's adopted son, Will, and how he had died from bites inflicted by the Goliath Bird Eating Spiders which he had been raising. She explained that subsequently Emily had married the Reverend Wilbur and they continued to mourn the boy, but she never mentioned anything about the Reverend having been Will's biological father. She didn't think that information was necessary to the story, which she was only telling to keep people from hunting for a killer who did not exist. Eventually, she had to explain Emily's obsession with being buried next to Will who was actually in her cellar; that is, both Emily's and now Elena Maria's cellar.

Why Theodore Mills was never able to bury Emily where she had requested to be, Elena Maria could not say. But she did believe that Teddy must have done for her the best that he could. Then Matt and Elena Maria made an unusual request of the coroner's office; would they release Emily's remains so that they might bury her next to her son?

Emily had no living relatives that the State of Connecticut could locate. Advertisements were placed in all major newspapers on three consecutive Sundays. No one came forward to claim Emily's remains. Therefore, Elena Maria and Matthew Nelson were granted custody of Emily Harrison Wilbur's remains to bury in accordance with the decedent's wishes as supervised by a licensed mortician of their choosing.

Elena Maria felt truly happy that they could make Emily's wishes come true. It wasn't until they were headed for a meeting with an undertaker that it dawned on her that this venture might also disturb the widow.

2.9

CARING FOR THE DEAD

As they rode into Willimantic to meet with the undertaker, and make arrangements for Emily's burial, Elena Maria suddenly blurted out, "But the person who does the digging will possibly be exposed to COVID if Joseph Macintosh had it!" Matt replied, "We have no reason to suspect that Joseph was exposed. He died before anyone in this country had hardly heard of the Pandemic. It's just that the State was shutting everything down at that time and no one really believed us. I guess it isn't every day that someone tells the police that a disturbed neighbor has been pulled into the ground in their cellar and murdered by a crazed skeleton. So, they probably were looking for any reason not to start digging thinking it a 'fool's errand'."

"Okay, I get that," said Elena Maria, "but this guy is going to find more skeletons than just Will. So, we are going to have to specify that we want Emily Wilbur buried next to the bones of the young boy, but that we want two other adult sized sets of bones removed from our home."

"Yes," said Matt, "that is what we should specify, and if there is any hassle for the undertaker, or extra expense, we might do well to have some cash on hand."

"It sounds like a good investment to me to be rid of those skeletons" concluded Elena Maria.

Then Matt, who was driving, also reached for her hand and added, "I hate to say this but please prepare yourself for the slight possibility that there may be some sign of your mother too."

Elena Maria turned to look directly at her husband and only added, "I've thought of that, and I am as prepared as I can be."

They parked at the funeral parlor and entered the office for their meeting, masks in place. While undertakers were very busy during this time of COVID, this one seemed pleased to get this business as it had received considerable publicity. Also, as the undertaker listened to the Nelsons, he realized it was possible they would be able to gain two more burials from this dig. Matt and Elena Maria had elected not to mention the possibility of her mother being buried there as it would introduce another layer of mystery that they were not able to explain. Of course, they were hoping that it would also be unnecessary.

It was agreed that the next morning the funeral home would retrieve Emily from the coroner's office, and since they had no other clients to serve that day, they would come directly over to the farmhouse on Cemetery Hill Road where the Nelsons lived. Matt would make certain to be home. Elena Maria planned to read a few words from the bible and to place a few fresh flowers on the new gravesite. Now her biggest concern was whether or not the widow would leave peacefully, and if she did not, just what kind of ruckus would she set off?

Two men showed up to exhume two possible bodies and to leave Emily in the cellar where those bodies had been. The older gentleman, who appeared to run the funeral home, told the Nelsons that he had contacted the town constable after they left him yesterday. He said if there were two bodies in their basement that did not have death certificates he was told to leave them with the town coroner. The coroner would have to determine each cause of death, especially in the case of a more recent corpse.

Elena Maria and Matt both understood this and certainly had no objection. They just thought 'please God; take these bodies off of our property'. They opened up the bulkhead doors and turned on all possible lights. Then they indicated the area of their cellar where they firmly believed Will's bones were located and where Emily would wish to be interred. The grave digging began with the slow and careful transfer of earth from this location to the tarp these men had placed on the cemented portion of the floor. After the dirt was piled up on the tarp one of the men said "I think we've got something here." And he carefully moved a head and neck, arms, shoulders and a rib cage to the edge of the tarp. Right after that he lifted out the pelvic area, legs and feet. It certainly appeared to be a whole body.

Elena Maria stared intently at these remains. They were definitely old and had been underground for some time. "I'm certain this is the widow," she whispered to Matt. "But why isn't she screeching or ranting and raving as she usually does?"

Matt said he "couldn't account for the behavior or lack thereof, but maybe she didn't like a large audience or wasn't a morning person." The men then set this body in a cardboard box and labeled it with the name Elena Maria provided them as the person it was most likely to be: Beatrice Loudon, deceased around 1800. They returned to the earth and continued to dig. Within a short period of time they uncovered casket remnants that were quite thoroughly rotted; and cradled within this wood were the bones of a half grown child. "This is Will," Elena Maria declared, "and we should not disturb him except to dig around him to see if others are also contained herein."

The men complied with this request as it had been part of the initial agreement. This, of course, was to be where Emily would be placed. Then the men put down their shovels and used hand tools to work in and around Will and what was left of his casket. They found bones almost immediately and these bones appeared young and sturdy but full sized. These were the remains of Joseph Macintosh, the neighbor who had stalked all would be buyers of his folks' land, and who had tried to rape and kill the Nelsons.

Elena Maria turned away in horror at seeing what was left of him. Matt told the undertakers what label they would need for his box. Then the gravediggers completed their duties by working their tools through the dirt and, when they found nothing, setting a simple box in the soil which held the remains of Emily. The needed dirt was filled in, and Emily was at last underground, in her old farmhouse, next to the boy she had loved so much and called "son".

Elena Maria read a bible verse and gently placed on the earth the flowers she and Matt had purchased. As they walked away with the undertakers, Matt turned and said "May she finally rest in peace."

When the others had left, Matt and Elena Maria allowed themselves a few moments of pride in what they had done to support Emily's dying wishes. They hoped there could be some happiness here, and that the evil forces which had resided in their home would be passive now, as good seemed to have triumphed, at least as far as they could see.

The young couple slept well and Elena Maria was comforted that her mother's body had not been found while the men were digging. It was a break from the constant pain and worry over her mother. They went to sleep and did not hear the sirens that awoke most of the town around midnight and continued for hours as a three alarm blaze was engulfing much of the village of East Apple. It seems the fire had started in the coroner's office, although no one could say exactly how.

It had been an intense fire and the result was that those old sheds from the 1800's, which had been incorporated into town offices, were totally destroyed. In fact, the two bodies that had just been brought into the coroner's office that afternoon were effectively cremated. Although not a huge loss, as the Town had insurance, it still meant that many old papers and documents were destroyed and anything significant about those bodies was gone forever.

But the one tragedy in all this was the loss of the coroner. It seems he had chosen to work late because of the unexpected finding of two bodies in town. He told his wife that one set of bones looked so old they were 'almost mean' he said. He concluded by telling her he'd only be happy when he had conducted his autopsy and dispensed with them. Sadly, his tape recorder, containing the work he had done that night, was also melted into a ball of plastic.

3.0

ARSON?

Life, or 'half-life', was quiet in the Nelson's cellar that first day. Outside the house there was an unmistakable smell of smoke in the air. The entire village of East Apple carried the scent of the fire from the town center; it added a sad tinge to the general atmosphere as everyone soon knew a life had been lost. The building that had burned, and those abutting it, had been so old that everyone seemed to accept this fire as the inevitable conclusion of advanced age. However, the fire chief had a different perspective. He believed that with no obvious cause for the fire, and with the loss of life, a full investigation was both warranted and necessary.

For the following week, fire department volunteers could be seen sifting through the rubble and sorting their findings. When they had completed the recovery of fire-damaged material they had enough bone fragments for more than two people but not for a full three. This then, necessitated sending the bones to the forensic laboratory down State. Three weeks later the newspapers had some additional headlines regarding this fire. It seems that the bones were identified to be: Harvey Desmond, MD, coroner age 53; Joseph Macintosh, 28; and a nondescript canine. None were the bones of a long deceased woman from the early 1800s who would have been in her early thirties. The conclusion was that either the bones of the Widow Loudon had decomposed in the fire, to nothing but ash, or they were never touched by the fire; they just were not there!

The papers went on to say that a furnace would have to blast human bones at a temperature of between 1400 and 1800 degrees Fahrenheit to turn human bones to powder. And even then there could be pieces of the bone that would remain intact. The most likely conclusion was that the third person was not caught in the fire and did not incinerate there. Reading the summation put a chill into Elena Maria's living bones. Although, each time she entered the cellar, and every evening when trouble might have been anticipated, all was quiet. Perhaps the widow had taken this strange opportunity to leave the area.

Elena Maria discussed the widow's potential location with Matt but, he was hoping that she had been eliminated in the fire, and there was just too much rubble and dust in those old sheds for her remains to have been discovered. That comforted Elena Maria but she was still wary that this hideous and hateful skeleton would return to plague them. Still, until there was some sign of her, Elena Maria decided she should just go about living her own life. She would be having a baby in just a few more months, and she wanted to find her mother.

Determined to find out something concrete regarding her mother, frustrated by the issues around the widow, and increasingly weary as her body grew in roundness, Elena Maria stomped into her parlor and stood before the portrait of the Civil War soldier, Benjamin Mills. "Well," she began, "we have relocated the body of your step-grandmother in-law, Emily Harrison Mills, to our basement. As your brother Teddy knew, she wanted to be buried next to the body of her adopted son which happens to be located in our cellar. Teddy had difficulty getting her into this area. Probably it had something to do with the widow, who haunted our basement, but now the widow is gone, and Emily is interred with Will where she had wanted to be."

"This has given Matt and me great comfort, to have set things right if you follow me, but my life remains heavy with grief as my mother was so soon taken from me. I want my mother back. She was closer to a saint than have been any of these other characters with which we are dealing. I want her back and I am determined that you are able to assist us and should do so!" Then she fell silent and just stared at the portrait.

After a few minutes she thought she saw a twitch in Ben's facial muscles and then he began to speak. His voice was very deep as though both distant in miles and deep within him. He admitted that he had not used his earthly sounds in over a century but thought it appropriate to respond to her now. Elena Maria gave a little shudder for the gravelly quality in his voice unmistakably called a grave to mind.

He said, "I will help you to find your mother but I cannot be certain that we will accomplish this. The person who did the most to extinguish her would be the one who could most easily reveal her location but, I'm sure this 'widow' will not wish to accommodate us. Still, your mother may not be too far away, so it is possible. And I should also warn you that her experience of being 'dead' may also have had an effect on her personality. It may be that the woman we bring back is no longer the woman for whom you yearn."

"Finally, I must extract a firm commitment from you that if we are successful, and your loving mother returns here to you to live out her normal life, you will do something for me, no matter how difficult my request may seem"

Elena Maria grew frightened. Could this brother of Theodore, and late husband of Victoria, actually be evil? Then she asked him, "Could your request mean that you will demand the life of my son or husband in return for my mother? I have already chosen to keep my boy when forced into this dilemma."

"No," replied the soldier. "It may be a difficult request but it will not force you to part with anyone you dearly love. I know too well the pain of such a sacrifice."

And so, there in her parlor, Elena Maria swore an oath to Benjamin Mills. She pledged to reward him with whatever request he must make of her in order to return her mother to the world of the living. After stating this she now said to him, "Where shall we begin?"

Benjamin Mills said he would pull into his inner world for a time and see what visions might appear that would either lead him toward her mother or to the widow, who had forced her mother to disappear or die. The widow appeared anxious to hold on to her power over Elena Maria's family. "But why is she tormenting our family?" asked Elena Maria.

"Because you moved into the house where she was murdered and where her son hung himself. This is the house where the devious judge mistreated the widow's family, causing her son to die, and showing no mercy to them when she was penniless and trying to support three children. The judge concluded by beating and raping her and, with the help of the constable, concealed his misdeeds and made her disappear, for his own protection. That is how she came to exist in such an aggressive and aggravated state in your dirt floor."

Elena Maria had been aware of much of this information before but, when laid out in this context by the soldier, she saw most clearly why the widow remained such an adversary. And like Victoria and Teddy before her, she wished to find some means of appeasing the widow for the ordeal through which she had suffered. But what could possibly compensate this widow for the loss of her family, her reputation and then her life?

Matt and Elena Maria spent many intense hours in conversation trying to hit upon an idea that might be used to appease the widow, if Ben Mills could even manage to reach her. But all they could think of were notions such as "you are all dead now" or "your children never stopped missing you" or even "we admire you for the fight you put up against so formidable an opponent". But none of these seemed as though they would assuage her anger.

Then Matt, as a psychologist, asked a profound question. "What is it she has always desired with her threats and fire attacks? She had done everything she could to frighten the judge's wife and to threaten his children, and any subsequent male children born in that house were cursed. What was her goal?"

Elena Maria answered; "She wanted to know that the judge had at least a taste of the pain and anguish she had been through."

"Yes, precisely," responded Matt. "Then we had better find out that something beyond horrible befell the judge after he and his family left East Apple."

"Yes," replied Elena Maria, "We had better find something horrible enough to appease the widow if there is any hope of getting my mother back!"

3.1

JUDGMENT DAY

Elena Maria awoke with a start in the middle of the night. Her mind told her that she and the captain had finally spoken as she stood before his portrait. He said he would be willing to help her find her mother as long as she pledged to provide him with a favor, to be determined, in return. Now she just prayed this recollection was correct because she was so anxious to bring her mother home. She lay there for a few minutes and, thanks to that conversation, reassured herself that she did have a way into the portal. However, first she must trace the steps of the judge who had started the trouble with the widow.

Judge Alexander Rider had been a fairly flamboyant character when he first came to East Apple and built his home in 1785. He enjoyed being elected to office and having a powerful role in town such that he could give or withhold from the citizens, and those who did not demonstrate their respect for him, would learn to regret this. Having the constable do his bidding, and the bankers wishing to be in his good graces, was a spot in which he relished being. When his life had taken a vile turn and the paper was raising questions regarding his judgment and integrity, he was most displeased. Soon he realized the only way to protect himself, his family and his office was to leave town with all due haste. This is what he did and the constable assisted him. He completed this move before the widow was barely cold in the ground.

Given that Judge Rider enjoyed being prominent within his community, it was not a surprise to Elena Maria that his name quickly resurfaced as she began her research. He and his wife were the proud owners of a grand colonial home in Deerfield, Massachusetts. The home still stood as a fine example of homes and furnishings of that period, and the name Alexander Rider was listed among the distinguished home owners of the past. However, most such citations included the respectable notation of "Mr. and Mrs." or "His Honor and Mrs." But this legend did not read as such.

Perhaps, thought Elena Maria, when we appear there in person we shall see a plaque on the homestead bearing both of their names. But, a few more minutes of research led her to conclude that such was not the case. It seems that Mrs. Rider was diagnosed with a nervous condition soon after joining Deerfield society. In fact, her behavior was so opposite of expectations that local gossips were quoted as saying; "She was fortunate that the Salem Witch Trials had ended one hundred years prior to her arrival in the area or she might have been suspect."

Good heavens thought Elena Maria, did she behave like a witch? Here are the things she learned as she read more deeply from the local press of the day, which apparently could print anything! "Abigail Lynd Rider who was raised as a well behaved young lady by her parents, Ebenezer and Hortence Lynd, even completing Miss Nathan's finishing school, has returned to Deerfield. She arrived last week in the company of her husband, the Honorable Alexander Rider, her son and two daughters. The family will be living with her parents on Main Street. The Lynds own one of the largest and most prestigious homes in our area, and it is hoped that having the younger couple in residence will open up the house, once again, to social events which have been missed as of late."

Another entry in the paper: "Mrs. Lynd has decided it is good form if she welcomes her daughter and son-in-law to the community and has announced a Gala to profit the Church Outreach Fund. This Gala will feature the entry of the Judge and Mrs. Rider into Deerfield Society. This event will be held in their home, 37 Main Street, on October 11, 1800 beginning at 8. Guests are encouraged to come in costume and leave a donation of $10 at the door. The Church Auxiliary will cater this event."

"And that is when the trouble began, at this very party. It seems Mrs. Rider was not at all interested in helping to play hostess for the community, whether the party was actually in her honor or not. When she discovered that her mother would insist upon her so doing, she must have decided to demonstrate her contempt. For, when she descended the grand staircase, at least forty minutes after her husband and children had been presented, she came dressed as either a scarecrow (as labeled by the charitable) or a corpse (which the more daring seemed to find obvious). In any case she was a hideous sight and caused both her parents and her stately husband to rush her back upstairs whilst making profuse apologies."

"Louise Masters, a childhood friend of the now Mrs. Rider, stated that this display was totally out of character for her old chum. She believes Mrs. Rider is suffering from a traumatic experience which occurred not long ago when the couple still lived in Connecticut. She would provide no further details. The family was also unwilling to offer any further information about the incident."

"Persons living in the Rider's former hometown of East Apple, Connecticut, who wished to remain anonymous, stated that Judge Rider had been accused of wrong doing by a local widow. This had led to the woman harassing the entire Rider family and eventually to their leaving town and returning to Deerfield. However, no one would comment on the record. A neighbor from Rattlesnake Hill Road in East Apple informed this reporter that Mrs. Rider had seemed to suffer a nervous collapse with regard to this incident with the widow. Certainly, that would help to explain Mrs. Rider's recent behavior."

Such information appearing in the Deerfield newspaper was very much upsetting to the judge who hoped he would now have a fresh start, politically and professionally. While the judge seemed to want to protect his wife from dispersions and gossip, he also did not wish to have the weight of the past rest upon himself. And somehow it became known that she had fled their home on several nights and caused disturbances as other families were sitting down to dinner.

She seemed to find it very humorous when she could cause children to run and scream.

Subsequently, when Mrs. Rider did not regain control of her senses, she simply seemed to disappear within their large home. Several years passed and the children went off to boarding schools or marriages. Then the older couple, the Lynds, passed away leaving everything to their daughter and the judge as had been promised since their return to the area. Then Mrs. Rider died in a tragic accident where she fell to her death out of a third story window in the home.

The catch here was that the upstairs maid swore that she witnessed Judge Rider coming up behind Mrs. Rider and providing her with a quick push out that window to her death below. He was indignant and he believed it would simply be his word, that of a court officer, against the word of a nearly illiterate house servant. But he was wrong. The maid had a brother-in-law involved with Massachusetts politics, and many friends who thought her a woman of integrity. The judge's past was also tarnishing him. Not only that, but all three of their children believed their father to be a flawed man beginning with a boy hanging himself in their Connecticut home. They believed their father made choices which inevitably led to the boy's demise and his mother's unmanageable reaction to the judge.

In the end, the judge was tried and found guilty of manslaughter and given a thirty year sentence. The Lynd/Rider estate was turned over to the three children of the judge and Abigail Lynd-Rider. He died alone in a jail cell, penniless and separated from all he loved. This story had nothing but victims.

Someone even brought up the case that had caused the judge to flee Connecticut. There was speculation that perhaps "His Honor" had not been so innocent in that matter either. But when questions were sent to East Apple the town constable swore by the judge's innocence and proclaimed it was a moot point as the widow was thought to have perished in a fire on a work-farm in the state of New York. Nothing further was investigated or done about this matter.

3.2

DEADLOCKED

Elena Maria was surprised by just how easy it had been to discover these stories regarding the judge. She realized, however, that anyone seeking such information prior to 1980 or so would not have been as fortunate. Very few smaller towns would have had their records uploaded to the internet. Yet today, her search for Judge Rider, simply by name, yielded significant information. Once the Riders left East Apple, if one had not known to where they had relocated, learning anything about them would have been extremely tedious and time consuming. If there were not many seekers involved in the effort, it is doubtful that they would ever have uncovered this information.

While she was gratified, she knew that the next step would be far more difficult. She would now present her findings to the Civil War portrait in her home and see if he had discovered a way of reaching the widow from whatever dark place she now inhabited. She had no notion of how communication occurred within or from the portal. All she could envision was from one of the articles a physics professor had written. She saw a deep, vast, black hole that was both empty and yet filled with everything spinning in a vortex. Could the captain simply call out within this hollow and reach whoever or whatever he sought? She hadn't an inkling of how this communication would transpire.

Elena Maria approached the portrait with a mixture of trepidation and excitement. Certainly she was pleased to know the judge had met a bitter ending to his self-centered and cruel life, but would the captain even think this worthy of persuading the widow to give back the life of Elena Maria's mother? If not, what recourse was left to her, if any?

Matt left for the university to participate in yet another Zoom meeting, wishing Elena Maria good luck as he kissed her goodbye. She then consumed a little breakfast, thinking to keep the baby appeased while she focused on the portrait. Finally, having procrastinated enough to build up her courage, she approached the painting. "I'm here," she announced, "hoping to discuss my findings with you. My hope is that the information I have garnered will be of use to you. I know you must find some means to convince the widow that she would do well to return my mother fully to the realm of the living."

Only a moment went by before she could then see the light return to those eyes within the portrait. He simply said, "I am listening." Elena Maria then repeated the tale of the judge's life in Deerfield, Massachusetts, ending with the tragic death of Mrs. Rider and the empty life the judge had to endure within a jail cell. It was indeed a pitiful and devastating ending for a man who had once seen himself as a pillar of the community. Elena Maria also tried to emphasize any points that might demonstrate Mrs. Rider's empathy for the fate that had befallen the widow's son. She hoped such empathy would feed the vacuum of pain that remained within the widow. It was so difficult to know what, if anything, could still reach that heartless body only held together loosely as a skeleton.

Before Benjamin Mills replied to her tale, he appeared to ponder her information for a considerable period of time. Then he echoed some of her thinking. "It is difficult to say what will appease this widow who has remained so distraught for so great a period of time. But if you speak the truth to me, and I am certain that you do, it will undoubtedly be valuable for her to know that he did not escape punishment without a blemish; far from it. What she wants done with this information, or what more we may offer her, is hard to say.

We can only move forward and see what she may offer. I will return to my world and attempt this communication." And with that, the picture went quiet and lifeless.

Elena Maria sat back on the parlor couch and noticed her breathing as it returned to normal. There was so much hope and fear within her it was difficult to wait quietly for an answer, or to imagine what next she might do to enhance the probability of reaching her mother.

All this investigating into Victoria's family history; the trips, if that is what they had been, into the portal; her review of the possibility of the portal concept being accepted today; and now investigating into the judge, had taken time. Waiting for the portrait of Captain Benjamin Mills to communicate with her had dragged on for considerable time as well. She now looked down at herself and realized there was very little time left before her baby was due, a 2020 baby who would be born during the pandemic. She wondered if her mother would be with her for this amazing time. Then the baby, who would be named for her husband, gave a fierce kick. She imagined little Matthew was saying, hurry up Mamma, hurry up!

She pushed her shoes off and, for a second time, fell asleep beneath the portrait. Again, she was returned to the Maryland coast. She began walking down the grassy path heading for the sea. She followed the path directly over the dunes and could hear gulls screaming and feel the heavy salt air blowing in her face. Her hair and clothing were instantly wet from the moisture this air contained. She was barefoot, and that greatly aided her traction. Suddenly she realized that it was more than gulls screaming. There was the voice of a little girl crying out for help. "Help, please someone help me" was the cry she heard repeated. She ran down the beach toward the voice and the distant imagine of a child waving her arms.

Of course, the child must be Grace, and something was terribly wrong. As she drew closer to her she saw that Grace was pointing out at sea and a small rowboat was bobbing up and down. Grace declared that four of the girls put out in the boat, but the sea suddenly started growing rough. The rope to the boat was yanked out of Grace's hands. Now she could not reach them. What could be done to save them, she begged of Elena Maria?

If it were modern times she would already have called 911 on her cell phone; or at least found a lifeguard stand with ropes, life rafts, or possibly even a full raft. But these aids were not available and a decision must be made immediately. Then she thought she saw the end of the rope bobbing up and down in the sea but not nearly as far out as the boat. With no further thought than to save the children, she ran into the water and swam with all her might toward the knot. If she had been asked to describe what happened next she could only have said a miracle transpired. She felt her body glide to the rope's end, despite the violent tossing of the water, and she had the tow-line attached to her wrist in no time.

Now she had to perform the truly heroic part. She began swimming back towards shore while every stroke of her right arm brought the boat along with her. She was struggling and worried. At times she couldn't avoid taking in a mouthful of water which certainly interfered with not only her ability to swim but her ability to breathe and continue. Then there would be moments when the boat lurched in another direction with such force that she had to flow backward with it. She came to a point when she could not tell if she had actually even gained any distance in the direction of the shore. She felt physically ill from the salt water and the incredible effort she was making. Elena Maria was just beginning to think she would become unconscious and drown when she felt a hand on her right arm relieving the effort of pulling and propelling her forward. Just before she passed out she thought she saw Grace saving her and the boat.

When she came to she was lying in the parlor on her couch. She was soaking wet and felt miserable. She thought perhaps her water had broken and she was in labor. Then she realized that she was covered in salt water complete with bits of kelp hanging to her clothing and hair. She began to panic wondering if the children in the boat had been rescued or not. She started to jump up off the couch, although she had no idea how she would find an answer to this question. Then a gravelly voice from just above her said "Worry not, they made it." There was a slight pause and then the captain added, "Good work." And then she fell asleep until she woke up cold and headed for the shower.

3.3
TURNING POINT

After Elena Maria was warmed by her shower, she decided not to get fully dressed again but rather to simply wrap her fleece robe about her. This last month of pregnancy was enough effort in the mornings; by late afternoon there was very little energy left, and Matt would not complain about her attire. She just hoped no one would drop in on them, but COVID pretty much eliminated that concern. Elena Maria also had no concern about how she must dress in front of the portrait. As a figure on the wall that had observational powers, he must have seen odd things for decades and simply ignored certain details. She assumed the portal was interested in more important things than attire.

When she returned to the parlor she noticed that the couch on which she had napped was quite unkempt with a damp feeling, disheveled pillows and kelp strewn about. She hastily swept up the mess, put the pillows out on the porch to dry off and stood the cushions on their sides to help the air evaporate the moisture. Then she looked up at the captain and asked "What happened?" To her surprise he was willing to answer saying "You came upon a moment in Grace's life when she truly needed help. Her friends would have drowned at sea if you had not intervened."

Elena Maria replied; "I did not know what to do but tried, in desperation, to reach the rope that had been swept into the ocean. My first thought was that Grace had let go of the rope but changed

169

her mind when she spotted me coming down the beach. Forgive me for thinking that of your daughter, but I do know she had been difficult and even sinister in her past."

The captain added, "I believe she might have thought to rid herself of those other children but she had a change of heart. Such a change is a miraculous step for a girl such as Grace. Obviously she is not pure evil but wishes to be more human. She even sought to rescue you when the struggle became over whelming. I think there is hope for Grace."

"Well, I am glad to learn this and very glad to have been rescued" rejoined Elena Maria. "What more may I do to encourage your cooperation in finding my mother or working with the widow?"

"I will be having direct contact with the widow within the day and will provide you with more information at that time" he said and then, once again, the portrait became only an inanimate object.

Elena Maria was so excited by this conversation, with its hope for a future with her mother that she could barely prepare Matt's dinner. She had a simple menu in mind of baked stuffed shrimp and a few reheated left over vegetables, but she was fumbling and dropping things on the floor. Fortunately, the lid was tight on the parsley flakes or the kitchen would have appeared to be moldy. Then she could barely hold the knife to chop her garlic so she decided to employ the garlic press, which, under the circumstances, she could not find. Eventually, she had all her ingredients prepped and lined-up so that dinner could quickly be cooked at the right time.

She fed the dog and cat, combed out her wet hair and set the table. As she bent over the table to line up napkins and water glasses, she felt a long moving pain creep up her lower back. This, she thought, must be what labor feels like as it begins. She caught her breathe and looked at the clock. When nothing more had happened for thirty-five minutes she decided it was a false alarm and she would resume her chores but try to take it easy. She then continued her meal preparations.

Matt was also excited by her news; both about the captain being closer to locating his mother-in-law, or the widow, or both; and the first contraction having made itself known as he would like to see this baby. They chatted amicably throughout dinner until there was a sudden flare-up in the kitchen fireplace.

They both moved to the front of the fire where they could make out the features of their skull-like nemesis. Her claw like hand appeared to beckon them to come closer. They held each other's hands and remained firmly in place some distance from the hearth. "Please tell us what you would like," intoned Matt.

"I wish to make things right with you if you will repeat, directly to me, all that you learned about the judge and his family. I have been informed through the portal but desire to hear it from you." And so Elena Maria repeated to the widow the many ways the judge had mistreated his family. It included how he had tried to manipulate everyone so that he appeared a thoughtful family man. Yet, in the end, he only sought full ownership of that fabulous home in Deerfield and to be free of his now troublesome wife.

Elena Maria finished by emphasizing that the judge had ended up alone and isolated in a jail cell with no friends or family nor any of the comforts to which he had become accustomed. The widow responded that this was a good story although, unlike her experience, he had deserved this by bringing all this disgrace upon himself. She said her plight had been completely unfair, but at least there was finally some comfort in knowing about his ending. And then the widow was gone and the flames grew smaller. Elena Maria turned to Matt and said, "Now what?"

Without speaking another word they both walked over to the portrait in the parlor. It appeared that the captain was waiting for them as his pupils moved and his entire face was animated. "Now," he said, having apparently heard the question, "we wait to hear that your mother has been freed by the widow."

"But where has she been held?" said Elena Maria.

"I do not know where, but if you are patient for a few more minutes we should know much more," replied the captain. And with that, they all three sat, more or less together, in the parlor to wait for something to happen.

They heard strange noises deep within the chimney and then a sound as though there were fireworks on the roof. There was an odor similar to old coal being burnt followed by flashes of light out near the barn. "That is where mother disappeared," stammered Elena Maria as she rushed to the window. But suddenly all was quiet and still. Then there was a knock on the side door; at first gentle and then louder and more insistent.

Elena Maria was the first to get to the door as she nearly flew toward it with apparent disregard for her safety and condition. She was so overwhelmed with her need to see her mother that rational thought had disappeared. She flung the door open and beheld her mother, seemingly in natural human form but surrounded by a bright light and smiling at her daughter. The women embraced and both collapsed into the house laughing and screaming and speaking two languages at the same time. Matt approached his mother-in-law and touched her shoulder. He exclaimed, "You do feel real!" And then he joined in their rejoicing.

They stumbled into the parlor so that the captain could easily see what had materialized. They laughed some more and thanked him in both English and Italian before he withdrew into the realms of the portal. He made one final short statement as he left, "I shall return soon to seek the favor I have been promised." And then he was gone.

Elena Maria and her mom headed for a cell phone to give her dad the amazing news. They spoke with him at length for he had difficulty believing this was true. He had not been aware of the hopes Elena Maria and Matt had harbored, as he did not know their beliefs in the portal. They had thought to spare him disappointment should it never work out. Now he could hardly comprehend this news while simultaneously pledging that he would be driving to East Apple that evening. When they hung up, Elena Maria felt her water break. Undoubtedly the excitement had gotten the baby to begin his decent into the world. When her dad arrived he would be there for a double celebration.

3.4

A BOY CHILD AT THE FARMHOUSE

When Elena Maria's father arrived at their house on Cemetery Hill Road later that evening, he could only think of holding his wife tightly in his arms. But part way to Connecticut he had realized he would have to convince them to let him in as he was crossing state lines and was not part of their immediate household. He hoped that they would believe him for he had been isolated for months. When his wife died, and the pandemic was in full force, he decided to withdraw to his beach home on Cape Cod and to only go outside for solo walks. He communicated with Elena Maria by phone. He ordered his groceries and all needs online, or via phone, and used his credit card. He immersed himself in research and writing and grieving. He had just reunited with his wife, and then she was taken from him. The pain was unbearable, except by withdrawing from everything.

Upon his arrival he spent his first few minutes at the door where a very happy dog and a very anxious son-in-law greeted him. He finally understood that Matt was going to let him in if he wore a mask, and that he was about to become not only a husband again, but a grandfather! His eyes leaked large droplets of joy down his cheeks. He had frankly assumed that he might never know joy again and then everything had seemed to change in an instant.

He saw his wife slip out of a room and remove a white gown, gloves and a mask hanging them on a hook in the hallway. Apparently

173

she was assisting with the birth. During this time of COVID, Elena Maria had a tentative appointment for the baby's birth but nothing about childbirth can be precise. With the events of the last day, of course, Elena Maria's body had been thrown off course far more than might have been expected so there was no bed immediately available for her delivery. But her delivery of little Matthew seemed imminent. Her mother, who had not as of yet, even had a moment to explain her ordeal or where she had been, went immediately to work preparing a room for birthing.

"This house has seen babies born before." Declared the nonna-to-be, "And if there are no complications we can handle this safely and free of the virus. If there is even a tiny little problem," she continued, "we will immediately call an ambulance." The fear Elena Maria had felt, coupled with the exertion from the recent swim and then the emotions of having her mother return, had apparently caused her body to progress rapidly toward delivery. She was already fully dilated when she began to actually feel the labor pains.

While her mother stepped into the hallway to hug and reassure her poor confused husband, the baby started to crown; and nonna returned to the delivery room just in time to catch the baby! When Elena Maria had felt the urge to push she simply held the hand of her husband and bore down. If this wasn't the easiest first time delivery in history it was among them, but the adrenaline caused by prior events must certainly have played a major role in preparation.

After a little time for cleanup and to catch her breath, Elena Maria asked that the door be opened to admit her father so that they might all rejoice together. The baby boy remained nuzzled into his mother's breast and the others stood around congratulating themselves and touching each other to make certain what they were experiencing was genuine. Elena Maria had just had a healthy baby boy and her mother was home from the dead!

Thus the questions began to fly. "Mother, where were you all this time? Were you in pain; were you frightened, did you know that you would come back to us?"

She began by saying she knew that there would be consequences when she had stepped in front of Elena Maria in order to forbid the widow from stealing and killing the fetus. She believed no grandmother would have done differently. It was necessary, but she had an added faith that throughout her life she had somehow been able to communicate, if not with the dead, then with those at another level. So, trusting in her own ability to communicate at this 'other' level, she had acted with bravery because she felt less vulnerable than others may have felt in the same situation. Then, when she had disappeared with a flash of light, it only confirmed in her own mind that she was in the hands of good rather than in evil.

She continued to explain that she woke up in a greenhouse. At first she was charmed. It was sunny, warm and she was surrounded by a great variety of plants. Some of the plants were consumable and some were simply pretty. She soon saw that she had everything she needed to tend the plants. But when she tried the door she realized that it would not open. She could entertain herself by caring for the plants but she must remain with them. She too was being treated like a hothouse plant. There was bedding and a small corner bathroom. From that she realized that she must still be human with normal bodily functions. But once she had cared for the plants each day she would have very little else to do. And that lifestyle was both her punishment and her joy. She received no communication nor could she send any. While she always believed that she would get back to her loved ones she had to survive on faith. That is what she did until that day.

Then the widow spoke to her, but did not appear to her. The widow sounded neither angry nor happy, just matter of fact about it being time for her to return to her daughter. She was very excited, thinking about the reunion and wondering about the baby, but uncertain if she had something to fear or not. Then the joyful moment of arriving at this house which she recognized well, and entering to find Elena Maria. She summarized by saying that she was never hurt but she was held a prisoner and could not reach those she loved.

When Elena Maria began to speak she was overwhelmed with joy to have her mother back and on time to be so involved with Matthew's birth. She said there would never be a reason for her to complain about anything again. She had everything a woman could desire: wonderful family including the new baby, a dear husband and parents who would give their lives for her if necessary. As Christmas was coming right up, and the difficult year of 2020 was nearly over, they should celebrate by decorating and cooking and enjoying the baby!

Elena Maria was so happy and high on life that Matt did not want to mention to her the reminder the Civil War Captain had given, of her owing him a debt for this good fortune. Matt put it right out of his own mind too as he knew she deserved some happiness free of worry. They all accepted duties to help prepare the house for the new baby and for Christmas. He went to get a hatchet and then out back to find a perfect little Christmas tree and he dreamed about hanging 'baby's first stocking' on the mantel.

Elena Maria was the most recovered new mother one could imagine. She was like a person out of a Perl S. Buck book who gave birth in the fields and then continued right on with the work of harvesting. When she wasn't cuddling or feeding Matthew, she was skipping around the house decorating. She was even so bold as to hang a piece of holly on the portrait and say "Merry Christmas, captain!" What she failed to notice was something she had, here-to-for, always been alert to observe. That was the captain's eye movements. This time his response to Elena Maria was not as cordial as it had been of late; this time he appeared to be wondering if she had lost her mind. But, perhaps in the spirit of the moment he simply quieted down.

Soon enough he would explain the price of bringing a dead mother back through the portal; soon enough.

3.5

AND THEN IT WAS CHRISTMAS

The following morning, when the house was all awake, they continued decorating and cooking. It was a bit wearisome for Elena Maria as she was breastfeeding and up, therefore, with every feeding. But, her mother also got up every other time her daughter did, and Matt was up with his wife when it was not his mother-in-law's turn. Since her dad had the most sleep the group nominated him to perform many of the most challenging tasks such as bringing in the wood for the fires and setting up the two trees Matt had selected. While they had trees in every room the previous year, they cut back to only two trees this year because there could be no real entertaining. This was simply decorating to please their little family, and it did.

Elena Maria was determined to make her own bread. The previous year, as they had their housewarming as a Christmas party, she had ordered many delicacies from an Italian Bakery. Then, she and her mother had baked Italian cookies and breads to go along with the antipasto, the melon and prosciutto, and fine cheeses. Naturally, Matt and Elena Maria had been generous with wines and all manner of beverages. This year it would be a party of four adults, one nursing so she would not be drinking alcohol, and one infant. Passing up a drink this Christmas was not going to dampen spirits.

The delivery truck pulled up to the house as often as three times a day with gifts they had in mind for each other and had ordered on-line. There was a slight undercurrent of mystery surrounding the arrival of each package as one of them would scramble to hide an item and to later make it appear under the tree in its fully wrapped glory. But as they bustled through the house none of the adults took this excitement and joy for granted; they each knew how lucky they were as compared to others going through the pandemic and how incredible was their own personal luck after the fears and loss of the recent past. Each delicacy cooked, each pinecone arrangement set up with candles, each brightly wrapped package, made them almost hold their breath to keep the joy inside.

Elena Maria and her mother even baked cookies and sent them to neighbors with notes promising visits as soon as possible after the pandemic and announcing the birth of baby Matthew. Matt and his father-in-law found enough Princess pine and pine boughs on the edge of their woods to create a large wreath which was hung on the barn and illuminated at night. They wanted to share the good cheer with all who passed by. Matt wrote a substantial check for the local soup kitchen and the five of them planned to attend an outside bonfire at the church, being offered just before midnight on Christmas Eve, to thank all possible for their happiness.

Music sung by Andre Bocelli was sent throughout the house via Blue Tooth. The home was in complete readiness for Santa Claus when they walked, arms linked and wearing masks, to the church. The plan was to hurry back, feed little Matt, open one gift each and try to sleep until Christmas Day when the unwrapping and eating would begin in earnest. They also planned to call Italy and many friends who would not yet know the miracles which had befallen them: Joy to the world.

They walked back to their house a bit subdued as so many memories flashed through all of their minds. How different this experience was than what it had looked like fate would give them. Not only did they have Nonna back, nearly from death, and on time for the birth; but they had a healthy baby; the evil bones had gone away and were swept out of the cellar; and Emily was where she had wished to be. Little wonder all looked so rosy for this holiday and for the next year.

Once inside they had their little get together in the parlor, for that was where the principal Christmas tree stood. Matt lit the fire and mugs of cocoa and hot toddies were passed. Baby Matthew suckled his Christmas beverage and then they all went up to bed. Matt remained behind to tamp the fire down for the night. As he turned to go upstairs he noticed motion behind him and the captain began to speak. "Be sure you remind your wife that I will soon be asking her for that favor," was all that was said. And Matt hurried up the stairs trying to decide when he might wish to deliver that message.

Matt had grown up with Christmas in an American tradition, as had his father-in-law so the little group planned to follow those customs. For them on Christmas morning it meant opening gifts after a light breakfast as baby Matt was so little. Once there were older children, gift opening would probably not be delayed, or emotions would run wild. But for now they nibbled on fruited breads, yogurt and coffee before coming to sit around the tree. Then, for a little time, they could all behave as children enjoying the surprises within each package.

They stacked new items under the tree to enjoy a bit later; fully unwrapping only games in which all might share. Then the women went about the business of finishing preparations on a sumptuous repast for the next meal. The men picked up the debris of things left by Santa and took what was appropriate out to the barn to wait for trash day. Of course the baby required attention throughout the morning but there were always a pair of hands at the ready to hold him. It wasn't long before food was being laid out and new games were being learned.

Among the gaiety of that afternoon it suddenly dawned on Elena Maria that the Civil War captain might be taking notice of them. She raised her glass of juice and asked her family to stand a moment while she made a toast to Captain Benjamin Mills. In her toast she gave him credit for this incredible reunion and stated how lucky she felt they were to be in his acquaintance. There was a resounding cry of "To Captain Mills" followed by clapping. No one had expected that the portal would open at this time and that the captain would address them all.

He began with "I thank you for considering me during your family gathering. This truly seems to be a loving family. In fact, Elena Maria reminds me very much of the woman I once married named Victoria. She has been gone for many years but I still love her. It was the war that pulled us apart. In any case, we had one child together, a girl named Grace. Grace was trouble due to the strangeness of her origins, which I shall not now get into, but it required that I remove her from this world when she was yet a young child. She has resided for decades in a place of half reality half spirit. She has not aged or grown in all this time. Some part of her spirit has matured and I know that there is hope for her to be happy back in this time. It will mean she will be mortal again but she will grow and have a life; perhaps even children of her own."

"I have watched how she interacts with Elena Maria and I think there will be a bond formed between them. In any case my wish and my request of you all is that you shall take Grace and raise her as your own child. She will gain good parents and grandparents and will soon learn to love her baby brother. So my request is quite simple. I wish you to raise Grace as your own."

Elena Maria was dumbfounded. She knew from her readings of Victoria's family history just how misbehaved and destructive this little girl had been. Her first instinct was to protect her baby and her family by blurting out "No", but she did not. She thought of all the joy that had just come their way due to this man, and knew they would have little or none of it without him. She had never told Matt the terrors Grace caused and suddenly realized she hoped she would never have to, but on this day, on Christmas itself, she would have to say "yes" to this request; and actually she had already pledged so to do.

She stood up straight and faced the portrait. "If you think we are the right people to raise Grace then I am touched and honored to take in this child and pledge to do all that I can, 'all we can', to see that she has a happy home in which to live. It can only be a blessing to have both a son and a daughter. Certainly we have adequate space and the means to feed her. It is settled then, Grace shall live here with us."

Her parents did not know what to make of all this and they knew that a good deal was owed to the portrait, so they modeled their affect and responses to match Elena Maria's. Matt had known that there would be a major request made of them. He had never imagined that they would be given another child to raise; but he thought, far better to be given a child then to have one removed or to lose Elena Maria's mother again. If our price for the miracles we have received is to contribute to the life of a girl named Grace, then we shall do it. He pledged to stand by Elena Maria in this decision and to be the best father he could be to this child. It sounded like Grace had a difficult time in the past and he wanted to make certain they would not fail her. Nodding toward his wife and the others he said "I'm sure we will all welcome her and put her safety, comfort and education at the top of every decision we make for her."

3.6

RAISING GRACE

E lena Maria was quick to add "And we also pledge to love her, for no child will flourish without love, especially one who has so long been deprived of family."

Nonna added "Then it is settled! When can we meet our new granddaughter or is that COVID dependent?"

The deep, distant sounding baritone voice of the captain replied, "It shall be soon." And the portrait was once more still, devoid of any human characteristics, simply a painting on canvas.

When they felt quite certain that they were alone, they all began to talk at once. Their voices were animated and excited. It felt as though they had just won the lottery to be handed this little girl. Elena Maria kept her trepidations to herself so that she would not spoil the mood nor jinx this fresh start for Grace. She only added, "Grace was born in the 1890s; she knew this street and neighborhood well. Now she will be lost, for her life has been frozen in time while all else moved on. She may also be confused as she starts to grow and mature, as nothing has changed in that way for her in decades. She may be fearful of cars and planes, of escalators and drive-up windows. How could she imagine pulling an automobile up to a window and getting food or money? She will, in fact, know nothing about currency, or television or computers."

"She may well look for the people whom she new here before, including her parents and siblings. This could be a very difficult time for her, although those acquaintances are long ago. A lot will depend on Grace's reactions and if the captain plays any role from here-on-in, as he is her actual father. We will all need to be understanding. We don't even know if she can read or write as education was so different in that time and especially for a girl."

Elena Maria's dad added, "And speaking of school, she will be shocked to see what one looks like today and the hours that are required. Not everything will revolve around crops and harvest time!"

Elena Maria moved the baby to her breast as he was just beginning to suck on his hand. Then she acknowledged just a bit of her fear. "What have we agreed to, this is going to be very challenging for all."

Heads nodded, "Yes" said Matt, "We will all have to work hard to make such a huge adjustment possible for the child."

"Well," said Elena Maria, "Little Mattie will be the only one for whom this will all seem normal." That caused laughter. Christmas Day was drawing to a close and food had to be put away and the dishwasher turned on. Showers were being taken and a light snow was falling outside, all in all an unforgettable Christmas. Soon the house was quiet except that Elena Maria was sitting in bed nursing Mattie as his father told him stories of all the good times he would have with their cat and dog, Sybil and Scruffy. Sybil and Scruffy had also both received gifts under the tree, so even they were content this Christmas night. And then the last lights were shut off in the house and not a creature was stirring.

As light dawned on the new day, everything looked particularly bright due to the perfectly white snow with its glistening crystals. The women and baby were the first ones up and nonna reset the kitchen fireplace to warm and cheer that room. They had just begun to discuss cooking eggs and bacon when there was a loud knock at the door. Elena Maria, with Mattie in her arms, was the first one to reach the door and swung it wide open thinking she was letting in the milkman. But there, on their side step which was a huge granite slab, stood a child in raggedy clothing holding a cardboard suitcase and a cloth doll. She was shaking from the cold so Elena Maria pulled her directly into the house and said "Welcome home Grace. Do you remember me?"

"Yes," spoke the child. "I am glad you are well recovered from the boating accident. You saved my friends and Papa tells me I will now live with you."

"That is right," said Elena Maria, "And this baby in my arms is your brother Matthew, and the lady standing by the fire is your grandmother whom we call nonna. Now tell us what you need for I am sure you are cold and tired. Wash your hands, and at least, put a warm sweater on, and shortly we will all eat eggs and cornbread."

Grace gazed around the house as though she was uncertain of her surroundings. Then she spoke; "This was my Aunt Esther's house. She lived here with Uncle John and their daughters. I was here just before my father, Ben, had to send me away."

Elena Maria interrupted, "I'm sure you have many memories, some of them fun and some of them dark. We will talk about them whenever you want to but first let us get you settled, warm and fed."

Elena Maria's heart was beating fast. In truth she was shocked to have had the girl arrive so quickly. She would have appreciated a little more time to prepare herself and the family but, Grace was with them already. She had interrupted Grace before she could speak of any of the details of her last night in East Apple. If Elena Maria had understood correctly, the captain had killed his daughter in order to remove her and to protect the family of his brother and the wife, Victoria, whom they had shared. This must be a most painful recollection for the girl, not something Elena Maria felt prepared to discuss with her nor was she even ready to try and explain it all to her own mother.

Instead of introducing the difficult subject of filicide, she asked her mother if she would mind preparing the upstairs back bedroom for Grace. It had a nice closet and two windows looking out on the barn and the woods beyond. She believed it would be a lovely and comfortable space for the child with easy access to a bathroom. It was also near to the master bedroom and the nursery so that Grace would feel connected to the entire family. Naturally her mother went right up to begin the chore and announced she would let the men know that "the rest of the family was with them".

When nonna exited, Grace reappeared from the downstairs bathroom right off the kitchen. She seemed to have cleaned herself up and was now wearing a large gray sweater that looked homespun. Elena Maria complemented the girl on this sweater which was apparently the correct thing to do as Grace grinned widely at the remark. She then asked "Where did the old lady go?"

Elena Maria took a deep breath and replied, "If you are talking about nonna you must try to be more respectful; she is to be your grandmother and her age, although she is still young, does not define her." "OK," said Grace, "where is nonna?" Elena Maria liked this as it appeared to reflect progress. Then she replied, "Nonna has gone upstairs to prepare your bedroom so that you shall be comfortable."

Elena Maria then continued; "When you feel ready I would like you to call me 'mama' or 'mother' if you prefer. We will make arrangements for you to have our last name and, as soon as the pandemic is over, we shall find a way to enroll you in school. Tell me, Grace, are you fond of reading?" To which the girl replied "Yes, mama." This pleased Elena Maria on two levels, that the girl could read and that she would immediately call her mama.

Then she asked her, "Do you know your numbers?" To which the child also replied in the affirmative. With a few more questions it became known that Grace could tell time on the grandfather clock in the living room, and she could read the numbers for time as they flashed on the microwave although this required a few minutes for her to figure out, but all in all she seemed an intelligent child. Elena Maria realized they would have some work to do to bring her up to par on history and science, but the pandemic would buy them a few more months to prepare.

Suddenly they heard a rush of feet on the stairs. Nonna was coming down with a crying Mattie and the men were ready for breakfast. It was time to serve bacon, eggs and cornbread, along with more introductions.

3.7

THE DAY AFTER CHRISTMAS

Usually, the day after Christmas Elena Maria had devoted to cleaning up the house, making a hearty leftover soup, and a little bit of bargain hunting in preparation for the next year. This year she woke up to feed a newborn and to begin discussing what they must all do to integrate Grace into their lives.

She began by asking Grace, over breakfast, what she would like to do on this sunny December day. Grace's response was that she had been living where it was always sunny and warm so she was happy for them if this was special weather. Elena Maria did not know if this was meant to be flippant but decided to let it go, not to start out defensively with this child. Then Grace added, "I would like to walk by my old house. Do you know the Chase-Mills farm? That is where I was born. Perhaps the current family would even allow me in for a quick look."

Elena Maria took a deep breath. She disliked being in a position to give the girl bad news but she knew the site of the Chase-Mills farm which had been torn down and the land behind it subdivided. Where the farm and outbuildings had stood, there was now a new library and a recreation area. The location was ideal as it is in the middle of town. She said to Grace, "That farm no longer exists, but its land was so special that East Apple built a new library there which is filled with important books and educational materials."

"Oh," said Grace, "Then I may go inside and just see what it looks like to be there again."

"Of course, we can even get you your own library card so that you may take out books yourself." And then others joined them, explained about library cards, and this discussion ended.

Matt asked Grace if she had any idea what grade she should be in. Grace laughed, "I didn't go to school very much, only when there was no work to do. And when I did go we were all in one room. You answered when you could or tried like hell when the teacher called on you. They didn't push me around much, that's for sure."

"I'm glad you didn't feel afraid of the teachers," reframed Matt. "But we will need to work with you, and them to discover where your learning level is, so that you can feel at home in school. In other words, what do you know already and what do you need to know next? Also, we don't use words like "hell" in school or anywhere. They make many people feel badly so it is not worth using them when other words work well."

"So what should I say?" asked Grace defiantly.

"Good question," said Matt, "What is best to say is 'we tried as hard as we could' when the teacher called on us; or we tried so hard that our shoes popped off when the teacher called on us." At that point they all began laughing and a possible crisis with Grace was averted.

Then Grace asked the kind of question they were all afraid might be on her mind. "So, mama," she said addressing Elena Maria, "are all the people who lived at Chase-Mills farm dead now?"

Elena Maria looked ashen. She went over to Grace and took her hand. She sat down next to her and replied, "Yes, I think they must be, dear, because you were born a very long time ago and those people continued to age. But when your dad, Benjamin, took you away, you ceased to age until just yesterday when he brought you here. Now we will all grow-up and grow-old together. You have become human and will have to learn to keep much of your past to yourself. In our family we will know where you came from but other people would not understand. So you cannot mention that this was your aunt's home, or that a very long time ago you lived where the library now stands."

"I guess I understand," said Grace. "I don't know if anyone will like me because they won't really know why I'm so different. I hope some of the girls will play with me."

"They will Grace, they will. It just takes a little time for everyone to get used to you and you to them. You'll have plenty of friends" said Matt. "We just have to figure out how to register you for school."

Elena Maria's dad had been on the periphery of this conversation, listening but not wanting to interfere. Now he believed he had something to contribute. "I've known some men who have the ability to be 'creative' regarding such problems; and their work is flawless. I'll be glad to contribute this as a new grandfather. We'll just have to know Grace's birth month and day and pick the year needed, maybe 2011? Then I think he finds the name of somebody approximately her age who doesn't need (and here he cleared his throat) identification any longer, and moves forward."

"You mean I will get some other dead girls birthday" said Grace. Her affect was flat as she said it, if anything, she was almost teary.

"Yes, dear," said Elena Maria. "You are a real person but we must have records that reflect your age as you appear to be so that you can stay with us and grow forward."

"And may I still be 'Grace'?"

"Yes, of course," said her grandfather. "People alter their first names for all kinds of reasons; we'll just note somewhere that your parents decided the best name for you would be Grace even though some other name may appear on the original birth certificate which we will have copied. It would be too much to have you learn another name." He did not add 'after all these years' but it was understood that he thought that.

And the day went on much in this vain. Grace had questions, worries sometimes, and the family did their necessary chores while assisting her to understand how her needs would be met. Her grandmother measured her, and the girl and two women looked through online catalogs to be certain she would have adequate and appropriate clothing. Just the notion of fashion was a difficult concept for Grace, never mind the internet. But this child was already aware of multiple worlds via the portal so she accepted these new things with, well, Grace. Step by step they seemed to unravel the mystery of how Grace would appear as a modern child.

Then it was time for the child to spend her second night in the 'real world'. She appeared to be learning how to wash with modern water, and where to place her clothing for laundry the next day. They had even cut and stitched two of Elena Maria's night gowns to work for Grace. She would soon have her drawers filled with clothing of her own.

The family was a bit on edge with so many changes happening at a rapid pace and as Grace seemed a bit different to them all. But when they spoke of her oddities they all attributed them to her being part of a bygone century. Only Elena Maria knew that there might be problems of a mental health nature but decided it was best to wait and see. They bid each other good night, and Matt carried baby Mattie into their bedroom. They were tired and knew the baby would wake them soon so they snuggled into bed.

Around midnight the baby woke once for a feeding which Elena Maria and Matt handled. Then the three of them fell back into a deep sleep. It might have been thirty minutes later when their bedroom door slowly opened as though without having been touched. A young girl in a white gown entered the room and went right up to the side of the baby's crib. She just stood there staring over to the bed at Elena Maria.

The sensation of eyes almost penetrating her skin awoke Elena Maria. She abruptly sat up seeking to see that Mattie was well. He was, but next to him stood Grace looking very trance-like, ghostly and eerie. She spoke a short sentence to Elena Maria and then walked out of the room. "I want to see my mother."

3.8
HERE KITTY KITTY

"Here Kitty, Kitty" shouted Elena Maria for about the one hundredth time that morning. She followed this by coughing so scraped was her throat. It seemed to her she was caught in a déjà vu. Hadn't her first days in this house, prior to any renovations, begun with her furiously hunting for a cat? And that had ended sadly to be followed by a time when they thought Sybil too was lost. But that had ended happily, so maybe Sybil still had some lives left. It would be tragic to lose the brave little kitty that had jumped on the skeletal remains in the basement and been willing to fight them. Sybil didn't have multiple personalities, but she certainly had multiple strengths and talents.

In the year that they had lived with Sybil she had enjoyed free run of the area. Generally she hung around with the dog, but Scruffy wasn't always spunky enough for her, and the woods and stonewalls were alluring with all kinds of critters to chase, then munch and crunch. It had happened that she would traipse away and miss dinner; however she always appeared at the backdoor the next morning. She would be purring and rubbing just to make up for worrying anyone. But this was day three of being AWOL. Where the heck was that darn cat?

Elena Maria had asked Grace if she had seen the kitty and been told they passed by each other only briefly some days ago. Grace was exploring the barn, and Sybil seemed to be on her own exploration headed out, according to the child. Matt had already performed the morbid task of slowly driving around the neighborhood to determine if any cat-splat could be found by the side of the road, but to date, no sign of Sybil.

Elena Maria had even called her parents to determine if, by any chance, they had accidently packed Sybil into one of their suitcases. Her folks had decided to go home for a few weeks, probably hoping to give the new family a little privacy and also to give them time for a honeymoon. Her parents had been through so much it seemed appropriate.

Finally, in desperation, Elena Maria asked Scruffy to go find Sybil. She had held back on doing this fearing the worst if the dog had to drag a lifeless body home. But this time Scruffy ran to the barn and commenced to barking fiercely at a cupboard. These were some very old storage compartments which they had endeavored to salvage when most of the barn was replaced. These cupboards worked well for things not needed often. They stuck once closed again and were difficult to re-open without a strong yank. Now, as she approached them, Elena Maria heard a faint "meow" emanating from within. She yanked the door open to reveal a starving, nearly dehydrated, Sybil, who fell into her arms. "Oh my God" cried Elena Maria, "How on earth did this happen, you poor little kitty," she said as she ran for the house.

With a new baby, Elena Maria had not wandered far from the house in days. She had believed that Sybil would make it back to them under her own steam. It never dawned on her that the cat would be closed in and practically locked up. She tried to keep certain thoughts from her mind as she continued to administer to the cat. But as hard as she tried not to think that Grace had done this, she really was convinced that Grace had! These were the kinds of acts Elena Maria feared most; random sadistic acts on helpless animals or even babies. If she totally lacked compassion for others, failed to see them as having feelings and needs, then she could evolve into a monster.

On the other hand, Grace had known a lot of loss and death. Perhaps emotional injury, rather than a personality disorder, had triggered this kind of thoughtless action toward an animal who she was too young to appreciate as having needs. Elena Maria did not want to make excuses for her new daughter, only to be cautious not to over react to an impulsive action a child might make. That was why laws had age related restrictions on penalties; kids did not possess the same judgment as adults. She and Matt would have to discuss this. Additionally, it would be nice to see how Grace reacted when she heard where Sybil had been found.

Grace was with her father at the moment. He took her along on some COVID safe errands he had setup. This meant that they were primarily doing 'curbside pickup' stops which included one trip to a farm that let you go in, take eggs from their refrigerator, and leave cash under a rock on the counter. Grace immediately asked Matt why he didn't just take all the eggs and leave only a dollar. He explained that the farmers were friends, and if they couldn't afford to buy food for the chickens then no one would get eggs. She seemed to comprehend this. They also carried on a running discussion over the age of the community. Matt thought it would help Grace to have a context of which buildings had been around when she was a kid the first time, and which were new. It also allowed her to reminisce and ask him questions as they occurred to her. Matt seemed to understand how weird it might be to die and then come back to the same place where no one else remained from your earlier time.

Grace did say that she "felt like a visitor who was allowed one last look at a place she had loved but all the people who had mattered were now turned into trees." A sad thought; he hoped other people would soon matter to Grace. He also knew when she felt a little more secure he would have to talk to her about the moral issue of 'taking the eggs without paying for them." He wanted 'his daughter' to be an honest and respectable person.

When they pulled into the yard Matt said gently "I hope Sybil has come home. Your mother really loves that little cat." He later would report to Elena Maria that Grace had looked down when he made that statement and walked immediately to the barn. A few seconds later she had run directly to the house as though she now knew that Sybil was out. Matt and Elena Maria sat by the kitchen fire with Sybil sitting on a cushion between them. She was licking cream off her paw and allowing them to take turns scratching her under her chin as she soaked up the warmth of the fire. The cat froze as Grace approached them. When Grace drew closer Sybil jumped up and ran into another room.

"Hello Grace," said Elena Maria. "I'm glad to hear from your father that you had a nice time together on the drive. You seem to enjoy automobiles. And thank you both for bringing home eggs."

"When you've washed your hands and had a snack we would like you to go out to the barn and clean the cupboard that Sybil was trapped in as the cat had no way to get out for the bathroom. We have already cleaned her but; she was in there so long she almost died. We want you to help us be sure she doesn't get trapped like that again. Can you do that; can you help us to take good care of the kitty?"

Grace hung her head. She said, "Yes ma'am. It won't happen again." And she went about following her new mother's directions.

The remainder of the day was uneventful. Elena Maria thought it best to postpone the discussion of seeing 'Grace's mother' as there seemed to have been enough turmoil already that day. Although at some point she was certainly willing to take Grace to the cemetery and let her speak with her mom in private, that way, she hoped Grace wasn't thinking she could use the portal to find Victoria, all these years dead and buried.

That evening the little family of four enjoyed a beef stew and biscuits for dinner, read stories and took their bathes in preparation for bed. All seemed to be quiet and relaxed with the only major interruptions from the baby. Soon the fire was tamped down and they were in bed.

Again, at about midnight, the door to the master bedroom opened wide and Grace, apparently sleepwalking entered her parents' bedroom and went to her mother's side of the bed. She spoke in a loud whisper without ever opening her eyes. "Mother, it wasn't my fault. The big boy who lives in the cellar told me I had to do it."

3.9

GRACIOUS

It took a long time for Matt and Elena Maria to fall back to sleep once Grace had spoken to them. Baby Mattie was sleeping better than usual, but his parents were tossing and turning. "How can she be talking to a boy in the cellar?" whispered Elena Maria. "We only recently watched the undertaker as he carefully laid Emily to rest beside his bone-filled coffin? That corpse is practically dust!"

"It must be her imagination," said Matt. "She has gone through multiple traumas; living but always in trouble; dying at her spirit father's hand; being brought back to life in the place where she had been born, and yet so much had changed in this place including everyone she knew being gone. We need to give her time, to help her through the trauma, to stabilize. So she made up an imaginary friend to take the blame for something bad we caught her at. That's all this is."

And so they agreed to talk to her in the morning but, just in case, Elena Maria asked Matt to simply check the cellar first thing and verify that the dirt floor was as they had left it. Matt came up the cellar stairs to join the other three at breakfast and shook his head while smiling. He let Elena Maria know that nothing was amiss downstairs. Then they had the task of bringing this all up to Grace without sounding like they were accusing her of a crime.

But, the surprise was on them, as Grace had no memory of entering their room and making that statement. Further, she said, "What

194

boy?" Which they hastened to say was the question they had for her because, of course, the cellar was just a storage area.

"Perhaps," added Elena Maria, "you are lonely for someone your own age to play with? There may be some kids in the neighborhood whose parents would allow them to play outside with you if you all wear masks and follow rules about distances between you. Would you like me to find out?" Grace said she would as long as Elena Maria promised her that these kids would not be mean to her. Her mother smiled and said, "Of course they will not be mean children. I will make some calls today."

Thus, by the following morning two girls about Grace's age, one just the same and one a bit older, plus their younger brother, showed up at the backdoor of Grace's house to see if she would like to go sliding. Grace knew how to ride a sled, and the farm still had one on hand, so the four kids walked over toward the parsonage which allowed kids to use their steep front lawn. Elena Maria said she would follow along shortly pushing Mattie in his new stroller.

When Elena Maria arrived she saw the little boy getting his nose administered to by his big sister. He had fallen onto his sled just before he had intended to go zooming down the hill; the sled took off and little Steve didn't stay on long before he tumbled, scraping his nose during the journey. There were tears, but it didn't look serious, and certainly his sisters didn't think it was a big deal. They intended to keep on sliding. But Steve turned toward Grace and, with his chin quivering, pointed a soggy mitten at her yelling "She pushed me!"

Grace's reply was that she "did not!" The exclamations went back and forth increasing in volume with each volley.

Elena Maria said that she was certain if Grace accidently bumped into Steve that she was sorry. Grace stomped her feet and said "No I'm not because I didn't do anything! I stayed six feet away!"

"Well Grace, do you want to go home or tell Stephen you'd like to be friends?"

There was a long pause. Grace felt caught like that little bit of eggshell in a bowl when the cook has finally got her finger on it, not much chance she could slide back down where she wanted to cause trouble; any choice could leave her out. "I'd like to stay," she finally said. "And I do hope we can all be friends."

"Is that okay with you, Stephen?" asked Elena Maria. He nodded his affirmation. "Well then I'll wheel the stroller around this area for awhile and pick Grace up after you kids slide a bit longer. I had forgotten how much I need her help to prepare lunch today."

With that, the children were seemingly left alone, although Elena Maria never went far from sight and certainly could hear their high pitched voices wherever she was. The kids could work things out for themselves pretty well, but she was fearful that Grace had to know the 'law' was close by.

After lunch, while Grace was playing somewhere else in the house, and Mattie was napping, Elena Maria called the neighbor kids' house. She explained to their mom what she had witnessed, and said she hoped her new daughter hadn't arrived with any rough or dubious habits. She wanted that mom to know she was apologizing for any injury to Stephen and that the family was working to help Grace adjust after the tragic loss of her parents.

Matt and Elena Maria, with Grace's help, were telling a tale to explain her suddenly appearing in East Apple. What they had rehearsed amounted to: a cousin of Matt's from Maryland had been killed in a car accident. The accident also took the life of his wife. Their only child, a girl named Grace, had survived but been traumatized. After several months she had been rushed out of a care facility as the virus raged in that state. Matt had been discovered to be her only living relative so the Nelsons were asked to take her. The agency made all necessary arrangements. The family was just trying to handle the social integration aspects and, be supportive of Grace's mental health issues.

The neighbor, and mother of the three other kids, could not have been more empathetic. She kept saying, "That poor little dear, of course she would have a rough time." And, as to the apology for Stephen, his mother insisted he had not been injured at all. She said, "I think his pride was hurt because he was the only boy, but he got the first boo-boo. Don't worry about it. We'll set up another play date in a day or two. They'll all be best friends soon enough."

When Elena Maria hung up from the call she wasn't sure if she was happy or fearful at the prospect of those four kids all getting together again. She guessed she would leave it up to Grace to decide if SHE could be nice to them. Then she began to wonder what was entertaining Grace at that moment.

Elena Maria first looked around the ground floor since she was already there. No sign of Grace who she thought might have become interested in the computer. She then checked all the upstairs bedrooms, in case Grace had a book or game, she might be quietly playing. Then she went out to the barn to see if Grace had found something unique to do there, other than trying to hide the cat. Finally she went back inside and called down the cellar stairs "Grace please come up I need you." And Grace came up.

"What were you doing down there," asked Elena Maria.

"Oh," said Grace, "the little boy is only allowed upstairs at night so I play with him in the cellar in the day time. His grandmother is nice too. She reads books to us, and they both like the big spiders."

4.0
TRUTH OR CONSEQUENCES

Elena Maria had been an emotional wreck over the loss of her mother. That pain had gone on for many months. Simultaneously, she had been pregnant and tired. Now she was living on severely truncated sleep due to feeding the newborn. On top of all this she had to accept a strange reality in order to connect with her mom, and this 'spirit' had forced her to accept a child who might well be possessed!

Hearing Grace say that she had been in the cellar playing with 'the living dead' was the last spark before the fire exploded! Elena Maria grabbed Grace by the arm and dragged her to a chair in the kitchen. Her touch was not gentle, and the child wiggled and made a face. Elena Maria did not mind being rough for she was sick of these spooky pop-ups, not on her computer screen, but in her daughter's actions. She meant to demand that Grace answer some questions.

"What do you mean you were talking to people in the cellar? What people? And are they down there right now?" Elena Maria said.

"Yes," stammered Grace. And that was all she was allowed to utter before her arm was pulled back in the direction of the cellar from which she had just exited. Elena Maria was going to see with her own eyes just what it was that so intrigued Grace.

Down the stairs they went, bumping first against the wall and then against the banister as they clomped down into the basement.

"All right!" shouted Elena Maria, "Where are they then?" But no one could be seen.

Grace stared back at her mother with her mouth hanging open. She seemed unable to speak. Then she blurted out "Well they don't want to talk with you. You are not like them, but I am, as I have been dead before."

Elena Maria said, "We shall see if they lurk around down here. Where are their books, why are the graves not open? Is there no evidence that you have friends down here?" And Grace only looked more shocked, more caught with the last cookie and company coming. She did not want to say more or could not think what story to tell.

But Elena Maria could not yet let go. She yanked the child through every nook and cranny in the cellar until they were back where they had started, having discovered nothing. "Grace," she said, "Why do you tell me such fantastic stories? Do you wish your dead friends from long ago would return? Would you prefer people from the old days rather than to make friends with those of us in current times? Are you rebelling against the plan for you to be part of this new age? Talk to me, Grace."

Grace truly looked stricken. The light in her eyes was dim, her hair was limp and she seemed to be hanging in an imaginary breeze. "I don't know why I said those things. But when I was here the first time, when I lived at the other farm and Victoria was my mother and Ted was my father, they were always over here worrying about my aunt and cousins. There was a cruel skeleton lady who tried to burn people and steal children. She lived down here. Then, when I went sledding, the kids told me that you and daddy Matt had been mentioned in the newspaper. You had allowed an old skeleton found near the church to be buried in this cellar. You did it because the woman who had been those remains had written a diary which you read. You knew she wanted to be in the earth next to her long ago dead adopted son, and you thought it would be a kindness to allow that. The kids thought I should know that there were bodies down here."

"Then, when one of them remembered that my parents had recently died, she said 'shut-up' to her sister and they wouldn't say anything else. So I figured maybe those dead people would talk to me because I have been dead, and I would like to know more about them. Not to make you angry, I just like to understand everyone's story so I don't feel so strange."

Suddenly, it all almost made sense to Elena Maria. She asked, "So you know that there are no dead people walking around down here, right? You just have a big imagination and like stories?"

"Well," added Grace, "I'm not completely sure about that because there was someone down here when I was first a kid; and my real father lives in an in-between world. I'm not able to explain everything."

"Okay, "allowed Elena Maria. "I can understand there is room for confusion and you haven't been in this world long. Just, please, come to me with questions the next time you are confused and don't tell me stories unless you know them to be true. Now, I hear Mattie crying, it's time you learned to change a diaper."

The woman and the girl went back upstairs and shut the basement door. It was time for Elena Maria to practice her maternal skills and to show Grace that she was not still angry with her. She felt badly about having lost her cool so completely with the child and to have even been a bit rough with her. Grace, on the other hand seemed slightly amused, as though she had just sold someone that first Connecticut nutmeg.

It turned out that changing a baby's diaper was not a reward for being a big girl but, in Grace's eyes, a punishment which would insure she never wished to become a mother. After that chore was over Grace sat and read a book while Elena Maria nursed the infant. They didn't speak much except to discuss what they would have for supper, but the atmosphere was pleasant. Finally, Grace said she wondered if she could have her bath before they ate; if it would be okay to come to the dinner table in her night gown. Elena Maria said, "It has been a busy day, you live here, please make yourself comfortable."

Once Grace was upstairs alone she started the water running in the tub but, under the cover of that noise, she decided to do some looking around. She went into her parents' room and looked through her mother's jewelry box. She saw a small ring and slipped it on her finger leaving it there. Then she looked at some sexy pictures of Elena Maria that were in the top drawer of what must have been Matt's bureau. She pocketed one of these.

Now she went to the clothing closet and began to paw through the items hanging there. It wasn't too interesting except her mother had a pale blue evening gown hanging there that had sequins all over it. She picked about ten of the shinny little discs off the gown, planning to do more, when she saw light through a crack in the back of the closet. She hastened to inspect this area and discovered that there was a backdoor on the closet which was slightly ajar. She pushed on it, and suddenly she was in a back chamber, like a hidden closet. There was a trapdoor on the floor of this closet. She knelt down and swung the trapdoor open. A set of stairs slid down to the floor way below; it went all the way to the basement. She was thrilled and fascinated; this is going to be fun she thought.

Then she decided the tub might be running over and quickly dashed to the bathroom saving the water from spilling by mere seconds. Next she returned to her parents' room and covered her tracks. She closed the trapdoor, made the closet neat, closed that door and returned the picture to Matt's drawer. The only thing she did not return was the ring from her mother's things.

Smiling with a crooked mouth, one cheek elevated and that eye closed in what made a sort of sarcastic wink; she danced her young self into the bathroom and shut the door. Grace was making some plans.

4.1

DOCTOR SPOCK

M att shook his head from side to side. Once the kids were in bed he was amazed at the story Elena Maria told him. Grace had actually claimed to be 'hanging out' with a boy and his grandmother who stayed in the cellar by day but came upstairs and used the whole house by night. What crap, he thought, and all because a kid in the neighborhood had revealed the recent news stories to Grace regarding the interment of Emily. These kids had no judgment on how to welcome a frightened little girl. He said these things to Elena Maria.

"I agree with you Matt. But I'm wondering how she got her information on the spiders. How is it she thought to mention that these friends in the cellar like big spiders?"

"The only thing I can think of," said Matt, "Is that our neighbors must have done a lot of talking about us a year ago when that exterminator nearly died from trying to fumigate the Goliath Bird eating Spiders in our cellar. They probably told their kids that they were lucky COVID would keep them out of our house because we have bodies buried in the cellar and an infestation of giant spiders!"

"Dear God," said Elena Maria. "What a reputation we must have. It is a wonder they would let their kids play with our Grace!"

And so, once again, the new parents found a reasonable explanation for Grace's actions which could have been viewed as normal.

Hopefully this denial of their daughter's abnormalities would not cost them too dearly.

The next morning, looking both sweet and perky, Grace joined her parents at the breakfast table. She had washed her hair the night before and now had a bouncy ponytail. She said "Yes please" and "Thank you" to ask for and receive food. Matt and Elena Maria looked at each other as if to say 'who could ask for a cuter child.' Then Elena Maria was off to give the baby his morning bath, Matt was off to the University, and Grace was asked to clear the table and read her first on-line assignment. Elena Maria added that she would join Grace shortly to review how the work was going.

When the morning was drawing to a close, Grace asked if she could again play with the kids next door. Elena Maria, hesitating slightly, said she would make a call to their mother. Their mother responded that they were still doing their on-line assignments but would come calling for Grace right after lunch.

Grace looked crestfallen when she learned of this slight delay. Then she asked if she could just explore the house some more before lunch, as she still didn't really know the whole place, especially since it had been renovated. Her mother agreed that was fine and emphasized that she should not leave the house, just explore indoors.

As soon as Grace was out of Elena Maria's sight she headed upstairs for her parents' bedroom. She knew it would cause trouble if she headed directly for the basement, but the find of that trapdoor off the bedroom closet, gave her easy access. When Grace got into the first part of the closet she stopped dead in her tracks. There, on the closet floor, were all the sequin pieces she had picked off the gown. Apparently no one had gone into this part of the closet last night so the broken sequins had not been discovered. Quickly she shoved every last piece into her pocket. She had a plan to bury them outside when she was finally alone with the kids; for now her pocket would do. Then she rushed to the trapdoor and began the climb down into the cellar.

When she arrived, Emily and Will were setting some rocks in a large terrarium not far from where the stairs met the floor. The three of them almost collided. "Well, look whose here," said Emily,

"Your little friend from the upstairs. Tell her you are happy to see her, Will." Then Emily went on to mutter, "You'd think Ben and I had taught him no manners."

The kids exchanged shy 'hellos,' and then Grace told Emily that she had a present for her. Grace held out her hand which contained the small ruby ring she had taken from her mother's drawer. Emily accepted it and it fit. She thanked Grace for thinking of her.

"I'd better get back upstairs," said Grace. "I just wanted to check in on you two. See you tonight." And then Grace ascended the stairs which led her back through her mother's closet and away from the cellar. She then traveled through the house arriving in the kitchen in time to offer her help with preparing lunch.

The neighbor kids arrived as expected, and Grace threw on her coat to greet them. She promised her mother that she would behave; no misunderstandings, no one should be hurt, and that she would come and find her if anything went wrong. Then the kids disappeared to play in the neighbor's yard where their mom had said she would keep a watchful eye.

The first thing Grace did, as she was crossing between the yards, was to dig a little hole with her heal and drop all the sequins into it. It was a warm day, and most of the snow had melted or blown out of this spot so she was able to go down several inches. Hurriedly, she then buried the hole with the remaining loose soil and snow. The other kids didn't have time to miss her. They then set up a game of hide and seek which Grace understood how to play.

But Grace had a different way of reacting to being found when it was her turn to hide. As the hunting child grew close to the spot Grace occupied, Grace would jump out at them giving a hideous roar. It was very deep throated and gruff seeming more like a wild and angry animal than a playmate. It scared the youngest girl so badly that she peed in her pants, burst into tears and ran in the house. Her older sister said not to worry, she was just going to change her wet clothing but, then she too went into the house to check on her sister with neither one of them returning.

This left little Stephen, who had not enjoyed his previous time with Grace, alone with her. To evade any rough stuff he feared she might try, he invited her into the house saying he thought their mom would make hot chocolate for them all. When they entered the kitchen Stephen's mom looked a little surprised to see Grace standing there. She had just dealt with her shaken daughters regarding how wild they found Grace. And, due to that, she had just placed one daughter in the bathtub.

When Stephen asked if they could all have cocoa, his mom gave up the idea of a little time to herself to catch up on work while the kids were playing. "Sure," she said. "And Grace, please call your mom so she knows you are inside our house and not in the yard where you could hear her calling if she wished to. I don't want her worried."

Grace didn't really know how to use a phone but, they showed her, and the number Elena Maria had insisted that she memorize, worked. Elena Maria thought the playtime was short but did not ask any questions. She simply agreed that Grace could stay for cocoa and then she would come over with Mattie and walk Grace home.

On the way over to the neighbors' house Elena Maria saw a muddy scuff mark in the soft snow and all around it she found sequins, sequins just like she had used recently to make a gown. How strange she thought. But later that night she would discover that much of her gown was now stripped of these adornments.

4.2

JUST KIDDING

They hadn't had a quiet moment all evening until the baby and Grace appeared to be down for the night. That was when Elena Maria told Matt of the strange way Grace had of playing hide and seek and how badly she had frightened the neighbor's youngest girl. He closed his eyes and shook his head as if saying, what are we going to do? Then he offered that perhaps it was too soon for Grace to go from one time in history to another and from a harsh altered state to life to life among the living. "Don't you think she needs more time to adjust before we allow her to play with regular kids?" Matt concluded.

"Yes," replied Elena Maria, "And maybe she is going to require some professional help before we permit that interaction. It is hard to know, however, how she will adjust to other kids if she cannot be with them." Finally, they agreed to give her more time around the house with their family before they even introduced therapy or 'professional day care' of some sort.

They would not have to explain this to the other kids' mother. She called them a short time later to explain that her kids might need a little more time to adjust to Grace. Elena Maria said they certainly understood and had just come to the conclusion themselves that she needed more time and more help in adjusting. She had to bite her tongue not to add 'and to the great time gap too' but fortunately left that off. Elena Maria wondered if this family was regretting their recent purchase of the house next door which the college students had been renting and which put them in such close proximity to Grace.

Then Elena Maria had a little more time to tell Matt of the purloined sequins. While it seemed trivial to worry about something so small, it was indicative of Grace's destructive nature or maybe her aggression toward Elena Maria. In any case they would have to set more limits and enforce them. Matt agreed it was not necessary for children to go through their parents' closets; it was better for them to know that their parents' bedroom was off limits.

Tired, yet pleased at having reached this firm understanding together as parents, they staggered up to check on the kids and go to bed. It did not take them long to wash a little and pull on their night wear. They knew tomorrow would be a demanding day in which they had to find the words to be firm with their new daughter, yet compassionate given her strange life and experiences. They wanted to show her love, and to be optimistic, while she had to accept that there were rules of conduct even a youngster must accept.

In the morning everyone met around the kitchen table in front of the large beehive fireplace. The baby had slept well so that they all felt refreshed. Grace was dressed in her new dungarees and flannel shirt looking like a very sweet farm girl. It was a pleasant scene as they ate oatmeal and drank fresh squeezed orange juice. Matt said he would be heading to the university just for the morning. He hoped they could all go for a walk that afternoon. He pointedly said that he wanted to play an important role in his daughter's life.

After Matt left for work Grace said she would like to go out and see if the other kids were in their yard. Elena Maria reminded her daughter that those kids had not enjoyed yesterday's playtime so they were not to see each other right away. There needed to be some time for everyone to cool off. Grace said she was fine with them, but her mother interjected that the other kids and their mom needed more time.

"Well, how much more time?" asked Grace. "We don't know yet," said Elena Maria. "Your father and I are working on a way to help things improve. You will need to just hang around here for a few days. When we have a plan we can discuss it."

"And will I be involved in making the plan?" said Grace.

"You will certainly be involved, but your dad and I will set the final steps before you, so that you can profit from our experiences and our love for you as our daughter." Elena Maria was pretty sure she saw a sneer pass quickly over the child's lips, but she decided not to make that the issue. The general behavior was the issue; Grace had to follow directions from them even if she didn't like it.

"Well, may I go out and just get fresh air in the yard then?"

"Yes, you may" said Elena Maria. "But you absolutely must stay in our farmyard and not wonder off into our woods or fields. Just the area inside the closest stonewall, and you may look around in the barn but do not touch the animals. Do you understand me, Grace?"

Grace swore she understood and just wanted to play in the yard. Her mother wanted to give her some freedom and not just be saying 'no' to her, so Grace was allowed outside. Her mother then frequently peaked at her out of the windows. After watching her doing some hopping game in the driveway, Elena Maria was distracted by Mattie and had to change her focus.

In that time period, Stephen from next door caught Grace's attention. Following the rules not to leave the yard, she ran over to the edge of their property. "Stephen, can you come over and play?" she asked.

He looked horrified and then said "No, my mommy doesn't want me to play with you anymore!" "Not ever?" asked Grace. "I don't think so," said Stephen.

"Well," said Grace "how about you just come over for a few minutes while no one is looking?"

"I don't think I should," said Stephen.

"But I have a baby goat, and it is the sweetest little thing. I can even give you a small bottle and it will drink right out of your hands. Come on, I'll show you." And with that Grace headed for the barn.

Stephen could not resist the invitation to feed a baby goat. "OK," he yelled "I'm coming, but just for a minute." Then he scampered over the wall chasing Grace.

She led him out behind the barn because she knew her mother would be trying to watch her. Then, she told him before she would get the kid; she demanded he tell her why he wasn't allowed to play with her anymore. When he said they all thought that she was too rough and too mean, she socked him in the eye and when he tried to run she grabbed him by his collar. She pulled him down and while sitting on top of him removed his scarf and began to strangle him.

Two things saved him; Grace still had her clumsy mittens on and Elena Maria came charging around the corner of the barn looking for the daughter who had disappeared from sight.

Elena Maria quickly ascertained that Stephen was not seriously injured. Fighting back tears she called his mother and explained what had happened and asked her to send one of the girls over to walk Stephen home. She apologized for not doing it but, she had to get back into her house before the baby woke up.

Stephen's mother came herself. She said, "I feel sorry for you but I cannot allow Grace to play with any of my children, ever again."

While Elena Maria was again apologizing and saying that she understood, Stephen asked "Is there really a baby goat in the barn?" Poor dear boy did not yet know how badly he had been treated but this would probably be the end of innocence for him.

4.3

A DEAL IS A DEAL

Matt arrived home thinking of lunch and an afternoon devoted to the family. He had not anticipated just how devoted he would need to be. Things began well enough with Scruffy running up to him for a pat, and he could smell onions and peppers frying in the kitchen. But one look at Elena Maria, and it was obvious that she had been crying or was close to tears. Her jaw was clenched, and her eyes were a little puffy but not red. Then he observed Grace seated at the table while she scribbled fiercely in a coloring book. She was not doing art work, she was working out aggression. The scribbles were dark colors, which went all over the pages and left deep impressions.

"OK, somebody want to tell me what happened?" He said.

"We had another problem with Stephen from next door," answered Elena Maria.

Grace looked up and shouted "It wasn't my fault; he followed me when he saw me in the yard. All I wanted to do was play outside for a little while. Then he was asking me to play some silly game, but he said his mother couldn't see us. She didn't ever want him to play with me again so we got out of sight by going around behind the barn. That's when he said all kinds of mean things to me."

"Grace," said her mother, "that is not how things happened. Can you tell your father the true version or should I?"

"You tell him!" Grace shouted. "You don't want him to love me anyway."

"That's not so Grace. I want all of us to love each other, but you need to play fair and honestly say to your dad how things happened." When Elena Maria could see that Grace was stuck, she began describing the events of the morning including the last sad little request of Stephen to 'please see the baby goats.' She was kind in her description but did want Grace to know that she had broken her promise to stay away from those kids, and Elena Maria knew it.

Matt turned to Grace and asked if she wanted to say anything. She certainly looked like she was feeling a good deal of pain over this. Her hands were shaking, and her breathing was rapid; then her lip started to quiver, and she blurted out a horrible question: "Will you be breaking my neck the way my real dad did?"

Both Elena Maria and Matt went to her side and each took a hand into their own. "NO, no, of course not, sweetheart" said Elena Maria. "But we do have to get you some special help to be certain that you adjust a little more easily to the people around here. Today could have been a tragedy. You have to deal with what you went through in your past in some other way. That is what Doctor April will talk to you about: How to recover from so much pain even if it were from one hundred and fifty years ago."

"You already know what you want to do with me?"

"Yes, dear, we do," said Elena Maria. "Your dad and I have been talking about what is best for you and this is our plan. We spoke with Doctor April, a psychologist friend. She will work here in the house with you so that we can all learn together as a family. She has had her COVID vaccinations, and we will all be safe and learn a lot.

"What if I don't want to work with her? What if I think she's something that would cause a horse to shit green and run through the streets?"

"Well, if she's that bad," said Matt, intentionally ignoring the vulgarity, "then we will all want to get rid of her, I promise you."

After Grace had been tucked into bed that night, Elena Maria and Matt sat close together on the couch while she nursed Mattie. Matt spoke softly speaking near her ear; "It is a good thing we had made a plan before today or I would have been in the parlor on my knees begging Captain Ben to please take his daughter back. The thing that still frightens me is whether she can be controlled well enough to guarantee this baby is never her victim."

"I understand completely," said Elena Maria. "We will have to watch her like cream about to boil on the stove. One bubble and she is shut off for good. No more chances; no curdled sour mess in our home. We have an obligation to be certain she doesn't torment our baby boy."

"So" said Elena Maria, "I will call Doctor April in the morning. She promised to be available on short notice and to stick with us. I know she is great with kids. We studied together for four years and she was a savant with troubled children."

"Our future is hers," said Matt.

Soon the whole family was sleeping. Matt was dreaming about taking his wonderful family to a faculty picnic once the pandemic was over. Elena Maria was dreaming about taking her new daughter shopping for summer clothing. Baby Matt only dreamed of drinking more warm milk. Grace was having more elaborate dreams: She was chasing two boys through the backfield; one was Stephen and one was Will. A close look at this scene showed her carrying an axe and yelling to them that they could not escape. She was faster and stronger. They were wailing for their mothers to please help them but Grace only laughed. This is when she woke up, and when she thought of the dream she only laughed some more.

Doctor April arrived at 10:30 the next morning. She asked Elena Maria if she would leave them to begin working on their own, to which she naturally agreed. It seemed only right that the psychologist should have an opportunity to get to know Grace in her own way. She needed to be free of any bias Elena Maria might transmit. She just hoped Grace would be honest.

Then Elena Maria placed Mattie in his snow suite and took him for a walk in his stroller. There was a little light snow and the air was crisp. She tried to think of the beauty of the area and the joys of motherhood. Unfortunately, the terror of raising Grace kept eating away at her mood. Every sinister book she had ever read about a child now struck up against her. Beginning with Rosemary's Baby, The Exorcist, and Carrie, she could only imagine that she was raising a potential Lizzie Borden. And she didn't know which way to turn; she just prayed that this would work out. She wanted a happy ending for all of them. She was also uncertain if the captain would, or could, place Grace back in limbo if they could not manage the child. The options seemed as narrow as the space behind the portrait and the wall where it hung.

Elena Maria walked until she was afraid the baby might freeze, and then she returned to her cozy kitchen. Doctor April was just saying that they had covered a lot of ground for one day and she thought it best to close. She also told them that she would move into the guestroom the next day so that they could function more like a complete family. She said that she had very much enjoyed working with Grace.

But when she called Elena Maria and Matt that night she reported that it was her firm belief that Grace needed medication to help eliminate her psychotic thoughts. She said that Grace believes that she has been murdered by her father in a gruesome manner as he simply snapped her neck. Further that she claims to have lived as a half-dead person, with other dead people, for one hundred and fifty years, and that currently her only real friends are others that have returned from the dead.

"Yes," said Elena Maria. "We knew she was talking like that. If you know a psychiatrist who can offer medication to assist her in giving up these morbid ideas and images, then we must try that."

4.4

THE COO KOO'S NEST

After they ended the conversation with Doctor April, they sat for several minutes, side-by-side on the couch saying nothing. Matt began by stating the obvious problem: "When Grace tells her truth, she sounds extremely disturbed. If Doctor April is going to live here for purposes of treatment does she need to know the REAL truth or the truth that will allow Grace to survive in this time and on this side of the world? And if we tell April what we believe to be true, does she lock us up, remove the child from our care, or get a court order to force us to take anti-psychotics too?"

"All important points" said Elena Maria. "The thing is; part of what Grace told Doctor April is not true. She only imagines that there are dead people in the cellar speaking to her, playing games and making plans with her. She remembers stories from her first childhood which included that horrible widow from the cellar, and she has embellished anything she heard about Will and Emily. Now she has romanticized them into friends from her past. What she really wishes is that Victoria and possibly Theodore would come back to her."

They agreed that this was very sad and they wished Grace could have an easier life with pleasant memories. Here-on-in they planned to provide her with a foundation for happiness but it would be tough getting her to build it over the old rough and haunted one. Before Doctor April arrived in the morning they would need to have another conversation with Grace to see what stories she felt necessary to elaborate on with Doctor April. Some stories Grace might just discuss with them, setting a goal of eventually closing those off, and enjoying some happy memories like the beautiful family Christmas they had just had. They would have to emphasize the very challenging concept of moving-on.

Grace was looking forward to seeing Doctor April again. She also was not afraid to meet another doctor and perhaps take some medicine to help her relax some of the memories that still made her angry. But she was resistant to saying that there were no people in the cellar who were her friends. She insisted that she had two friends down there and they were very much like her. Her mother said, "If you want to discuss them, that is okay with us. Thinking those friends are real will be a reason the doctor will want to put you on medication, that medication is designed to help you with those thoughts. There is nothing wrong with taking medication to help you."

"But, although dealing with the horror of how your last life ended is, sadly, not a fantasy, it may be necessary not to speak of it. We know Captain Ben felt he must immediately remove you from the world you were in. He acted as he did to save other lives. Could you keep those memories to yourself and when you must talk about them, please turn to your father or me, but no one else, not even Doctor April?"

Grace said she would like to talk about Will and Emily and she wanted to hear what Doctor April would say. Also, if they, her parents now, would listen to the memories she had about her first childhood, she figured it could do her some good to understand how they had agreed she must go away. She also wanted to understand how her family had agreed to let her father kill her. That was a place her brain got stuck. She said she was pretty sure she wouldn't have to speak to Doctor April about her murder, or the world in which she had recently lived, she just wanted to know how Victoria and Theodore had let her die.

When Doctor April arrived Grace led her to her bedroom and assisted her in unpacking. April suggested that they go for a walk to begin their first session of the day. So, with masks in place they headed out the farmhouse door, both appearing animated and friendly. Doctor April knew that one of the reasons she was to live here was to help keep track of Grace's whereabouts so that Grace could not get into trouble or possibly injure another person. April could sense many things about this girl without having been told the full history. Of course, there were likely things no one knew as the girl had only recently arrived in East Apple after the tragic loss of her parents. Naturally, Grace wanted to imagine dear friends in the basement. Maybe these friends were so special that only she could see them or that they only wanted to be seen by her. Friends like these were harder to take away and Grace didn't want any more loss.

After they had walked about half a mile Doctor April asked Grace to describe her friends in the cellar. Grace said that they were both nice and that they had been through a great deal of loss themselves. "The boy had not known his real mother but the elderly lady is his adopted mother and she loves him with all her heart. When he had died at age 12 she had spent the rest of her life mourning him and had worked out a plan so that could both live again in the future, which is right now!"

"The boy had been bitten to death by a spider which he had raised. That spider was known as a Goliath Bird Eating Spider and was so large that it fascinated the boy and many scientists. He had studied the spiders, and researchers had written to him about the arachnids, and even visited his collection. Due to his pride in these critters, and the fact that most had been born in his house, which is the house we live in," Grace continued; "he had not been particularly careful to their potential for escape. In fact, over the first few years he had let a few go free just to see what would happen."

"What happened was that they had adapted to the colder climate and resided in many of the farm's outbuildings. So it had been particularly important for him to return just to see how his clan was doing. But for a variety of reasons he could not recycle back to life for about one hundred and fifty years. And this," Grace announced with a flourish, "is precisely the time of their return! They had made a few appearances over the years but they are now jumping up like toadstools after a rain. They are very hungry at this stage, and he finds them gregarious so he and his mother are enjoying their company."

"They have cleaned the old terrariums which were hidden in the back of the barn. This allows the young ones, just emerging from their eggs, to be safe. Then the boy, Will, and his mother, Emily, forage through the house at night for scraps to feed them, or with which they may entice their prey. Emily is still helping Will to study science. She enjoys his company and when I came along and could see them, they were delighted to let me join in the lessons. They also talk more the way I always did. Well," Grace interrupted herself, "that's another story, but I am glad they are around."

"Do I need medicine to make them go away?" said Grace.

"I'm not sure yet," said Doctor April. "It may be that your ideas about the boy and his adopted mother will help you to accept your adopted mother. You see how much they love each other and help each other? Maybe you and Elena Maria will be just like that."

"Maybe," said Grace. "I would like it if she and Matt, and even the baby, would be proud of me and love me. Then I could be happy."

"Well, let's work on that; your happiness. After a while we can decide together if medication would help you or if you are quite happy enough without it. My only advice for you, Grace, is that you try to be gentle in all the things you do. Do not overly react to anything that happens around you. Check-in with me or your mother if anything takes you by surprise. Even the neighborhood kids will come around and love you if you just give them enough time. And at your age, dear Grace, you have plenty of time!"

Grace wanted to tell Doctor April just how much time she had already had but thought it was one of those things to keep to oneself.

4.5

PANTRY MOUSE

Doctor April decided to leave them after only two weeks. Grace had not acted out in anger, been aggressive or violent in any way during that time. She said that Grace was doing so well there was no reason for the Nelsons to waste their money. Further, Doctor April had other clients who had been waiting. Grace would have twice weekly appointments with Doctor April for as long as they were needed, and she had begun talking to Grace about the possibility of seeing a Doctor Edith. Doctor Edith was a psychiatrist who specialized in treating adolescent females and she was aware that someone named Grace might be calling her. Matt and Elena Maria were not happy to see April go but they were encouraged by Grace's behavior.

While Doctor April had been staying with them, Elena Maria had been a bit surprised by how much this thin young woman had eaten. Every morning when she opened the refrigerator she discovered appreciable quantities of food missing. Sometimes it was just a few eggs and toast, sometimes cheese and one morning most of their leftovers from a large roast chicken dinner which Elena Maria had intended to turn into a curried chicken salad for their lunch. But, no matter, she told herself; her support with Grace is worth at least this on top of her salary.

Yet, with April gone, food still went missing. Now, Elena Maria was considering the possibility that Grace was a nocturnal eater. She had always heard that teenagers had enormous appetites; Grace was just eating extra food ahead of her natural growth spurt. Well, good for her, Elena Maria thought, she certainly did not want to contend with an anorexic child.

It was time to see about enrolling Grace in hybrid classes in grade school. She would have to test up to her actual level as the Nelsons could not produce records from her previous school. They would have to discuss Grace having sort of amnesia as a result of the trauma she had experienced with the loss of her family. Doctor April had promised to write a letter of support for Grace so her situation might more readily be accepted. The conclusion of the school staff was that Grace should enter the fourth grade and work to keep up with others. They thought she was bright and did not want her to get too far behind her age group. In fact, it was possible, Grace could move up quickly if she felt comfortable and did well.

Grace explained to her parents how strange this system was. In her old school everyone was in one classroom, and you did all the things you could do and listened while older kids did more advanced things. She said that encouraged learning and you moved at your own pace. Very wise, her folks thought, but they spent time helping Grace to accept the school as it was now set up. They did not want Grace to arrive in class and to start telling her new teachers how they should do their jobs; or to slip and say 'we used to do it this way right here in the town!'

All the preparation was done so that Grace could have a fair chance at enjoying her education. One of the variables which could not be controlled was just who those other students would be, and the middle child of the next door neighbors was a classmate of Grace's. On the first day when they saw each other in school this girl simply tried to ignore Grace. But by midmorning the teacher had pointed Grace out as a new girl who was now living in East Apple. She asked the class to introduce themselves to Grace, one at a time. When it was the neighbor's turn she said, "I already know Grace. She lives next door to me, and she is so strange that my mother won't let any of us play with her."

The teacher quickly intervened and said "We want to be welcoming. That means as you speak to Grace you should say something

219

to help her feel that she can be a part of this class. If you have an outside relationship with her, just please keep that separate from how we behave in school."

"Well what do I tell my mother?" piped up this little neighbor.

"Just tell her that you and Grace are now classmates, and you will have to do some school work together, but that Mrs. Jameson will guide you in this relationship. She can call me after school tomorrow if she has anything to say." And that seemed to be that.

The class broke for recess. The playground was the pavement around the school which was also fenced in from the outside world with an eight foot high black wire fence. There had been so many school shootings in recent years that this was one attempt to keep anyone out who did not belong at school. Grace was obviously on the inside, but she was also obviously isolated from her class. The other children had started up a game of kickball but no team had chosen Grace nor had she been given a role to play. Grace leaned against the old brick building and stared at the kids as they ran and played.

Her little neighbor friend appeared to be a leader. She pitched the ball and she called out orders to the other children. Grace hadn't known what an evil force this girl cast upon her when she spoke against her that morning. She might as well have said 'Grace brought the COVID virus to this community and if you touch her you are dead.' That was how well everyone avoided Grace and how alone she felt.

When she got home that afternoon she did not want to deal with her mother about her social problem at school. She simply said "It was fine. I'd like to take a nap." And she disappeared upstairs. Elena Maria felt a twinge of worry but decided to give Grace some space.

That evening Grace came down for dinner, offered to help, and then went back upstairs 'to read a book they had been assigned.' Clearly, she wasn't excited about the next day, but she said enough about the teacher (a huge bosom on which she rested her hands much of the time, and could have used this chest as a portable desk), her classmates (all good pals with each other but not interested in her although they wanted to know how her parents had died) and the school itself (must have been pretty once but the paint is gray and peeling on the ceiling, there is mold in the girls' room, and the thing they call the 'intercom' squeaks so much that you cannot tell most of the messages).

Matt and Elena Maria demonstrated interest and humor at these descriptions. The three of them agreed that tomorrow would be another day, and things would get easier for Grace. Then she went up to get ready for bed as the bus arrived early each morning.

After the house was quiet, Grace got up to help Emily and Will find food for the arachnids. She told them all about the mean girl from next door and how she wished that kid would leave her alone. Will said he had an idea how they could arrange that, or at least give her a little something to worry about other than picking on a nice person like Grace. Grace was very excited; no one had ever really stood up for her before. When things had been difficult she had been eliminated. Casually, Will asked if Grace knew which bedroom belonged to this girl.

"Her name is Kate," said Grace. "She has her own room on the second floor, first door on the right at the top of the stairs. Her room is all frilly and pink. What are you going to do?"

"Oh, nothing much," said Will. "I just think my biggest spider needs a little room of his own, and this house is getting low on food scraps. I'll let him visit for a couple of days. I don't think he has ever had a little girl to play with all by himself."

This idea seemed to charm Grace. She felt warmth flow toward Will, and the excitement sent flashes of joy into her brain making thoughts of school tomorrow most exciting. She announced to her friends that she would have to go lay out her clothing and get a good night's rest. She thanked them for being there for her and promised to come back the next evening to find out how things had gone for the Goliath, and she would report on happenings at the school.

4.6

CANARY IN A COAL MINE

Elena Maria and Matt were sitting at the kitchen table just beginning their breakfast, with Mattie nursing in his mother's lap, when in charged Grace. Her hair was fixed prettily with ribbons in her pigtails, and she had on a new pinafore. She set her backpack down by the door toward the driveway and announced that she was starved. Then, without asking for any help, she went into the refrigerator for milk and helped herself to oatmeal off the stove. A banana and brown sugar were already sitting on the table next to her placemat. She asked her father if he could drop her at school on his way to the university.

"Well, certainly," said Matt. "Someone is pretty anxious for her day to begin. Did you make a boyfriend yesterday?"

Grace was fighting a smile. She was actually playing along with his little teasing. "Maybe I did and maybe I didn't. Perhaps your new child is simply interested in her education."

They all smiled. Elena Maria said, "Your lunch is waiting in the refrigerator. I added Baby Bella's and grapes today. Don't forget to put it in your backpack."

"Great," said Grace. She finished her last piece of the banana and asked to be excused. Then she rushed down the hall where they heard the sound of running water and teeth being brushed. In a flash she was back in the kitchen standing by the door as she pulled on her bulky jacket.

Matt's chair made a scraping sound as he rose. "I guess that means I'm late." He then proceeded to organize his things a bit and grabbed his keys. "We wouldn't want our wonderful student to be late on her second day." With that remark he kissed Elena Maria and the baby, then steered Grace out the door with a gentle push on her wool hat.

Elena Maria felt buoyant. What a nice way to start the day and after they had been so worried. Then she went about her chores and even turned on some music to accompany her steps about the house. Dancing through housework took away any drudgery.

Grace was one of the first two kids to take her 'distanced seat' in the classroom. Her mask was on, and she was tapping her toes in anticipation of the morning before her. The teacher entered the classroom, bid those assembled "Good-day" and lined up her notes. When the bell rang, the class, now nearly full but spaced, stood and recited the Pledge of Allegiance to the Flag. The teacher then took attendance. She noted Katie as absent with a raised eyebrow. It seemed Katie never missed school.

Shit, thought Grace. If she doesn't show up I won't find anything out until tonight. Then there was commotion in the hallway and Katie and her mother were standing there with the principal. She called the teacher out. The group conferred, and then Katie, with circles under her red eyes, came in, and took her seat. The class was buzzing and staring.

"Now people," said the teacher, "Katie has had a bad experience last night and we need to be kind to her and not bother her with questions. She just wants to pay attention to her studies. Her mom has asked that I tell you all what happened and then we leave it alone. Am I clear? No further questions."

"All right then. Poor Katie was sound asleep last night when some kind of a giant spider came into her bedroom. It surrounded the cage over her bed where her pet canary was sleeping and shot its venomous tongue into the hapless bird killing it, and then consuming it! When Lucky let out a terrified chirp, Katie awoke to the gruesome sight of the bird's last struggle. Her screams made the spider leave but it was too late for Lucky. Katie and her family are very concerned as the spider disappeared within their house. So again, no questions but please be very kind to Katie!

One close friend of Katie's blurted out, "Oh, poor Lucky, she was such a happy bird."

And a boy in the back snickered "Lucky? I guess his luck ran out."

The teacher bellowed "That will be enough people! Perhaps I made an error in trusting you with the information. Now take out your history books. Someone tell me where we left off."

Grace hastened to keep up with the class as she certainly didn't want to stick-out today following that conversation. But it took all the self control she had to avoid looking at Katie, and enjoying the pain she saw etched on her face. She couldn't wait for midnight when she was planning to see Will and congratulate him on the adventures of his arachnid. She just hoped no harm had come to the poor creature as Katie's family pursued it. Rather she hoped it had found a lot of great leftovers.

While Grace was enjoying the drama at school, Elena Maria had a visitor. It was the children's mother from next door. She inquired as to Grace's health; and said she was pleased to know that Grace could handle the fourth grade curriculum; that Katie had thought it so nice that they were classmates. Then she dove into the matter that had actually brought her over.

She explained about a commotion last night while they had all been sleeping; including a dead canary, and a hysterical fourth grader who could not sleep the remainder of the night. She said she was telling all this to Elena Maria for a few reasons. First, she wanted to warn her in case these spiders traveled easily from house to house.

Second, she had been told, when they had first moved in next door, that the Nelson family had made the newspapers when a man from a pest control firm had been all but asphyxiated in their basement. It seems he was hired to rid the home of giant spiders, big enough to kill birds, but the fumigation process had gone wrong nearly costing him his life. So, did he get rid of those spiders, and in any case, might there have been a few left who migrated to their house next door?

Finally, and she apologized in advance for how this might sound, could Grace, whom they all knew had problems, possibly have wanted to do Katie harm? At this remark Elena Maria drew her breath in sharply. She quickly and forcefully defended her daughter saying Grace wanted to get along with everyone at school. Grace needed friends, and Grace had been tucked in her own bed all night.

From there, Elena Maria did back track, and admit that the Goliath Bird Eating Spiders may have adapted to this area and could be living almost anywhere. She would gladly provide them with the name of her former exterminator so that they could decide on hiring him or not. They might also learn more about the spiders by asking his group what they had learned about them.

When Grace got home from school she and her mother had a story to share. Elena Maria never indicated to Grace that she might be under some suspicion. Grace never indicated to her mother that she might have some inside information as to how this arachnid had come to be next door. With these two secrets left unspoken, the mother and daughter passed a pleasant late afternoon together. In fact, there was a bit of pleasure felt in both their hearts over the facts of this story. Neither mother nor daughter appreciated being seen as not quite doing the right thing.

Grace asked what was for supper. She was pleased that it would be a main course of meatloaf, for meatloaf was easy to crumble and stretch when she wanted an offering to bring downstairs later for the arachnids. They were extra hungry these days. They were growing.

4.7

LITTLE MISS MUFFIT

Elena Maria and Matt were up early the next morning because Mattie had decided that he needed a 5:30 feeding. He had slept through a typical feeding time of three AM so they were pleased to sleep this late. In another hour Grace would need to get ready for school so they decided to simply stay up. This way they could be organized for the day and have her lunch ready. Matt said he would make his famous banana nut pancakes since they had the time.

All seemed normal until Elena Maria reached into the refrigerator for the leftover meatloaf. She could not find it. She moved bottles and jars around in her admittedly crowded GE, but the meatloaf was not there. Then she saw the dirty pan soaking in the sink. "What the hell is this?" she uttered. "We had enough leftover meatloaf from last night to feed us all for lunch today, and it is gone!"

Matt walked over to the sink and replied, "It sure is."

They launched into a discussion of how Grace could eat so much, first for dinner, and then again a few hours later. "It would make more sense," said Elena Maria, "If one of us was sleepwalking and consumed the food. She is still a small child."

Matt suggested that perhaps it was one of them, and since they were asleep at the time, of course they did not remember. Elena Maria thought that was improbable, since three of them slept in the same room, but she said she would really like to know. Matt walked around the corner to his study and came back holding a small contraption.

"I have this field cam," he said. "I was going to set it up over the stone wall and see what varieties of animals are out there at night. It is triggered by motion and will click every three seconds if a group of critters are out there or moving around. But I have never gotten around to setting it up. I think I'll place it up here on the mantel, behind the old vase, pointed at the refrigerator. I'll turn it to the on position when we go to bed, and that will activate it. It also has a function that will link it to my Fitbit so that I will receive a buzz when it snaps a photograph. This must have been designed for hunters so they would be awakened if they fell asleep in their blinds. I never expected to use it, but why not?"

"If I get a buzz and catch myself with a plate of ice cream, the only dilemma will be do I confess or not?"

"Well," said Elena Maria, "food has gone missing for many days now and I would like an answer."

They left the matter at this point, and a short time later, Grace appeared. She seemed happy enough with the big breakfast, and ate well, not like someone who remained overstuffed from the previous night. She demonstrated none of the intense anticipation for school that she had displayed the previous day. She rather begrudgingly got dressed and gathered her books, then allowed that she would catch the bus that day.

Once Grace got to school things did not go well. Before attendance was even taken, there were whispers and pointing aimed toward her. Finally, she caught the gist of what was being said 'those huge spiders are from her house' and 'my mother says it is her fault that Katie's canary got eaten.'

Pretty soon the physical harassing began: a yank of a few strands of her hair as someone passed by her desk; a sudden bump with a sing-song apology also delivered as someone else passed by; then she observed the 'juice-duty' girl trickle spit into the cup which was delivered to her; and finally she was knocked flat on her face going out the door for recess. No one apologized for that last move; it seemed the entire class had gone blind in terms of witnessing anything.

Her knees were both bloodied and her new pants torn by this last action. Grace could no longer play it tough and act above them either; she began to cry when she saw the crimson stains. She asked the teacher to please call her mother. The teacher was quite dismayed that anything like this could have happened with her students since she was sure that they were all socially distanced. So she sent Grace to the nurse's office. The nurse sent Grace home because the cuts were rather deep. Elena Maria had to pack Mattie into his baby seat and drive over to the school.

On the brief ride home Grace didn't say much. Elena Maria advised her to take her pants off while she washed, disinfected and bandaged her knees; then Grace could put on any comfortable clothing she wished. Grace remained withdrawn, not caring to let her mother know any details connected to the morning's events; not bothering to thank her for the ride or for the clean-up. Elena Maria simply continued to speak calmly and kindly to the child. She reassured Grace that she could get the blood out of her slacks and mend them without leaving any sign of the repairs. Still Grace acted aloof. Perhaps her pride was wounded too deeply for discussion, at least yet. Elena Maria told Grace about her own childhood in which her grandmother would offer to kiss the injuries, called booboos, and" make them all better". She asked Grace if she could kiss her knees. Grace almost smiled but held back with a simple 'no thank you.'

Finally, Elena Maria suggested that Grace rest in her bedroom until she felt strong enough to explain what had happened. Grace disappeared upstairs shutting her door with unnecessary zeal. After she lay on her bed for a while she decided she needed to speak with her friends. She quietly moved from her room to her parents' bedroom, through their closet, and down the trapdoor stairs into the cellar. Within moments she saw Emily and Will working on a new terrarium. They used glass which they had scavenged from something in the barn, added wooden pieces across the glass and brackets to hold all corners taunt. This would be for a larger nest.

"What are you doing home at this hour?" said Emily.

"Yes," said Will. "We enjoyed your school stories last night but did not expect to see you so soon today."

Grace said she had an awful day at school and wished she never had to go back there. Her friends replied that they were sorry if she felt stuck, but she should stay and help them right now, and try not to think about her problems. So Grace spent a pleasant afternoon learning how to use a little hand saw, and to pack dirt, moss and wood pieces into the terrarium. As a reward at the end they taught her how to play with the spiders so that they would not bite. Grace just wished she had a picture of herself doing all this to show those kids in her class.

Then she got worried about the time and went back up the ladder and through the trapdoor. She spent a few minutes in her bedroom, and then went down to explain the morning to her mother. Soon her dad was home and they were all working on dinner preparations. Grace peeled potatoes for meat hash, her father ground an oven roast from a couple days back along with a fresh onion, and Elena Maria made a salad. Baby Mattie interrupted when he needed to.

A few hours after dinner they were all in bed. But just before they started for the upstairs Matt reached to the top of the mantel and switched on the field cam. They would see what types of creatures roamed the kitchen at night.

4.8

SOLITAIRE

It was just minutes past midnight when Matt's Fitbit buzzed. He was so solidly asleep that it took him a few moments to realize what was going on and what he needed to do next. After observing his surroundings, he knew for certain that not he, not Elena Maria, nor the baby was downstairs raiding the refrigerator. Then he quickly and carefully made his way down the stairs that led into the kitchen.

Once in the kitchen he was in view of Grace holding a small serving tray and ladling leftover meat hash, bits of bread, and a little lettuce onto the tray. But, instead of sitting down with a fork, or warming most in the microwave, she was tiptoeing to the cellar and then down the cellar stairs. Matt decided he had better follow.

Grace arrived at the basement level and a conversation ensued. Matt could only hear Grace's side. She announced that she had brought down enough food for the brood. That the spiders should be very happy with the great leftovers from upstairs, and she began reciting what treats she had.

Then she said, "Oh no trouble at all, we have so much food you wouldn't believe it. Shall I feed them for you?" And with that she banged on part of the stone cellar wall and along the dirt near the burial area and out marched at least fifty Goliath Bird Eating Spiders. According to the books, they were probably about half grown, currently the size of two chipmunks each. They seemed to be tame or at least nice to Grace for she was calm with them.

Then she sat down while the critters feasted, and had an apparent conversation with two other people. Every little while she turned her head from one place to another; she smiled and laughed at something. Finally, she said, "Well I'd better get some rest. Thank you again for being my friends." She picked up her tray which was now empty, gave a little curtsy to her friends, and headed for the staircase. Matt scooted out of her view. While he was surprised to see her actually feeding those hideous spiders, what bothered him the most was that he could not see, or hear the people with whom she was conversing.

Matt got back up to bed without running into Grace. He had an interesting tale to tell Elena Maria in the morning once Grace was gone to school. Elena Maria found it very sad that Grace was so needy for friends that she had totally fabricated these two long dead souls as living friends. She planned on calling the school nurse later in the morning to see what they could work out as a plan to combat the bullying that was befalling Grace and maybe triggering some of this reaction. She wanted to do all a mother could to protect her frail daughter. Also, she would call the exterminators to see if they would come out even in the midst of a pandemic.

Then she cuddled and played with Mattie to be sure her dear boy was happy and stimulated too. She still hoped they could be a happy family of four if only Grace could manage to fit in and make even one friend. She and Matt would go with Grace to see Doctor April in a few days; maybe they would gain some insights to help with this school issue. They had to keep trying.

Grace still did not know that Matt had witnessed her feeding the arachnids the night before. They thought to wait for Doctor April's opinion before admitting that they had spied on her and what they had discovered. Tonight, Elena Maria planned to wear Matt's Fitbit to bed so that she would receive the buzz, and be the one to follow Grace as she fed the spiders. Elena Maria just had to see it with her own eyes.

When spaghetti was served for supper that evening she thought she saw Grace wince. Elena Maria hadn't given the meal selection much thought except that she had premade sauce in the freezer and needed something easy to cook. Well, knowing that Grace was resourceful, she had every confidence that she would find a way to scoop it up and push it onto the floor for the spiders.

After they ate, the evening seemed to drag on; all Elena Maria could think about was tracking Grace into the cellar. Then, finally, it was time for bed.

Elena Maria had fallen into a deep sleep after Mattie's eleven o'clock feeding. Surprising, based on her excitement, but when the Fitbit buzzed she woke as though someone was banging on the door and yelling 'Open up, Police!' Her feet were on the floor and her robe over her shoulders. A hasty glance back showed both her husband and son continuing to slumber.

She knew Grace was already in the kitchen, or the Field Cam would not have triggered the Fitbit, so she quickly, but silently, slithered down the stairs pausing in the entry to the kitchen. She didn't know how Grace could have gathered the spaghetti, sauce and all, so rapidly but Grace, with her arms full, was just starting down the cellar stairs. Elena Maria paused for a moment in order to avoid detection, and then she followed.

It took a moment for her eyes to adjust to the darker lighting in the cellar, but she soon saw Grace over at the side of the cellar wall nearest to where they had interred Emily with Will. Her back was to Elena Maria and she was holding her offering for the arachnids. Then she kicked at the stone wall and made a sort of chirping sound in that same area. To Elena Maria it sounded more like the final squeal of a mouse caught in trap, but if it worked for Grace, so be it.

Before she could note anything further, the Goliaths, no doubt greedily anticipating their meal, came creeping up and out of the cracks in the wall and dirt floor. Elena Maria recalled them from a year ago. They were large, hairy and vicious. One had chased her out of her shower and through the house. They were capable of eating birds or small mammals. The adults were wider than Matt's two hands together with his fingers spread. They seemed to fear nothing and had adapted to the cold New England climate even though they were originally from deep within the jungle.

It was then that Grace set their meal on the cold floor before them and Elena Maria saw, to her horror that Mattie was wriggling at Grace's feet! Her darling tiny baby was to be a substitute for the meal Grace wished to offer? Without a thought, except to save her baby, Elena Maria shrieked and ran forward roughly shoving Grace out of her way in the process. She grabbed up, into her arms, the now screaming baby before a single spider had begun to feast. In one so small a single bite could have been fatal.

Elena Maria began stomping as many spiders as were directly under her feet while simultaneously yelling at Grace to "Get Out, Get the Hell out of here!" And then she pushed a shocked Grace toward the door to upstairs and charged along behind. Soon she would say soothing things to the baby but right now her terror was too great, and she wanted Matt to wake up and help them. Of course, as they entered the kitchen, Matt, Scruffy and Sybil appeared, perhaps anticipating that they were the rescue team. The tale Elena Maria was telling them made them all sit down.

Elena Maria was having a very difficult time calming down. She continued in a tirade aimed at Grace: "How could you do this? How could you even think to offer your baby brother to those hideous critters to eat? What in God's name is the matter with you?"

Grace blinked away a few tears and said, "But they don't like spaghetti, it has too much garlic for them so I thought they would like a fresh meal. I'm sorry."

But neither Elena Maria nor Matt could say anything to Grace that sounded like forgiveness. They ordered her to her bedroom until they could all cool off and figure out what steps needed to be taken next. When she was upstairs Elena Maria said, "I will need to discuss this with Captain Ben. We cannot live like this any longer." Then she sobbed into her baby's tummy and said, "How could that girl, who has been told that we all love her, have absolutely no feelings for baby Mattie and no sense of what he means to us?"

When they finally went upstairs to catch a few hours sleep, they noted a pillow had been placed in Mattie's crib, no doubt to delay their detection of his loss.

4.9

CLEOPATRA

They did not send Grace to school the next day. Her transgressions had crossed so far over the line into tragic behavior that they dared not have her around other children. Matt also took the day off. He sat in the bedroom with Grace and had hoped to talk with her about her actions, but she was so detached from the reality of her wrongdoing that Matt could say nothing to her that she might understand. Instead, he asked her what stories she liked, and they read them together. While they were so engaged, he forgot her insane actions and thought again, but only for a moment, 'maybe we can make this work'. Then his eyes filled with tears and he knew Grace would never truly be his daughter.

While Grace read with Matt, Elena Maria was downstairs in the parlor begging the portal to open to her. They had not communicated through that means since Grace had arrived. Elena Maria went to great lengths to try and get the captain's attention, but he would not appear. Finally, she said, "If you do not respond you will leave me no choice but to kill your daughter with my own hands. It would be almost the worst thing I can imagine doing, for a part of me truly loves Grace and saw her as a permanent part of our family. But I could never allow her to live with the risk she presents of committing the homicide of my son, or the children of neighbors. The worst thing I could ever do would be to allow her to live, and to commit murder."

Once she had said these last words the captain reacted to her by seeming to stand a bit straighter and she knew he was listening. "What would you have me do?"

"You must remove Grace from this house, from this town, from this time in history!"

"And do you want her dead?" he asked.

"Dead if necessary, or just away where she cannot come back into our lives ever again."

"And do I let you off your commitment to do me a favor?" he asked.

"Yes," she said. "We have done our utmost to make a life for her here with us, with our family, but she is too damaged for that to be possible. I consider our debt paid."

"Perhaps it is," he said, "Perhaps it is." Then he was gone and Elena Maria wasn't sure what she should expect to have happen, or when.

Lunch time came and the family met in the kitchen. Nothing had been planned for lunch as the shock from last night was still too great to allow for mundane thoughts. Elena Maria made toast and they would slice cheese to microwave between the slices. It was all she could manage to serve. None of them appeared to have much appetite. Then Grace asked to use the internet, and they allowed her to go into the study. They were in the room that led to the cellar, and baby Mattie was with them so they felt this was safe, even though they could not see Grace's every move.

Once they were alone, Elena Maria described her conversation with the captain. Although he had not said much, it appeared that he understood the predicament in which they found themselves. It seemed he would find a way to relieve them of this impossible burden; he had just not yet said how it would be done. Elena Maria concluded by repeating to Matt what she had said to the portrait: "If you do not do something, then I will kill her with my own hands!" Saying this she broke down in tears but vowed to Matt that she really meant it.

Matt too was much shaken and had been teary all morning. He said, "I am so unbelievably sorry that it has come to this, but she has left us no choice."

Then they settled into a work pattern of cleaning up after their meal and preparing the fires for later in the day. Elena Maria said she would take baby Mattie into the parlor with her while she called her mother and father and attempted to prepare them for the change that was imminent. It was inconceivable to think she could find words to plan her daughter's removal or demise.

What the couple did not realize was that Grace had positioned herself to listen in on their conversation while they believed she was on the computer. She was shocked, tearful, and then angry to think those who had claimed to love her could turn on her so completely that they would even wish her dead. "So much for love," she muttered to herself.

Grace entered the kitchen and asked her father if she could go up to her room as she felt tired. He said, "Alright, Grace, just check in with me when you wake up."

Once she was upstairs, Grace hesitated a few minutes to be certain they would not immediately check on her, and then she made her way to their bedroom, through the closet, and down the trapdoor stairs to the cellar. She wanted to ask her friends what she should do. They were now the only ones she could trust.

Emily and Will were playing cards when she arrived. They said they were taking a break from studies for a little while, and asked if she would join them. Grace said that she wanted to join them but not necessarily in a game of cards. Then she told the whole sad story of her real father, the captain, now agreeing with Matt and Elena Maria, that she was too dangerous to live. She ended by saying she wished that she could live with them even if they were dormant for long periods of time. At least, she said, you have freedom when you do reappear and you have each other.

Emily told her she could join them as it was almost time for them to have a big sleep again. The Goliaths were growing and would soon lay eggs. They could all have a nice twenty year nap and wake up right back in this cellar again. They would not have changed, but everyone else would have aged twenty years. Certainly all hard feelings would have passed.

"How do I join you this way?" said Grace.

"Go call up the arachnids," said Will. "They are hungry right now and will gladly bite your wrists, drink your blood, and leave you in a dormant state to sleep with us."

So Grace approached the wall where she had been feeding the little beasties. She only hit the stones twice and many of them scampered out of the earth and rocks. She bared her arms and hung them down at an easy level for the spiders. They pounced upon her, ravenous after missing out on a meal the previous night. Their venom was meant to stun and she was soon totally relaxed and then unconscious.

Elena Maria had just tried to find Grace. When Grace wasn't in her bedroom she looked for her throughout the upstairs. Coming to her own bedroom she quickly noted that the closet door was ajar and rushed through to the trapdoor. She did not want to travel down those rickety old stairs with a baby in her arms so she ran back down through the house, shouting for Matt, and together they entered the cellar.

The spiders receded immediately when the commotion began. Matt and Elena Maria were able to pick Grace up and rush her upstairs where they called 911 and began CPR.

But try as they might, and as the EMTs did, there was no reviving the little girl. Grace was pronounced dead upon arrival at the hospital.

5.0

SHERLOCK

The death felt almost as tragic to Matt and Elena Maria as though Grace had been their true daughter. They did love her and had formulated dreams and plans around this girl. They had begun to integrate Elena Maria's parents into her life and believed that they would be loving grandparents to her. They had decorated a room to her liking and purchased a wardrobe of which she had approved and was enthusiastic. They had only come to believe it would not work out with Grace for approximately the last thirty-six hours. This left her death as a shock. They would come to ask themselves if it had been a suicide, an accident, or had Captain Benjamin Mills orchestrated this death based on what he had agreed to do for Elena Maria? Was this his way of eliminating the problem without forcing Elena Maria to actively kill the child?

A dead child drew a lot of attention in the community, with her classmates, and certainly from the State Police. The Nelsons had to use her acceptance into the local grade school as proof that she was their ward, for no other records were accessible. A superficial review would have backed up their creation of her credentials; deep scrutiny would not have held up as well. Thankfully, the school and neighbors felt sorry for the young couple with their cute baby and heartbreaking story of family loss. No pressure was added by these factions.

It was documented that Grace had been having trouble in school and in getting along with her peers; that she had become despondent and that her folks had hired a psychologist to treat her. Certainly, Doctor April spoke well of the parents' intentions on the girl's behalf. All of these things were recent so it could not be expected that Grace would have had time to be "cured". The authorities were leaning toward "probable suicide" as the conclusion of their investigation.

Then one officer noticed the Field Cam still perched in the kitchen and pointed toward the refrigerator. "Food disappearing," he asked. "Yes," both Elena Maria and Matt said. They had not had time to consider this question in advance.

"Mind if we take it in and review it," the same officer asked.

"Go right ahead," said Matt a little too quickly. "Just be prepared for lots of shots of us in our pajamas."

So the troopers left with the camera.

The next day the troopers returned. They said they were ready to close the whole matter, with a verdict of suicide. Nothing unusual had showed up in the photos; just the immediate family going in and out of the refrigerator and Grace taking things to the cellar. They even had shots of Grace carrying the baby down the cellar stairs with Elena Maria in pursuit. It all appeared as it had been described.

Outside the kitchen window, in the grass up close to the house, sat two people. One was Emily dressed in her old cotton housedress and wearing an apron, the other was Will wearing short pants, soft boots, and a coarse cotton shirt. They began laughing when they heard that nothing unusual had showed up in the pictures. "I guess we aren't very photogenic these days," said Emily.

"Yes," said Will, "it can be comforting to be invisible to most people."

Then they continued to listen as Matt and Elena Maria explained to the police officer that they had decided to bury Grace in the graveyard at the top of Cemetery Hill Road so she could be with family. What the Nelsons didn't tell the officer was that the family she would be interred with was her original legal parents, Theodore and Victoria Mills, along with their other two children and children which they had had. It seemed fitting to Elena Maria that Grace be brought home to them in this way.

"Oh" said Emily, "It is good to know where she will be. I will tell the pets."

And so a few days later, after a solemn service attended by many school children, neighbors, and Grace's new grandparents, Grace was left in the ground at the top of the hill. But she wasn't alone for long.

At midnight on her first night in the earth, a troop of nearly grown giant Goliath Bird Eating arachnids marched in the dark to the crest of Cemetery Hill. Their outline could have been seen as they scampered up the hill, for the moon was bright. They proceeded to the freshly laid gravesite covered in highly scented flowers. They knew their mission. Soon they had burrowed into the earth and brought forth the body of a young girl. They placed her upon pine boughs and, as a team, dragged this sleeping beauty to the cellar down the hill. Here they would all lie in rest for twenty years until they could be active again.

ADDENDUM TO THE BOOK

www.Amazon.com/Books-Cynthia-Adams/s?rh=
n%3A283155%2Cp_27%3ACynthia+Adams

If the reader will kindly go to this link, you will see stars and a rating area where customers are encouraged to rate this book. By rating it you will help others interested in horror and suspense. It also helps the author. Thank you, Cynthia H-B Adams

Made in the USA
Middletown, DE
30 July 2024

58251638R00149